Praise for Por

'Smart, funny and always bri......,
from Portia becomes my new favourite rom com.'
Shari Low

'I laughed, I cried – I loved it.'
Holly Martin

'The queen of rom com!'
Rebecca Raisin

'This book made me laugh and kept me turning the pages.'
Mandy Baggot

'A fun, fabulous 5-star rom com!'
Sandy Barker

'Loved the book, it's everything you expect from the force that
is Portia! A must read'
Rachel Dove

'Fun and witty. Pure escapism!'
Laura Carter

'A heartwarming, fun story, perfect for several hours of pure
escapism.'
Jessica Redland

PORTIA MACINTOSH is the bestselling author of over 30 romantic comedy novels.

From disastrous dates to destination weddings, Portia's romcoms are the perfect way to escape from day-to-day life, visiting sunny beaches in the summer and snowy villages at Christmas time. Whether it's southern Italy or the Yorkshire coast, Portia's stories are the holiday you're craving, conveniently packed in between the pages.

Formerly a journalist, Portia has left the city, swapping the music biz for the moors, to live the (not so) quiet life with her husband and her dog in Yorkshire.

Website: portiamacintosh.com
Instagram: @portiamacintoshauthor

Met Your Match

PORTIA MACINTOSH

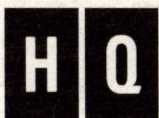

ONE PLACE. MANY STORIES

HQ
An imprint of HarperCollins*Publishers* Ltd
1 London Bridge Street
London SE1 9GF

www.harpercollins.co.uk

HarperCollins*Publishers*
Macken House, 39/40 Mayor Street Upper,
Dublin 1 D01 C9W8

This paperback edition 2026
1

First published in Great Britain as *Make or Break at the Lighthouse B & B* by HQ, an
imprint of HarperCollins*Publishers* Ltd 2020

Copyright © Portia MacIntosh 2020

ISBN: 9780008761950

Printed and bound in the UK using 100% Renewable
Electricity by CPI Group (UK) Ltd

MIX
Paper | Supporting
responsible forestry
FSC™ C007454
FSC
www.fsc.org

For Bambi Brambles-Brown & Teddie Charles Bear.

Chapter 1

Mrs Gia Delaney's wedding has been the wedding to end all weddings.

Seriously, if you're planning your wedding right now I probably wouldn't even bother because today has been a day that would put most royal weddings to shame. Gia's nuptials made Meghan Markle's look like nothing more than a piss-up down the pub!

She had a swan ring bearer, for crying out loud. How do you even coerce a swan into performing such a duty? A cute dog or trustworthy relative, sure, those are things that can be worked with, but a swan? I've never met a swan that didn't want to kill me. Still, I booked it for her, like she asked me to. Being chief bridesmaid left me standing awfully close to the angry bird (not the bride, although she does seem especially hot-headed today) and I was absolutely petrified. It sure will look good in the pictures, though.

Gia and her husband Kent, the spoilt son of a dotcom million-aire who managed to survive the 2000 tech bubble burst (because people will always want, ahem, adult material, but that's nothing to talk about at a wedding), have gone all out, all day.

The wedding ceremony took place at an enormous castle, belonging to a friend of the family who is something like ninetieth in line to the throne. It's gorgeous, like something out of a fairy tale. Honestly, it's like the kind of building you usually only see in romcom movies – or horror movies, depending on whether the venue is playing host to a lavish wedding with a Matthew McConaughey-type groom or a petrifying poltergeist with a smoky glow and chains hanging from it.

Speaking of dripping with chains, Gia's bling is like nothing I have ever seen in real life. It's the kind of diamond necklace you would expect to see the likes of Margot Robbie wearing on the red carpet at the Oscars – and even a mega star like her would only be borrowing them. Honestly, it's all I can look at right now. Then again, I am jammed into a toilet cubicle with her, carefully holding her dress up while she has a wee. I didn't really realise, when I agreed to be her right-hand woman for the day, that I would be taking on many of the duties of her actual right hand, but these are the kinds of things we do for our best friends, right?

'Are you having a nice day?' I ask her.

'God, Lola, seriously, it's amazing,' she says. 'I knew it was going to be amazing because, you know, I planned it, and because Kent has spent a fortune on it. Like, honestly, you could buy a house with the money we've spent. Not one that I would live in though.'

I laugh. Even when she's on the toilet, Gia is a snob. She's my snob though.

'You deserve it,' I tell her.

'Thanks, babe,' she replies. 'And thanks so much for all your help with the planning – I can't wait until I can return the favour for you. Any chance Patrick will be popping the question soon?'

'Gosh, I doubt it,' I say with an awkward chuckle. 'We've only been together for nine months, and we hardly see each other with him being away for work so much. Things are going great, we just need to work on our schedules . . . but anyway, when I do get married – if I get married – then you will absolutely be right there by my side, and you can hold my dress in the air while I use the loo.'

'Thanks so much for this,' she says. 'You can get these . . . I don't know what to call them, sort of weird pant things that you can wear under your dress, that you can kind of bundle your dress up in while you use the lav.'

'That sounds like a really good idea – why didn't you get some?' I ask.

Well, money was clearly no object, and I don't mind doing this for her at all, it just sounds like a much better system, with much less awkward eye contact.

'They were a little . . . granny pants-esque,' she says. 'Very ugly. I'd rather have my bestie do it.'

'Aww, thank you,' I tell her, only a little sarcastically. 'It's the closest I'll come to wearing a dress like this anytime soon.'

'You look hot in your bridesmaid dress,' she tells me, as I sort out her dress by the sinks. 'Patrick won't be able to keep his hands off you.'

'He looks amazing in a suit, doesn't he?' I say. I'm not usually one for boasting, but Patrick looks incredible when he's all dressed up.

'If I weren't just married,' Gia jokes as she washes her hands. 'Right, let's get back out there, get some more champagne.'

'You don't need to tell me twice,' I say. 'Let's go.'

Gia and I have always enjoyed the finer things in life. Our friendship was formed over £12 cocktails and lengthy shopping trips. We would frequent the Sky Bar, an exclusive rooftop cocktail bar in London, which is where Gia met Kent – it's also where I met Patrick. Gia is basically my brunette counterpart. She's like the sister I never had. It actually made me a bit emotional today, watching her get married. I've never had a friend I felt so close with and I was genuinely delighted. I was so proud of how beautiful she looked; like wow, that stunning babe is my best friend, and I'm helping her celebrate the best day of her life.

Gia kisses me on the cheek before getting back to her rounds, circulating, checking on all the guests, thanking them for coming.

This quick break in bridesmaid duties allows me to hurry over to Patrick, to steal a quick kiss.

'Hey, handsome,' I say as I sneak up behind him at the bar, wrapping my hands around his waist.

'Hey there, sexy,' he replies. 'God, look at you in that dress. Every time you walk away, when I see you again I convince myself more and more that we should sneak off upstairs to our room, see how you look out of it.'

I feel myself blush, just a little, as a massive grin spreads across my face.

Patrick is so confident and it's ridiculously sexy. He's self-assured, but in the best possible way. It's like he knows who he is and what he wants and he's not afraid to get it. On the first day we met, he just walked over to me, bought me a drink and asked me to go on a date with him. He reckons he just knew that I would say yes – and I did. Imagine having that much self-confidence! I know all the right things to say and do when approaching the opposite sex but I could never have that level of self-possession fuelling it. Patrick has so much it's spilling out of his pockets – and he has so much to spare, he isn't concerned with picking any up.

I unsubtly bite my lip. I am more than tempted to take Patrick up on that offer; he looks *so* good today. His pompadour haircut is so stylish, as is his trendy, neat beard. He's tall and muscular and there's just something about his posture . . . so relaxed, but so confident.

I do wonder, as you do when things are going well with someone you are seeing, whether or not Patrick is the person I'm going to spend the rest of my life with. I would absolutely love to get married one day – though I'd probably be a little more low-key than Gia is being. I'm not exactly shy, and I know that you are supposed to be the centre of attention on your wedding day, but even so, this is a little much for me.

I got a real lump in my throat, watching her and Kent exchanging the vows they had written for each other (or paid a

4

professional writer to pen, in Gia's case) and it made me wonder what I would say about Patrick, if it were us. Only in a just-wondering-to-myself kind of way – there's no way we're ready to get married anytime soon. With Patrick working as a stockbroker, and spending a lot of time abroad, I don't get to see him as much as I would like. We've got a trip planned in the not too distant future, just a little break away, but it will be some much-needed time alone together. I worry about him, working so hard all the time, travelling so much, doing such a stressful job. He loves it though; he loves the risk and the action – somehow this only makes him seem sexier to me.

'How are you doing?' Patrick asks me. 'Are you having fun?'

'I am,' I say. 'So, so much fun . . . I'm really hungry though. I was so nervous when we were eating – I think I was worried I might spill on my dress or something else classically clumsy me.'

'I hear they're doing the rounds with dessert items,' Patrick tells me. 'And apparently the disco is about to start, if you fancy a dance?'

It isn't long before Gia's favourite song, 'Stop' by the Spice Girls, starts playing.

Gia charges towards the dance floor, a champagne glass in her hand, without a care in the world. Her dress cost more than most people's annual salaries, yet she's carrying herself without a care in the world; she may as well be in her pyjamas. Whoever said money can't buy you happiness obviously never tried to eat a three-course dinner in a dress most people couldn't afford to dry-clean – I know I couldn't. I'm going to lock it away in its protective box as soon as I take it off.

My gaze shifts from Gia to the waiter behind her, carrying a mountain of profiteroles around. And they're not just normal profiteroles, they are salted caramel profiteroles – I know because I helped Gia choose them, and they are incredible.

'I'm going to grab some dessert, then we'll dance, OK?'

'Can't wait,' Patrick replies.

Gia has put so much time, effort and money into making today the happiest day of her life. She really has thought of everything. There is one thing she hasn't considered though: that her best friend might fall flat on her face on the dance floor.

I was making a beeline for the profiteroles, heading across the dance floor – not dancing, I hasten to add – balancing on the pin-like heels I've been wearing all day (the ones Gia insisted I had to wear, even though I said they weren't the easiest of shoes to walk in), and I was doing a great job of balancing on them until about ten seconds ago, when I stacked it in front of everyone. Still, I suppose you can see the red soles now that I'm laid out on the floor, which was the main reason Gia wanted me to wear them in the first place.

Patrick comes running over and tries to help me up, but as soon as I try to move my leg, I cry out in pain.

'Shit, shit,' I blurt out.

I watch as one of Gia's aunties ushers one of her young cousins away from me, her hands placed lightly over their ears.

'Sorry,' I say. 'It's just . . . I've never felt anything like it . . . It's . . . God, I think I'm going to be sick.'

'We'd better take you to hospital,' Patrick says.

'I'm sure I don't need to go to hospital,' I insist, trying to get up, but this only makes me cry out again.

I look for Gia in the crowd around me. There she is, with a face like thunder. Hell hath no fury like a bride upstaged at her own wedding. I swear, the way she's looking at me, it's almost as if she's jealous. Like she wishes it were her, sprawled out on the floor, trying not to cry all over her £1,299 bridesmaid dress (for some reason, I think Gia thinks reminding me of the price might encourage me to get up quicker, but I can't). If she knew how much pain I were in, she'd be happy where she was, even if everyone's eyes are off her for a fleeting moment.

It takes a few people to help me up from the floor and it is the most pain I have ever known in my life.

I feel bad for Gia. I know that she knows I can't help it, even if she does look upset, but it's bound to ruin her day a little, having her best friend carted off to A & E. I'll just get it checked out and try to get back here ASAP. I hate hospitals but I'm sure it will be just a quick in and out. I'll find out that I'm a big baby, I'll walk it off, I'll be back on the dance floor in no time.

I'll probably get my flats on the way back though.

Chapter 2

'OK, Lola, you are not going to like me now,' the radiographer tells me.

I didn't realise I liked him before. Well, what's to like? So far all he's done is talk to me like I'm a clumsy child and ask me a bunch of personal questions about my menstrual cycle.

'I'm going to have to move your leg into the right position for the x-ray,' he tells me through an incredibly forced smile.

'OK,' I say, taking a deep breath. I already know how this goes. It's been two hours since I fell, and the majority of those two hours have been spent slowly transporting me to the hospital, because the slightest movement of my leg causes me the worst pain I have ever felt in my life.

The radiographer begins moving my leg into position.

'Shit, shit, shit, shit.'

'I'm sorry,' he says. He sounds like he means it.

'I'm sorry for swearing,' I reply.

'It's OK, you have a free pass in here,' he assures me. 'And I've heard much worse.'

That's fortunate, because I know much worse. I wish I'd had a free pass to swear on the journey here. I kept getting these stabbing pains in my leg, and every time it happened, I couldn't help but drop S-bombs, and each time I did, you could guarantee there was a child lurking around. We had to apologise to a lot of parents on the way here – at the hotel, as the paramedics did their best to carefully get me off the dance floor and into the ambulance, and then at the hospital as they wheeled me to A & E.

'Well, I can see the problem here,' he finally says after taking my x-rays. He doesn't say much more than that though. I wait with bated breath, until he comes over to move my leg again, making me (as) comfortable (as is possible right now) in my wheelchair.

'You've broken your leg,' he tells me.

'What? Really?'

'Really,' he replies.

I mean, it is *very* painful, more painful than anything I've ever felt in my life, but I didn't think it was broken. In fact, after I fell, the first thing I did was insist that I didn't want to go to hospital. Even when we arrived here, and the nurse asked me to rate my pain on a scale from one to ten, I gave it a six and turned down painkillers because I didn't actually think it was broken. I thought I was just being a big baby.

'You're not actually a doctor though, are you?' I say. 'You could be wrong?'

The radiographer's eyebrows shoot up. I wasn't trying to offend him, I just meant that, maybe he could be wrong? He *has* to be wrong. I really, *really* can't have a broken leg right now.

He wheels me across the room, in my wheelchair with my leg sticking out in front of me, sticks my x-ray on the wall and flicks a switch. As the x-ray comes alive, my hope dies.

'See that there,' he says, pointing to a bone that is broken clean in half.

'Yes,' I reply softly.

'That's your fibula,' he replies. 'And yours is screwed.'

'Are . . . are you allowed to say that?' I ask, a little taken aback.

'Everyone gets a free pass in here,' he replies moodily.

I guess I must've offended him when I said he wasn't a doctor.

I wasn't being sassy with him, I was just really hoping he might be wrong.

As he wheels me along the corridor, I spot Patrick.

'Hey,' I call out.

'Hey, what's cracking?' he asks, looking up from his iPhone.

'Her fibula,' the radiographer tells him. 'You can take her the rest of the way back.'

'Thanks for all your help,' I call after him guiltily.

'You've broken it?' Patrick asks me in disbelief.

'Now that I think about it, I did feel a sort of . . . popping sensation.'

'Christ,' he replies. 'Well, let's get you to the doctor, get you patched up.'

I puff air from my cheeks as Patrick wheels me back to the minor injuries unit. We've had nine amazing months of going out on lovely dates, enjoying romantic evenings in, entire days in the bedroom . . . This is our first trip to A & E though. I suppose all couples have to have one eventually, right?

'I still don't understand how you did it,' he says.

'I just lost my footing,' I say. 'I wasn't exactly diving for the bouquet. It's these silly bridesmaid shoes Gia made me wear.'

Patrick sighs. 'Women and shoes,' he says as he wheels me back to see the doctor.

'So, it's broken,' the doctor says, appearing from behind the curtain. 'Fancy that codeine now?'

'Yes please,' I reply.

Now I know I'm not going to be able to shift the pain with a bag of ice and a couple of days off my feet, give me all the drugs.

'Here we are,' she says, handing me two paper cups: one with a tablet and one with water.

I knock it back.

'So, you've broken your fibula, I'm afraid,' she tells me. 'I'm just going to run your x-ray by the orthopaedic surgeon, see what he says.'

'OK,' I reply. My heart is in my mouth.

'Surgeon?' I say to Patrick. 'Am I going to need an operation?'

'Calm down,' he insists. 'We're . . . it's going to be OK.'

Is it?! It doesn't seem like it is.

I can't help but notice Patrick's bedside manner – or lack thereof. He isn't being very patient or reassuring. He isn't rubbing my shoulder or holding my hand. He seems deeply uncomfortable with the hospital generally. I suppose some people are just like that.

'OK,' the doctor says as she reappears through the curtain. 'So, we've had a chat and, as you're relatively young, an operation probably isn't necessary. You should heal just fine in a cast.'

I can't help but take issue with her use of 'relatively young' – I'm only thirty-two, for Christ's sake. Don't tell me I'm on the verge of old, brittle bones yet!

'OK,' I reply.

'I'll get you a prescription for some codeine to take home, OK?'

'OK,' I reply.

Why does everyone – myself included – keep saying OK? This is absolutely not OK, and repeatedly saying it's OK isn't going to make it O-*bloody*-K.

My cast goes much higher up my leg than I expected it to. It's big, and bulky, and I hate the way it smells. It certainly doesn't match the stocking on my other leg.

I notice Patrick staring at it with a look of discomfort. He winces, as he watches me shuffle to find comfort in my wheelchair.

Patrick wheels me out into the hospital reception. It must be quite late now. All I want is to sleep. If I sleep, things might feel easier in the morning.

As he manoeuvres me through a doorway he catches my wheelchair on the frame. The jolt sends a wave of pain around every nerve ending in my body. I turn my head to look at him, only to realise he's looking at something on his phone while he pushes me with one hand.

'Patrick!'

11

'Sorry, sorry, it's work,' he says.

It's always work with him. Being a stockbroker is, apparently, a twenty-four hour a day job. I say apparently because I honestly have no way of knowing whether this is true or not. Aside from the most basic knowledge of stocks, I don't really get what he does. I just know that it makes him very angry, and he's always on his phone. So perhaps it is a twenty-four hour a day job, perhaps I shouldn't be so hard on him.

'I'll go book a taxi,' Patrick says. 'Get you home to your bed.'

'Can I come to yours?' I ask him.

'Wouldn't you be happier in your own home?' he replies.

'Perhaps, if I didn't have a stupid bloody step up into my bathroom.'

I curse myself. When I was flat hunting, I thought the cute little step up to my bathroom was, well, cute. It made it look like a mini spa. I never imagined I'd be wheelchair bound. Now I'm kicking myself . . . or I would be, if I physically could.

'Oh, right.' Patrick scratches his head. 'Yes, OK then.'

As he wanders off to book us a taxi, a wave of cramp grips my broken leg, just like it kept doing on the walk over – I suppose from holding it in one careful but awkward position for so long.

'Shit, shit, shit,' I can't help but blurt out.

Right on cue, a toddler waddles out from behind one of the pillars.

Every single one of my excruciating agony-fuelled outbursts so far has had an accidental audience of someone who shouldn't be watching anything more than a PG, at best.

There's nothing I can do but watch, as the giddy little boy's legs turn to jelly underneath him and he flops to the floor with a clap, in that way toddlers always seem to go down. As he bursts into tears, his dad finally appears and picks him up. Poor kid, I know just how he feels (let's casually gloss over the fact that I have thirty-two years' experience with my feet, compared to his maximum of two).

His dad dusts him down and his crying stops all at once, as though someone has flicked a switch. The little boy is absolutely fine. In fact, it's only a matter of seconds before he's waddling around again.

Somehow, I don't think it's going to be quite so easy for me.

Chapter 3

Bloody men and their bloody sex drives!

I have it on pretty good authority – from my Auntie Val, of all people – that these are the days of our (sex) lives.

She had a few too many drinks at my twenty-first birthday party and took it upon herself to sit me down and tell me about the facts of life. Not the usual facts of life though, *her* facts of life, the supposedly real ones.

Auntie Val told me that, once men hit middle age, they're not worth bothering with. She said my Uncle Robert was 'fantastic in the sack' when he was younger, but that his 'tackle' could no longer rise to the occasion, and that they slept in separate rooms. Auntie Val might've had a fair bit to drink, but she and Uncle Robert did eventually break up, and she has only been known to date wildly age-inappropriate younger men ever since.

With that to potentially look forward to in my future, you'd think I'd take whatever I could get now . . . except right now, my leg is *literally broken in half*.

'Boy, are you out of your mind?' I ask Patrick. He's lying in my bed next to me, caressing the thigh of my good leg. I know he isn't comforting me though, he's caressing with intent.

'What?' he replies innocently.

'Are you seriously putting the moves on me right now?'

'I thought you'd welcome the distraction,' he says.

I slowly eject every drop of air from my lungs.

'I've been awake almost all night, in so much pain, unable to get comfortable, and you think thrashing away at me is going to make me feel better?' I reply in disbelief.

'Usually you like my thrashing,' he replies. 'Plus, I'm going to Amsterdam for work for a few days, so . . .'

'You are?'

'I told you I was.'

'You absolutely didn't,' I reply.

'Hmm.' He ponders whether he did or didn't tell me for a moment. 'Yeah, it's for work. For a few days.'

'Oh,' I reply.

'Did you think I was going to be able to look after you?'

'I did . . .'

'Sorry,' he says. 'Maybe ask your friends?'

'Erm, yeah, OK.'

I don't really know what else to say. If he has to work, then he has to work.

'I should call work, actually, explain what has happened,' I say.

Patrick plants a peck on my forehead.

'I'd better get ready for work,' he says, hopping out of bed. I can't help but envy the ease with which he is able to switch from lying to standing. For me, it feels like a distant memory – and it's only been ten hours! 'I'll leave you to your call.'

Patrick has always slept naked. I think he'd prefer to be naked all day long, if he weren't so into fashion. I like that though, that he cares about what he wears and how he looks. He works hard to keep in shape, and he has a beauty regime to rival my own, but he looks incredible for it, with his rippling muscles, his £60 pompadour haircut, his neat, short beard and his threaded eyebrows.

I can't help but admire him as he walks across the bedroom. I don't think that I'm out of his league, or anything like that, but

15

I do know how lucky I am. Women just seem to fall at his feet.

I carefully reach for my mobile, to call my boss. My plan is to – hopefully – take a couple of days off, just until I get the hang of the wheelchair, and the pain settles down, but then it will be business as usual, as far as actual business is concerned, at least.

'Hello,' Andrea pants down the phone.

'Oh, erm, hello . . . It's Lola James . . . Sorry, did I wake you?'

'No, no, I'm in the gym,' she replies.

That's a huge relief. It would be so like my randy boss to answer her phone while she was at it.

We both work for the Beautiful People Agency, which manages a range of clients who are either rich, famous, or an obvious combination of both, giving perfect people their perfect lives. We handle finding them work, advertising deals, we manage their appearance (both how they look and how they come across) – we even have an in-house estate agency, to make sure that they live in the perfect place for them. And then there's the department I work for, handling their relationships. I play cupid to the rich and famous, not only finding them their perfect matches, but also advising them on all areas of their love lives. It's a strange job sometimes, but I absolutely love it. How many people can put on their CV that they gave rock star Dylan King advice on a particular aspect of his lovemaking game? It's got to be fewer than five.

'Oh, on Friday, did you find someone for Kelly Parker in the end?' she asks me.

'I did, yes.'

'Someone from the Bin?'

'Yep. Fabrizio Napoletano – he was on *Love Island* last year . . .'

The Bin is a particular category of client we talk about in the office, referring to someone who we signed (usually off the back of a reality TV show), who we are thinking of dropping. Before we do so, we'll keep them in the Bin for a while, until we can match them with someone of a higher calibre (dictated by our guidelines). It sounds awful, but I do take pride in my work, and I will absolutely not pair up anyone who I don't truly believe belong together. My job is to find perfect relationships for people who find it hard to meet people. It's not easy, being rich or famous – there are thousands of people willing to date you (or even marry you) simply for your money and status. But I can spot a fake from a mile off, and I have a one hundred per cent success record. I'm so good that my company offers a money-back guarantee.

'Great,' she replies.

I hear a few beeps coming from whatever machine she's using. It sounds like she's getting faster.

'So, what couldn't wait until you got to the office tomorrow?' she asks.

'Oh, God, it's Sunday, isn't it? Sorry, I get so confused with Patrick working seven days a week. I thought I was in work today.'

'Not today,' Andrea says with a snort. 'Don't worry, I was up for my workout anyway. Can it wait until tomorrow?'

'Well, I'm not going to be able to come in tomorrow either,' I start.

'Oh. It's not like you to take sick days,' she says.

'I know,' I reply. 'But, well, I've broken my leg.'

'Oh, no, that's terrible,' she replies.

'Yes, it's not ideal. I'm in a wheelchair, actually. I'm not allowed to put weight on it – they didn't even give me any crutches for these first couple of weeks.'

'Oh gosh . . .'

'And my silly apartment has steps in it, so I'm going to have to find a friend to stay with.'

'Lola, listen, it sounds like you've got a lot on your plate right now.'

'I am figuring it all out, don't worry.'

'It's not just that,' she starts. 'You know, having you in a wheelchair in the office, it's just not practical. You're not going to be able to get around to clients, you're going to need ramps and whatnot – it's going to be a logistical nightmare.'

'So . . .'

'So, I'm going to hand over all your work to Angel, until you're back on your feet, and I won't hear another word on the subject, OK?'

Pssh. Angel. She isn't like any angel I've ever heard of, she's more like a devil. She's my office frenemy, the thorn in my side, the one always vying for Andrea's attention and trying to pinch my high-profile clients, because hers are all from the Bin. I always knew she was after my job, I guess now she's going to get it. At least it's only temporary.

'OK then,' I reply, but it's absolutely not OK.

'You rest up and take care now,' she insists, before hanging up the phone.

For a moment I just stare into space.

Andrea is right: I don't ever take sick days. I work myself into the ground for that company. Suddenly, because I'm in plaster and being pushed around in a wheelchair, I'm, what, not cool enough to be seen around the office? Andrea always tells us that we're selling a sexy lifestyle, so it's important that we look sexy. While I'm not entirely sure how legal this might be, female employees have to adhere to an office-wide ban on ponytails, trousers, and natural-look make-up. I don't mind too much. I like to have my long blonde hair flowing, wear nice clothes, and spend time applying my make-up each day. I do it for myself, not because Andrea tells me to. I feel like I really fit in there, which is why I'm so gutted to be put on the bench.

My next order of business is to find someone I can stay with. Patrick might not be able to look after me but, lucky for me, I have a lot of friends.

I call Gia, my best friend. I'm sure she'll be dying to know if I'm OK, but with last night being her wedding night, I didn't want to put a downer on things.

'Heeey,' she sings down the phone.

'Hey, how was last night?'

'Oh, amazing,' she replies brightly. 'Just . . . magical. Where did you end up?'

'I fell.'

'Yeah, I saw,' she replies. 'After that?'

'The hospital, Gia . . .'

'Oh, wow, how you feeling now?'

'Not great,' I confess. 'I've broken my leg.'

'No way!'

'Way,' I reply. 'I'm in a wheelchair.'

'Ah, Lola, that's awful. I'm so sorry.'

'Thanks,' I reply.

I'm so lucky, to have a best friend like Gia.

'The worst thing is, Patrick is going away for work, so he can't look after me. And I've got that silly step in my apartment.'

'Oh, gosh, yeah,' she replies. 'I forgot about that.'

I hear Gia giggling.

'Stop it,' she whispers.

'Do you want me to let you go?' I ask.

'No, it's just Kent, being a randy newlywed. Get off, Kent, I'm talking to Lola. She's broken her leg.'

'Get well soon, Lola,' he calls down the phone.

'Tell him thank you,' I say. 'Anyway, Patrick can't look after me, so I'm just trying to work out what to do.'

'Oh, well, Lola, you know I'm going on honeymoon,' she reminds me.

'Yeah, in three weeks, right?' I reply.

I wasn't necessarily angling to stay with her – I get that she's a newlywed – but I'm surprised she hasn't offered. She's my best friend, and she and Kent live in a massive house. Everything I could possibly need is downstairs in her house. I thought she might have suggested I look after the place while she's in Bali for three weeks or something. Just offered, even if she knows I'll say no. All the more reason to ask, right?

'Well, yeah, but . . . I mean, we're just married. It's not really a good time for guests, you know?'

I swallow hard. I'm not a guest, I'm her best friend. I'm the person who basically organised her entire wedding, right down to that stupid ring-carrying angry swan she insisted she needed me to arrange. When Gia asked me to help plan her wedding, she said she needed my organisational skills . . . I can't help but feel a bit used.

'Oh, no, I totally get that. I wasn't expecting you to look after me,' I insist. Well, I wasn't, I'm just shocked by how not her problem this is sounding.

'You're a star,' she replies. 'You'll land on your feet – oops, poor choice of words.'

'Drinks tomorrow,' I start, remembering our plans.

'Yeah, no, let's just . . . put a pin in that until after my honeymoon? I'm sure you need the rest.'

'Erm, yeah.'

'Maybe try your parents?'

'Yeah, thanks,' I reply.

And now she doesn't even want to hang out with me?! What, just because I'm in plaster, is that not cool? Is she really that superficial?

'You all sorted?' Patrick asks, walking out of the bathroom with a towel wrapped around his waist.

As he runs a hand through his hair, I notice his bicep wiggle. Something I suspect he does on purpose, either for my benefit or the mirror's.

'Erm, not really,' I reply. 'Work have told me not to go in until I can walk, and Gia doesn't want to know.'

'Shit, that's awful,' he replies. 'You'd better get calling someone else, or you're in big trouble.'

Wow, even Patrick doesn't have much time for injured me. It's like everyone is happy to have you around when you're all dressed up and socialising, but when the shit hits the fan and you need help, no one wants to take time away from their awesome, easy life to help out.

'Yeah,' I reply. 'Thanks.'

I frown.

He's right, I guess. I'd better start working my way through my contacts. There's absolutely no way I can cope on my own, at least to start with. But if you can't rely on your boyfriend or your best friend, who else can you ask?

Chapter 4

Life, it turns out, is a pretty fragile thing.

I don't mean in terms of life and death, although I'm sure that's a realisation we all come to eventually. I feel very grateful to have not lived through circumstances to cause me that epiphany yet.

What I actually mean is that, having a life is a fragile thing. Having a rich, full, happy life, with everything you've ever hoped for, everything you've dreamed of . . . just one little accident, and it falls apart like a fibula on a dance floor (hmm, perhaps that metaphor is a little me-specific to use here, but you know what I mean).

Yesterday I had it all; today none of it is anywhere to be seen. I'm stuck in this wheelchair, I can't go to my own home, my boyfriend is too busy to look after me, my best friend is too wrapped up in her own stuff, all my other friends are too busy with their own lives too. I rang round every single one of them, but none of them wanted to know. We're all BFFs when there are fancy nights out and showbiz parties to go to (parties that *my* job gets us entry to), but now I need a favour from them . . . nothing. And I call it a favour, like it's help moving house or a lift to the train station, but I'm here, in this chair, with nowhere to go, and no one to look after me. I don't need a favour, I need a lifeline. How can they all just leave me to it?

Ordinarily, I would throw myself into work, because I love my job so much, nothing makes me happier than helping other people find happiness . . . and I can't even do that. Even work doesn't want me.

I wiggle carefully in my seat. I'm not all that comfortable at the best of times, but sitting in the back of a car with my broken leg stretched across the seat feels especially awkward. Not just because it makes my break feel especially painful (although it does, everything does, even breathing makes my leg hurt) but because it is an ambitious stretch at the best of times. All this does is rub in my face the fact that I probably do just go to yoga because I think it's trendy, and because all my friends go. It turns out I'm not actually gaining that much flexibility from it. I suppose I knew, deep down, that I didn't take it all that seriously. I was in it for the chat with my friends, the funky, colourful yoga pants, and the drinks we would go for after. Now I kind of wish I had taken it more seriously – it might make this drive more bearable.

'I have to say, your mum and I are over the moon,' my dad chirps as he drives.

I can see his face in the rear-view mirror and he certainly looks overjoyed.

'That's great,' I reply, but I can't muster up much conviction. Not in these circumstances.

'I mean, your mum and I are sad you broke your leg – obviously.'

'Obviously,' I echo.

'But over the moon,' he insists again.

'OK, Dad, calm down,' I say.

It's not that I'm not grateful. It's unbelievably kind of him to drive all the way to London to pick me up, only to hit the road again straight away. It must be at least a ten-hour round trip he's making. But he could at least sound like he isn't delighted I broke my leg.

'Sorry, love,' he replies.

My dad, Paul James, gives me a reassuring smile in the mirror. One that I imagine is supposed to put me at my ease, but I still suspect he might drive into a tree if it means I have to stay with them for longer. He's your typical broad Yorkshireman, with an angry brow and an even less friendly resting face. He's a big softy, of course, but I did find it an advantage, growing up with an intimidating-looking dad. I certainly won every single 'my dad is bigger than your dad' standoff, that's for sure.

That's what I'm doing, by the way. I'm moving back in with my parents.

It's only temporary, may I add, until I'm back on my feet, and with this being very literal in my case, I know how long it will be – six weeks. That's what they told me when I went to have my temporary cast swapped for a regular one, before we hit the road today. They didn't even say I'd be better in six weeks, they said I could hopefully swap my cast for a brace then, so at least I'd be able to put some weight on it.

So, that's my countdown. Six weeks. I don't think I've spent six days at my parents' house since I moved out, with me only popping back for Christmas or encouraging them to visit me. It's hard for them though, running a B & B, because at the times of year when people have time off and usually want to get together, that's when they are busiest.

Anyone can survive six weeks back home, right? It might be kind of nice, taking in the sea air, eating my mum's cooking, watching TV with my dad. It's been ages since I had some time off, not without a holiday to jet off on. Yes, it will be great, just the chilled-out break I've probably been in need of.

I look out of the car windows, admiring the greenery on one side and the sea on the other. We must be nearly there now.

'It's a shame Mum couldn't come for the drive,' I say.

'Yes, but you know what she's like,' my dad replies. 'She's washing the windows and doing the stairs down.'

Almost all of my significant memories involve my mum on her hands and knees, with a cloth and a bucket of warm soapy water, starting at the top of the stairs and working her way down, scrubbing each step along the way.

'I can't even go up the stairs,' I laugh.

'Oh, she knows, but you know what she's like. She's just excited, her baby is coming home.'

I want to remind him that it's only for six weeks, but he knows. No sense in reminding him and bursting his bubble.

'How's the work coming along?' I ask.

When I was home for Christmas I made a few suggestions about the B & B. Just little things here and there that needed a fresh lick of paint, or new ideas for how to drum up more business.

Driving through Marram Bay, where I grew up, always feels like looking through an old photo album. You know how sometimes you remember how things were when you were a kid, and even though they look different now because of time or advances in technology, they remind you of the good old days? Well passing through Marram Bay is nothing like that. I always come back to find this place exactly as I left it.

I would hazard a guess there are a few reasons nothing changes in Marram Bay. First of all, it's a tourist hotspot. People travel from all over the world to visit expecting a Yorkshire seaside town, cute and picturesque, with quirks aplenty.

There are lots of weird and wonderful events that people flock here for. In December, Marram Bay plays host to the Winter Wonderland Festival down by the beach. We have rides, stalls, and performances, but the pièce de résistance is without a doubt the Christmas tree maze. I would always look forward to getting lost in the maze when I was a kid. It's funny, because I would try so hard to learn the layout so that one year I could walk it – I don't know how many years it took me to figure out that the layout is different each time.

In summer we have the 1940s weekend, which we take seriously

– and I mean *very* seriously. It's exactly as it sounds too. The entire place hops into a time machine and goes back to the World War II era. Locals cover their windows in white tape, hide their cars and dress up in their 1940s' best, and if you even think about breaking character, they probably force you into moving house.

Other annual events include a hot air balloon festival and a Valentine's Day Festival, dedicated to all things love. It's no wonder we get so many tourists.

People in little towns like this are always so set in their ways. They don't want things to change. They *hate* change. New builds, Tesco Expresses, Nando's – no one can get a look in.

As we drive through Marram Bay I spot the Little Acorn Primary school – the first school I attended – before passing the small park where I had my first kiss. I can pretty much map my pre-London-move life events across this small but beautiful stretch, although I'm not sure how much interest there would be in a tourist pamphlet like that.

'Oh, just in time,' my dad says as we approach the causeway to Hope Island. 'It closes in ten minutes.'

When I was growing up on Hope Island, I didn't give the causeway much thought. I was just so used to it that it became little more than an annoyance that stopped me getting to see my friends or returning home after. Now that I'm older and it isn't something I get to see very often, it absolutely captivates me.

Twice a day, when the tide comes in, the mile-long road that connects Hope Island to Marram Bay will be completely covered by the North Sea, isolating Hope Island from the rest of the country. Then, when the tide goes back out, and the road beneath becomes visible, the tidal island is connected again.

So, what used to just be a road closure that annoyed teenage me is now a real marvel of the natural world that I can't get enough of. That said, if it had been closed just now, I would have been annoyed at being stuck on the mainland for even longer – hours probably – because I really need the loo (which is an absolute ordeal that I'd rather not go through with my dad in a public lav) and I'm so uncomfortable in this car.

'Thank goodness,' I reply as we drive along the causeway. I look out of the window only to see the water edging closer at both sides of the road. It's fascinating, how it just looks like a centimetre or two of water creeping in slowly, but come high tide this road can often be under six foot of water. The locals know the causeway and the tide like the backs of their hands. They know how long they have to drive the mile-long road and they know what will happen if they drive when it isn't safe.

Tourists, however, who aren't familiar with our tidal island, will often think they can take a chance and cross, either expecting the road to keep clear for them, or that it will only be like driving through a big puddle. Of course it's nothing like that; it's so dangerous, which is why people get halfway across and realise the tide has them surrounded, leaving them marooned in their car, but not for long. Soon the sea takes their car too, and that's when they wind up in big trouble.

Growing up here, the risks with the tide were always made very clear to us, and I remember the consequences – along with the costs involved – clear as day. A sea rescue costs £2,000 whereas an air rescue costs £4,000 – and of course you're in danger if you need rescuing, and then there is the damage to your car, so why even risk it?

'Hopefully your mum will have finished tidying and we can have a nice cup of tea,' my dad says.

The thought of sitting there in pain while my mum tidies around me makes me anxious. I know she's just trying to make the place nice for me, but all I care about is getting comfortable in a room with an adjoining bathroom that doesn't involve any steps.

Hope Island is gorgeous, packed with cute little cafés, homely-looking B & Bs and plenty of tourist hotspots, like the old abbey ruins, but I've no time to stop and admire them today. I'm really starting to regret keeping hydrated on the drive here.

'Home sweet home,' my dad says as he pulls up outside the Lighthouse B & B.

On the coast, looking out to sea, sits the old converted lighthouse that my parents live in. Their bed and breakfast is in the newer building attached to it. I grew up in the lighthouse – the tall, slightly off white, weather-battered building with the red stripe across the middle.

Growing up, my old bedroom was on the top floor, which was as magical as it sounds. There's no chance of me getting up there today though so the bottom floor – also known as the family living room – will be my bedroom for the foreseeable future. Thankfully there is a bathroom just off the living room, so I'll be able to roll between the rooms with ease.

As my dad helps me out of the car and up the path, my mum runs out to meet us.

'Lola, darling,' she says excitedly.

'Hi, Mum,' I reply. I allow her a moment to kiss my cheek before wheeling myself past her. 'I need the loo, then we'll talk.'

'She didn't even mention the new curtains,' I just about hear her say to my dad as I struggle to close the door behind me.

It's just six weeks, I remind myself. Just six weeks.

Chapter 5

'Lola . . . Lola, honey, time to wake up.'

When I hear my mum's voice my first thought is that I'm going to be late for school. I always had a tendency to oversleep but she would talk me awake ever so gently.

It only takes a few seconds for me to realise that I haven't travelled back in time to my teens. I am here as a thirty-two-year-old grown person – one who has nothing to get up for.

'Just five more minutes,' I plead. Well, old habits die hard.

'Nope, I won't let you be an invalid,' she insists. 'I've made you some breakfast, come on. Do you need me to help you up?'

'No,' I insist, pulling myself into more of an upright position. 'It's OK, I'm a fully grown woman. I can do it.'

If there's one thing I don't want, it is to feel like a child again.

To prove a point I shuffle from the sofa into my wheelchair, being as careful with my leg as possible. I am most definitely overdue some painkillers because an agonising electric shock type pain shoots up and down from the break.

'Shit, shit, shit,' I say as I settle into my chair. I exhale deeply as I realise I'm going to have to move from my chair to the toilet. Perhaps I'll wait until after I've had my painkillers, before I attempt moving again.

'Oh, love,' my mum says. 'Please let me help you. Can I help you to the bathroom? Do you want to get changed?'

I remove a scrunchie from my wrist and scoop my long blonde hair up into a bun on the top of my head.

'I'll have something to eat and take my painkillers first,' I say. 'But then that would be great, thank you.'

Well, I can't do it on my own, and a little help isn't exactly going to make me feel like a big baby, is it? I do have a broken leg; I need to cut myself some slack.

I grab my phone from next to the sofa before my mum wheels me from the lighthouse into the B & B. We go through the door into the B & B office where there is also a door into our private family kitchen, separate from the bistro kitchen where food is prepared for the guests.

A quick glance at my phone turns up two surprising pieces of information. First of all, it's only 8:30 in the a.m. – way earlier than I want to get up when I don't have work, but also evidence that my mum has allowed me to sleep in. She's probably been up since 5:30 a.m., getting ready for a busy day in the B & B, working on her permanently flawless hair and near invisible make-up.

I've never really pulled off the natural look like my mum does. I have to spend time on my hair – lest it look like a bird's nest, like it does today – and it pretty much always takes a full face of make-up to get me looking well rested and healthy. I need to contour and highlight and open my eyes up. Otherwise I look like I do today – old, tired and like I just don't care anymore. That's not to say I do it because I think I have to though. I've always been a girly girl who loved doing her hair and messing around with make-up; it would just be nice to be a little more effortlessly polished like my mum is.

The other piece of disappointing information gathered from my phone is the fact that Patrick hasn't sent me so much as a text to see how I'm doing. I know he's in Amsterdam and I know he's working, but his phone is never out of his hand, and it wouldn't take him more than thirty seconds to punch me a quick text to see how I'm feeling, or if I got home safe.

'There's my two favourite ladies,' my dad says as my mum wheels me into the private dining kitchen, parking me at the table.

'Morning, Da . . . Oh my God.'

My sentence is derailed by the breakfast on the table in front of me.

'What?' my mum asks.

'Is this for me?' I reply.

'Yes.'

'All of it?' I check.

'Of course,' my mum says. 'We need to get your strength up, get you back on your feet.'

My mum, Linda James, has always taken a very domestic approach to any problem she's ever encountered. This kitchen is her Situation Room and her weapons of choice? Usually food. Today that food is scrambled eggs and toast, but not just any scrambled eggs and toast, a mountain of scrambled eggs and a stack of smiley face toast. She used to make me this when I was younger. I think it came from my obsession with the Teletubbies, but that was over twenty years ago, and I was probably too old for it even back then.

Ordinarily, I'd probably find it cute that my mum has made me my favourite childhood breakfast, but now, in these circumstances, it just makes me feel even more like I've regressed.

'There's no way I'll eat all that,' I blurt out.

My dad chuckles from behind his newspaper. 'Told you, Lin.'

'Shush, you,' my mum ticks him off. 'This is just what she needs to get her life back on track.'

'Eggs?' my dad asks in disbelief.

'Home cooking,' my mum replies. She gives my wheelchair another short, kind of sharp, push towards the table. 'Eat up, baby.'

'I'll give it my best shot,' I say.

I twist my body around awkwardly to try and eat from the table. The eggs are kind of on the cold side and the toast is definitely cold because it is rock solid, but I can see the love that has gone into making it, from carving the faces to including finely chopped chives and pieces of smoked salmon because she knows that's my favourite. I owe it to my mum to eat as much as I can, without throwing up from the pain coming from my leg. I just need to eat enough to take my painkillers; once they kick in I won't feel so tetchy.

My mum watches me like a hawk as I eat. She nods encouragingly as I raise my fork to my mouth.

'It's so good to have you home,' she tells me again. 'Isn't it, Paul?'

My dad reads his newspaper with that dad brand of harmless ignorance. You know he's in his own little world, no longer listening to either of us. I suppose that's a defence mechanism he's developed over the years, living in a house with two women. Whether my mum and I were at odds over me wanting to go to some house party or other, or if we were just having an in-depth natter about *Emmerdale*, my dad has perfected the art of tuning out. The only problem there is that he doesn't always tune back in when we need him to.

'Paul,' my mum snaps.

'What?' he replies with a similar faux anger.

'I said it's nice to have Lola home,' she tells him.

'Lovely to have you home, love,' my dad says, suddenly all warm and welcoming. He immediately goes back to his newspaper.

My mum and dad have always had a happy marriage, but the two of them couldn't be more different on paper. My dad is, for the most part, the strong silent type. He likes to keep himself to himself and he'll mostly keep his nose out of other people's business too. This makes him the perfect B & B owner really, because he isn't just discreet, he's oblivious.

My mum is the exact opposite. My dad always jokes that my mum doesn't have an off button, which is why she's always talking.

She loves nothing more than a good chat, and if she can sort someone's life out while doing so then she will be even happier.

When I lived here I felt like I acted as a sort of buffer between them. Someone to play the middle ground, bring my dad out of himself a bit, rein my mum in as much as possible. Since I moved out, I'm not sure how the balance is maintained but my parents have been married for nearly forty years. They are living proof that opposites do actually attract and I've always taken comfort in that. It's always filled me with hope that, if I ever do meet someone who isn't exactly like me, it's not like we're doomed. Thankfully I'd say Patrick and I are quite similar – well, except for the fact that since I had my accident he's been far too busy with work to care about me.

'This is lovely, Mum, thanks,' I tell her. I don't suppose I'll be able to force too much down, but I'll do my best.

'Good girl,' she replies. 'Let Mummy take care of you; you'll be back on your feet in no time.'

'You want to be careful,' my dad chimes in. 'Make sure she isn't whacking your leg with a hammer while you sleep, just so she can keep you here longer.'

I know that he's joking, but this triggers my mum.

'I already have a helpless lump to look after,' my mum points out. 'I'm certainly not in need of another.'

'Ow, ow,' I say, dropping my fork to grab my leg. It hasn't actually got worse, but acting like it has seems like a great way to defuse this situation.

My mum jumps up from her seat at the table and rushes round to me. She strokes my hair as she asks me if I'm OK. My dad puts down his newspaper, which is his equivalent.

'It's OK, darling. It's OK,' she reassured me. 'You'll be back to normal in no time at all.'

'I'm worried it's going to be a long recovery,' I admit. 'I'm scared I'm going to go out of my mind with boredom, without my job or my friends or any aspect of my day-to-day life at all.'

'We'll keep you busy,' my mum insists. 'Everything we talked about, for the B & B, is in place now, and it's all been great.'

'Really?' I reply.

'Oh, yes,' she insists. 'We've had a makeover. We've expanded the dining room so we can have more diners – we're more like a small hotel now. We've hired an extra chef – Robbie, such a lovely young man. Vince is training him up.'

'Oh, that will be nice for him,' I say sarcastically.

Over the years we have had a few chefs here at the Lighthouse B & B. Vince is the most recent, and he's very highly strung, very snobby and far too easily angered. He is a great chef though, so I think everyone has adopted a general rule of thumb to just leave him alone and let him do his job.

'Yes,' my mum starts. 'He's not happy to be sharing the kitchen with an up-and-comer, but everyone needs to start somewhere. And Robbie is so lovely. If you were single . . .'

'Ah, but I'm not,' I remind her. 'So don't go trying to play matchmaker while I'm unable to run away.'

'Would I?' my mum asks with a faux innocence. 'Anyway, if you let us meet this Patrick, then maybe I'd see how settled you were.'

I'm not really sure Patrick is a meet the parents kind of guy, not too early at least. I'm sure we'll do it when the time is right for both of us. My mum will just have to be patient.

'And then there's the fact that he isn't looking after you, in your time of need,' my mum adds.

'The man has to work,' my dad insists from the safety of behind his paper.

'Too busy for your little girl when she needs help?' my mum asks him.

'Ow,' I cry. 'Shit, my leg is really hurting.'

This time I'm not pretending.

'It feels really tight and warm,' I explain. 'Is that right? They told me to watch out for things like that.'

'It could be a DVT,' my mum says, going from nought to a medical emergency in a matter of seconds. 'That's it, we're getting you dressed and taking you to see the doctor.'

My mum wheels me away from my breakfast and back towards the living room (which is currently serving as my bedroom). She begins sorting through my clothes, looking for something for me to wear, before dressing me in them.

I have never felt more like a child.

I grab my phone to call Patrick. He told me he'd call me this morning, so I should probably let him know that I'm going to the doctor's, just in case he tries to call.

After a couple of rings someone answers. It isn't Patrick though, it's a female voice.

'Erm . . .' I look at my phone and realise that I've actually called Patrick's home phone by mistake. Still, there shouldn't be someone else answering – especially not a woman. 'Is Patrick there?'

I feel like an idiot for asking this random woman if my boyfriend is home.

'Not at the moment,' she replies. 'Can I take a message?'

'Erm . . . no . . . I'll call back later,' I say before hanging up quickly.

Who on earth was that? Why is she answering Patrick's phone while he's away?

I suppose I could text him, tell him that my mum is taking me to see the doctor and that I'll call him after. I don't want to seem like I'm keeping tabs on him, and I really don't want to seem like I'm trying to worry him, as some sort of kneejerk reaction, just because I heard a woman's voice on the other end of the phone.

Now I'm more worried than anyone, and not just about my leg – although it is frustrating to be going back to see another doctor. Like it's not bad enough I thought I was going to be stuck on my arse for six weeks, now I have to go and be poked and prodded again.

But I'm not just worried about that. Now I'm worried about Patrick too, because unless something bad has happened, things are starting to seem a little fishy.

Chapter 6

'I can't believe how much your accent has changed,' Kim, the local nurse, says.

Kim isn't just the local nurse though, she's my childhood best friend. In fact, I've known her since the day after I was born (if, you know, a new-born baby can actually know another one) because our mums were in hospital together, with Kim being born only a few hours after me. I was a night owl, she was an early riser, traits that followed us way into our teens.

So our mums became best friends, which meant that we became best friends, and we did pretty much everything together until after our A Levels, when our different studies took us to different ends of the country. The main difference though is that Kim moved back to Marram Bay, whereas I decided I liked life more in London. Up until the moment our lives went in different directions we were inseparable. We always looked alike too – at least we used to. People would often mistake us for sisters, or cousins at least. Perhaps that has more to do with the fact we were always together.

We definitely don't look alike anymore though and it is down to just one thing. We're both still the same height (a just above average five-five), both a not-thin-but-not-fat build (although my mum keeps harping on about something called a middle-aged spread that she reckons I'll fall victim to in under a decade) and we both have blue eyes. The only difference now is our hair colour – I am still blonde (with a few helpful highlights to make it more vibrant) with long hair almost to my elbows, but Kim has gone for a chocolaty brown long bob. It really suits her and I can't imagine how much courage it must have taken to get the chop. I'm too scared to do anything wild with my hair because there's no taking a style like that back in a hurry.

'I didn't realise my accent had changed that much,' I reply. 'I don't suppose I notice my own voice.'

'It definitely has,' she insists. 'You don't sound like a cockney geezer though, don't worry about that. You've just lost your Yorkshire charm.'

Kim gives me a sympathetic smile, as though she feels sorry for me for losing part of my identity. My regional accent made it hard for people in London to understand me, so it had felt right to gravitate towards something that sounded a little more universal.

'I can't believe you're sitting here in front of me,' Kim says, hugging me again. 'I see bits on Facebook and always tell myself we need to find a way to meet up, but you seem so busy. How have you been?'

I look down at my leg.

'I've been better,' I joke. 'Other than the leg, things are good. I have a nice place in the city, I love my job, I have a boyfriend. What about you?'

'Well, I'm a nurse, you'll be relieved to hear,' she jokes. 'No boyfriend though, and I'm just living with my mum but, well, my dad has dementia, so it felt right to move back in and help out. My mum doesn't really want him going into a home.'

'Oh my gosh, Kim, that's awful. I'm so sorry,' I reply. 'I had no idea.'

'Yeah, I didn't think it would make the best status update,' she replies. 'Are you in the Marram Bay Facebook group?'

'I'm not,' I reply. 'Should I be?' I know Mum is part of the group but I've never seen the point in joining it myself.

'One of our neighbours shared a Just Giving page on there, raised nearly £5,000 so we could make the house more safe for him,' she replies.

'That's incredible. I'll have to join.'

'Otherwise it's just missing cats, *found* cats, people complaining about the length of other people's grass, blah, blah, blah – probably not worth joining.'

I laugh, but then all at once my thoughts jump back to my leg, as a pain shoots from the break right up into my thigh.

'So,' I say, nodding towards my leg.

'Oh, right, yes,' she babbles. 'The real reason you're here. Well, I think perhaps you need to see the doctor, so I'm going to go and get him.'

'Oh gosh, is it bad?' I reply. 'Is it a DVT?'

'No, it's nothing bad,' Kim quickly insists. 'I just . . . I really think you should *see* the doctor.'

Kim gives me a wink, which I find confusing.

'Do you remember Will Coleman from school?' she asks.

'I do,' I reply.

Will Coleman was a quiet, nerdy kid. He was quite chubby (which is apparently the worst thing you can be in the eyes of your fellow fifteen-year-olds) and massively into Dungeons and Dragons (which also does not make you all that popular amongst your peers). I liked him though, because he was funny and he always seemed to be genuinely interested in what girls had to say, rather than just trying to grab their boobs while they shared a cigarette behind the IT building.

Kim wiggles her eyebrows and leaves me in the examination room on my own. It's nice to see that she hasn't changed much;

she's still the same fun-loving, kind of kooky girl I grew up with – except now she's a grown-up and doing a job that changes the world. Thinking about what her life is like makes me feel like a big woman-child. Well, I'm not exactly a grown-up, living in my flat, relying on cleaners and restaurants to keep me alive, and my job isn't exactly changing the world. All I do is make sure that footballers get dates with girls who aren't going to try and extort money out of them over an ill-advised (usually poorly executed) photo of their genitals.

I examine the posters on the walls, all dishing the gory details of a variety of diseases and medical conditions. As I read the symptoms for various lists, I check a few of them off. Tired – yes (but I've always slept less than most). Losing weight – yes (but I have been on a diet to try and look better in my bridesmaid dress, because Gia looks like a Victoria's Secret model). Aches and pains – yes (then again, I did fall flat on my face a matter of days ago).

The posters amuse me, in a weird way. It's a bit like, while you are here and unwell, have you considered these illnesses? It reminds me a lot of the 'customers also bought' bit on Amazon.

I'm going to stop reading them. I've already got a broken leg, I don't need to find out I've got psoriasis too. Not today.

'OK, the doctor will see you now,' Kim sings and she enters the room. 'Lola, this is Dr Will.'

It takes me the longest thirty seconds of my life to realise that the man standing in front of me is chubby, dorky Will Coleman from school. Except he isn't chubby *or* dorky anymore. He's kind of dishy now. He's tall and lean with neat, dirty blond hair. He's wearing black trousers and a tight, white shirt with the sleeves partially rolled up. Of course he's got a stethoscope hanging around his neck, making him look like a fake sexy doctor from the cover of a Mills & Boon novel.

'Lola James,' he blurts out.

From the look on his face, it doesn't seem like Kim told him I was the patient. He looks like he's seen a ghost. I feel sort of like I've seen a ghost . . . just a surprisingly sexy one.

'Hi,' I say.

'It's been years,' he says. 'How are you?'

I nod down at my leg again.

'Oh, God, right, yes,' he babbles. 'The broken leg.'

'Here's a letter they gave her at the fracture clinic in London,' Kim tells him. 'I've actually got to go do something else but, Lola, you're in very safe hands now.'

I watch Kim leave through the door behind Dr Will's back. Out of his line of sight, she gives me another wink. Now I understand exactly what she meant before. I don't need to see a doctor about my leg, I just need to see *this* doctor – literally just cast my eyes over him and see what kind of man he's grown into.

'OK, let's take a look,' he says.

I feel a strange little tingle as he lightly touches my toes.

'Well, I'm sure Kim was just being vigilant, but everything looks as expected to me – I'd be hesitant to say it looks fine, because, you know, it's broken in half, but yes, it looks as I'd expect.'

'That's a relief,' I reply. 'Good to know it's all as it should be, even if it sucks.'

'How are you coping?' he asks.

'Well, I've had to move back in with my mum and dad, and that's as fun as it sounds, and I'm stuck on my butt with nothing to do . . .' I soften a little. 'But my parents are being a huge help, and I don't think I'd be coping without them.'

'You're never too old to be looked after by your mum,' he tells me.

'That's true,' I reply. 'I definitely think there's an age limit on being washed though.'

Will laughs.

'Perhaps,' he says. 'OK, well . . .'

Will pulls a prescription pad from his pocket and writes on it. 'Your prescription,' he says, handing me the piece of paper. I notice it has a mobile number written on it. 'That's my mobile number. There are lots of things I could drop by with, to help you cope a little better, so if you're struggling just give me a ring.'

'Ah, damn, I thought it was more codeine,' I say with chuckle, to make sure he knows that I'm just kidding.

'I'm sure they've given you plenty,' he replies. 'Unless you're selling it on.'

'Well, you remember my mum,' I joke.

I'm sure he probably does remember my mum though. I think she probably scarred him for life. Will came over to help me with my biology homework once (not a euphemism) and he was curious about the lighthouse so I took him upstairs to look out. My mum caught us and thought we were up to no good, and politely asked Will to leave and not to come back – I say politely, but it had the low-key anger that bubbles inside an overprotective mother.

'I do indeed,' he replies. 'And, of course, I'm her doctor now.'

'Hmm, I'm not sure you're supposed to tell me that,' I reply – and if I didn't know better, I'd think I detected a flirtatious tone to my voice.

'Probably not,' he replies. 'But I'm also not supposed to keep a room full of patients waiting while I'm in here dealing with a fake emergency.'

We exchange smiles.

'Call me if you need me, OK?' he says.

'I will do, thank you.'

Once Dr Will has gone back to work, I feel an enormous grin spread across my face. Wow, I can't believe that's Will! He looks so different. I mean, of course he does, the last time I saw him he was a teenage boy and now he's a man, but he looks *really* different. Kim's hair looked very different, but she still looked like Kim. I can't believe Will grew up to be a hot doctor – I'll bet everyone who bullied him at school (especially the ones who still live locally) are kicking themselves now.

One thing I can't help but think though, is that if I don't call Will and hang out with him more while I'm here, I'll be kicking myself – well, I would be if it were physically possible.

Chapter 7

Day three stuck on my arse, trapped in the little lighthouse on Marram Bay: I'm going mad.

So apparently, at the moment, the town hall is undergoing some major refurbishments, so my mum and dad have kindly offered the B & B function room as a space for those who usually rely on the town hall for their events.

Ordinarily I would say this was a great thing. Great for the community, great for business, great for raising the profile of the B & B . . . It isn't great for me though. From where I'm (stuck) sitting, all I can hear is the local line dancing group practising. It's a group of mostly retired women, all of whom can move a lot better than I can right now. They're having fun, which is all that matters, but they're practising the same song on repeat. If I hear 'Elvira' by The Oak Ridge Boys one more time, I'm going to lose my mind.

Bored out of my mind, uncomfortable, and hungry, I decide to venture into the B & B and see if I can get something to eat. My dad is out running errands and my mum is upstairs helping the ladies who clean the rooms and change the beds – my mum is such a perfectionist, and it doesn't matter to her whether there are employees who are paid to do these jobs;

she likes to make sure they are done right, and she's happy to get her hands dirty. It's one of the reasons I look up to my mum, but today it's the reason I don't have a sandwich in my hand, and what else do I have to live for right now? I want a sandwich of white bread, a little butter and a full packet of salt and vinegar crisps crushed up. A crisp sandwich might not be very refined, but it's what I want. It's the thing that's going to make me feel better today. It's also only available in the B & B restaurant kitchen, which is far enough away from the function room that I won't be able to hear the line dancing crowd, the rhythmic pounding of their feet on the floor, the excitable woos, and that bloody song that I must have heard five times today already.

I'm getting a little better at wheeling myself around. I've never had much upper arm strength, but my dad reckons that will change after several weeks in this thing, and then even more on crutches, when I'm eventually allowed.

It's a little tight, wheeling myself through the doorway into the kitchen, but staff will be between meals so I'm not likely to get in anyone's way at least, and someone will have some time to very kindly make me some lunch.

'Get out,' Vince says the second he claps eyes on me.

I frown at him. Vince is a short, bald man, but what he lacks in height he makes up for in Gordon Ramsay style aggression.

'It's health and safety,' he insists, wildly gesturing towards the door with his hands. 'You'll be under our feet.'

I glance over at Robbie, the new assistant chef. He's a tall, skinny twenty-something with his longish brown hair pulled into a man bun on the back of his head. He rolls his eyes behind Vince's back, which makes me feel a bit like I'm getting a telling-off.

'I'm not sticking around,' I quickly explain. 'I'm just hungry and my parents are busy. I hoped I could order some lunch.'

Vince looks down at my leg sympathetically and visibly softens. 'What can I get you?' he says, crouching down in front of me.

45

'I won't take up too much of your time,' I reply gratefully. 'I just want a salt and vinegar crisp sandwich.'

Vince's eyes widen and he pulls himself to his feet. 'Absolutely not,' he insists. 'I did not train in Paris, under Chef Grégoire Trémaux, so that I could spend my day making . . . crisp sandwiches.'

Just saying the words 'crisp sandwich' clearly leaves a horrible taste in his mouth.

'But . . .' I protest.

'No, absolutely not, I will make you something that is worthy of my talent or I will let you starve,' he insists.

Bloody hell, why do chefs have to be so dramatic?

'I'll make it,' Robbie offers. 'OK?'

'Of course you will,' Vince replies. 'I'm going for a cigarette. There better not be so much as a sprinkling of salt on that worktop when I get back.'

On that note Vince storms off, leaving me alone with Robbie, my saviour, the man who is going to make all my sandwich dreams come true.

'He seems in a good mood,' I say sarcastically. 'Has he won the lottery or something?'

Robbie just laughs. 'It's comforting, to see him talk that way to everyone,' he tells me. 'I thought it was just me he hated.'

'How are you finding the job?' I ask.

'I love the work,' he replies. 'It's a stressful environment though. Vince likes things the way he likes them, but sometimes he inexplicably likes them the other way. He doesn't tell you though, you're just supposed to know.'

I laugh. 'Yeah, he's definitely the most highly strung chef we've had,' I reply.

'You must be Lola then,' he says as he gathers ingredients to fix my sandwich. 'The bosses' daughter.'

'Is it the family resemblance?' I ask.

'No, it's the broken leg,' he replies. 'I'd heard you were coming to stay for a bit. Until you're . . .' His voice trails off.

'It's OK,' I assure him. 'You can say "back on your feet". Everyone else keeps saying it.'

I watch a wave of relaxation spread through Robbie's body. Vince must have him so on edge. I can't imagine trying to do my job under pressure like that, constantly walking on eggshells – I'd imagine because Vince has been chucking eggs around in temper.

'I didn't want to sound like I was taking the mick,' he replies.

'Are you a local?' I ask.

'I lived here until I was ten, then I moved away with my mum, then I wound up working in the kitchens on a few cruise ships.'

'That sounds fancy,' I say.

'Believe me, it wasn't,' he replies. 'It's fancy for the guests, it's *Titanic* third-class conditions for the staff.'

'Is Vince better or worse?' I ask.

'That's like asking me which one of my legs I'd rather break,' he replies absent-mindedly. 'Sorry, sorry, that wasn't a joke either.'

'It's fine,' I insist. 'Or at least it is until you pass me that sandwich. Once I secure some food, I'm never speaking to you again.'

He laughs. Robbie cuts my sandwich diagonally before garnishing my plate with a small salad and a few extra crisps.

'That looks amazing,' I reply as he places it down in front of me.

It's so great, to have my appetite back. It's one of those things that you don't realise you'll miss until it's gone. When I was trying to shave a couple of inches off my hips so I didn't look like a disproportionally stuffed sausage in my bridesmaid dress, I would've probably given anything to curb my appetite and stop me craving Chinese food or red velvet cake or a simple crisp sandwich, but when my appetite was taken from me after my accident all I wanted to do was eat and I just couldn't face it.

I give the sandwich an unladylike squash with my hands to make sure the crisps are as fragmented as possible, because that's the way to do it. I squash it so hard I leave fingerprints in the soft white bread before lifting the almost paper-thin triangle to my mouth. I taste it and it's everything I hoped it would be and

47

more. I feel like I'm eating for the first time in years, even if it has only been a few days that I've been off my food.

'Is that OK?' he asks me.

'It might be the best sandwich I've ever had,' I reply, and while it might just be because I'm so happy to have my appetite back, I actually think I might be telling the truth. 'So, what made you give up a life at sea to come here and be beaten and scrambled by old Vince?'

'You know what Hope Island is like,' he replies with a shrug. 'It just drags you back. You know what they say, people go elsewhere, but they never leave. Their heart is here and at some point they have to come back for it. They can't live without it.'

'Well, I live in London,' I point out. 'And nothing is dragging me back here.'

Robbie raises his eyebrows and gives me a smug smile. It takes me a moment to realise what he's getting at.

'Oh, OK, I know what you're thinking,' I start, a little defensively. 'I do realise that I am technically back living here now, but it's only temporary, only while my leg is broken – only six weeks, tops.'

'You think breaking your leg was an accident?' he asks.

'Are you suggesting . . .' I pause, to gather my words. I'm about to say something so stupid I can hardly even bring myself to do it. 'Are you suggesting that the island broke my leg? Of course it was an accident – I know it was an accident because it happened to me. I fell on the . . .'

As I notice Robbie's serious expression melt into something more playful, I realise he's winding me up.

'Oh, hilarious,' I reply. 'Very good. If this sandwich wasn't so good I'd have my parents fire you.'

I'm kidding, of course, but he doesn't even entertain for a second that I might be serious.

'Lola, there you are,' my mum says as she bursts into the kitchen. 'I've been looking all over for you.'

'Well, you know I couldn't have got far,' I remind her.

'Well, your Auntie Val is here to see you and . . . What is that?' she asks, nodding towards my sandwich.

'It's a sandwich, Mum,' I reply.

'Bread?' she says.

'Yes, that's what sandwiches are made of,' I confirm.

'That's not what you need,' she insists.

'You literally made me five slices of toast for my breakfast my first day here,' I remind her.

I hear Robbie sniggering. He quickly tries to wipe the smile off his face. My mum is, after all, his boss.

'By the time I removed the eyes and the mouth it was more like three slices,' she says, like it's the most normal thing in the world. 'Where's Vince? You could have had him make you anything, something helpful, like with carrots in.'

'Carrots?' I ask, instantly wishing I hadn't.

'Yes, isn't carotene good for broken bones? I thought everyone knew that.'

'I've never heard that,' I tell her.

'Well, what am I thinking of?' she asks, a little frustrated.

'Calcium?'

'Anyway,' she says, changing the subject as she grabs the handles of my wheelchair to take me into the other room. I quickly grab my sandwich, so that I can bring it with me. 'Auntie Val is waiting.'

'Thanks for the sandwich,' I call to Robbie as my mum wheels me away.

'You're welcome,' I just about hear him call back.

'He's single, you know,' my mum whispers into my ear as she pushes my chair from behind.

I wasn't expecting to hear her voice so close to my ear. It makes me jump.

'Bloody hell, Mum,' I say. 'And anyway, I have a boyfriend.'

'Oh, yes, the one I'm not allowed to meet,' she pointlessly reminds me. 'The one who you haven't heard from.'

'Erm, I have heard from him,' I reply.

I've had a few texts from Patrick, which has made me feel a little better. He explained that he is really busy with work, and without me prompting him he mentioned that he'd hired a cleaner to take care of his flat while he's away/busy/I'm not there to help out with jobs. I think being stuck up here is messing with my head and making me paranoid. Well, I hope that's all it is. For someone who is supposed to be a relationship expert, I feel uncomfortably confused about my own right now.

One thing I'm absolutely not imagining though, are the photos of my friendship circle on Instagram, showing everyone out partying together, having a lovely time. So much for Gia insisting she wanted a few weeks of married bonding time with her husband or whatever line it was she fed me. She just didn't want to look after me. I suppose at least Patrick has work, maybe, I don't know. I'm trying to give him the benefit of the doubt but I keep feeling like maybe he doesn't care as much as he should either.

One person who does care, more than I'd like, is my mum.

'There's my little showgirl,' my auntie greets me.

Auntie Val has referred to me as showgirl for as long as I can remember, which I'm sure is a weird thing to call a child, but it's an obvious riff on my name so I can let it slide.

'Hi, Auntie Val,' I say. 'How are you?'

'I'm doing better than you, love,' she points out. 'Although your mum was just trying to convince me to join the biddies in the line dancing room.'

'I just thought it might be a more age-appropriate activity,' my mum says.

My Auntie Val is my mum's younger sister, although not by much. She's nearing the end of her fifties but you'd never guess if you spent a little time with her. She certainly doesn't look or dress her age, with her peroxide blonde hair and her trendy high-street clothes that she travels all the way to Leeds to buy. Otherwise Val is in great shape (she loves her yoga) and I suppose without the

50

stress of a family or a man in her life, she dedicates her time to looking after number one, which I really respect her for. Lots of people need an other half to feel whole, but not my Auntie Val. Ever since she and my Uncle Robert broke up, she's either been happily single or just casually dating.

'A more age-appropriate activity than what?' I ask.

'She's . . .' my mum lowers her voice. 'She's trying to boink the roofer.'

'Boink the roofer,' I can't help but repeat back.

'I am a vibrant woman in my sexual prime,' Val insists. 'And Ben is a single young man who just so happens to be doing my waterproofing.'

'Is that what the kids are calling it?' I joke.

'I haven't done it yet,' Val insists. 'But Auntie has needs, and things didn't work out with Karl.'

'The man who fitted her new kitchen,' my mum tells me with an uncomfortable yet satisfied I-told-her-so kind of tone. 'I did warn her not to boink where she eats.'

I'm not really sure whether my mum means she advised my auntie not to sleep with the people working on her house renovations, or whether she literally just warned her not to have sex in her kitchen. Either way I wish she would stop using the word *boink*.

'If you're looking for someone to spend some time with, why don't you let me help you?' I suggest. 'I literally mean to spend time with though – I'm not helping my auntie find hook-ups.'

'Really?' she replies.

'Yeah, why not?' I say. 'I'm bored, I'm stuck on my arse – and matchmaking is my job. You might not have been on *Love Island* but I'm sure the same rules apply for finding love for the general public.'

'Oh, Lola, you always were my favourite niece,' she insists, gently hugging me.

'I'm your only niece,' I point out.

Well, I am bored out of my mind, so I may as well help my auntie out. Just because my own love life seems like it's a bit of a mess, doesn't mean I'm not still amazing at putting other people together.

Chapter 8

I am feeling the best I have felt in days and it's all thanks to love. Well, love and maybe having my appetite back. Oh, and I suppose the codeine is probably helping quite a lot too, but really it's mostly love.

I had a long chat with my Auntie Val, over multiple cups of tea and far too many custard creams, about how she can attract and potentially keep men around for longer. With my mum giving us some peace and quiet to get on with work (not sure if she meant me or her) we had a natter about the ins and outs of my auntie's love life. Sure, at first it seemed a little bit odd, but as soon as I put my working head on, that's when we started making progress.

Understandably, since my auntie and uncle broke up (which it turns out was down to infidelity on his part – no pun intended) her man-eating ways are really just a front. Of course she wants to someone to spend her time with and of course she doesn't want to grow old alone, but she's scared about getting hurt again and so she puts up this tough front. Men being men, they don't see this as a front, they just see my auntie as a woman out to have a good time with them, not a long time with them. Once we realised this (it's amazing how much a sympathetic ear and a packet of biscuits can draw from a person; I might retrain as a therapist) it was easy to offer advice to my auntie from there. All she needed to do was change her approach – not the way she dresses or her young personality, but just the way she interacts with men in the initial stages.

It might not be immediately obvious to women that if you go in all guns blazing, spilling with sexual innuendo and blatantly flirtatious touches of their arm, you might be giving men the wrong end of the stick. We're brought up to be under the impression that men need things spelling out for them, that they're visual and overly sexual, and that giving up the goods is the only real way to show them that you're interested but that's just not true. I explained to my auntie that if a man approached her in the street and told her she had 'nice tits' she'd probably slap him, or at least assume he just wanted to sleep with her, and that's a fair assessment. Sure, you could do it, but you wouldn't hop into bed thinking something long term was going to come out of it, would you? This works the same both ways. If you come on too sexually strong with a man, sure, he'll probably be into it, but he might not necessarily assume you want anything more than sex from him – and he probably won't mind that, but he also won't call, and he won't even think that you expect him to call.

Men don't need a blatant sexual advance to know you're interested; they need a hint, a suggestion, something that starts the chase in a way that makes them not even all that sure if you're interested at all. Give a man a come on and he will have sex with you for a day, but give a man the mere suggestion of something he has to work for and he will pull out all the stops to try and spend his life with you.

Armed with this knowledge, my auntie went home and started the groundwork with her roofer. I wasn't expecting her to text me back by tonight, saying he had asked her out on a date (or 'a proper date-date with dinner and drinks and dancing' as she relayed it to me) but he has, much to her delight and much to my mum's too. I'm not sure she's ever really understood my job. I always wondered if she thought I was just some kind of overpaid madam, but today she saw me in action and she seems weirdly proud.

In other news, Patrick called. We had a long chat and everything was fine. He was home and knackered after his business trip, so it must have been pretty full-on. I feel guilty, for feeling the way I did, thinking he should have been checking up on me every few minutes. The poor man had work and he knew I was in safe hands here.

He sounded exhausted, yawning every other sentence, so I told him to get to bed and that we'd talk tomorrow. The last thing he said to me, before we said goodnight, was that we would go on a proper holiday when I was back on my feet, as a treat for me, and a break from work for him. This really lifted my mood but it's also given me something to do for the past hour, hunting for somewhere for us to go, checking the calendar for important dates.

I've found a gorgeous little island, just off the coast of Italy, which looks like the most gloriously romantic, luxurious destination – perfect for what we want, but as I check the calendar for work commitments, birthdays and friends' weddings, I realise the most important thing I am forgetting to check.

I fire up my period tracking app. I hate that I have to do this, it seems so unfair, but I also know that I don't want to go somewhere hot for two weeks and spend most of the time in big knickers, sobbing over a hot water bottle. A quick scan over the forthcoming months shows me when I'm free to go, but something doesn't seem right. I scroll back to the current date and realise something I had no idea about . . .

I'm late. I should've had my period days ago. I mean, it's not that I want it, it's the last thing I need on my plate right now, but even so . . . if it's late, it must be for a reason, right? And there's only one reason I can think of . . .

Chapter 9

If you think physical pain is the worst thing to contend with when you're trying to sleep, you've obviously never tried mental torment.

When I started worrying that I might be pregnant last night, the first thing I did was panic. This was in no way planned and it is absolutely not the right time. I know I'm in my early thirties, but I am sure I still have plenty of time for this stuff, right? It's not like it's now or never . . . right?

As my rational thoughts kicked in, I decided that it might help to call Patrick and talk to him about it. Not just because he's involved, but because he's my boyfriend. I just knew that talking things through with him would make me feel better.

But he didn't answer.

I felt guilty, calling him when I knew how tired he was, and that he'd probably been asleep for a couple of hours, but when he didn't answer his mobile I felt my stress levels creeping up again so I called his landline without a second thought.

No answer though, not from him or a random woman.

So I tried my best to sleep but I had a terrible night, and by the time it turned morning it was just a matter of counting down the minutes, holding off for as long as possible to call him without waking him up too early.

When I did call, his mobile went straight to answerphone which was odd. Then he didn't answer his landline, which worried me. By the time I'd called his office and his secretary had told me that he wasn't in work yet – but he's always in work at this time – I was really concerned.

Thanks to my overactive imagination I am already panicking about being a single mum, which is definitely jumping to a few more conclusions than I ought to. I'm sure he's fine; I'll just feel better when I hear from him.

I don't want to be that girl, the one who seems like she's keeping tabs on her man, but I'm legitimately worried about him. What if something has happened to him? What if he needs help?

Patrick has two best friends: Brandon and Evan. The three of them – or the three amigos as they call themselves – all work together, all wear the same suits and the same watches. I doubt they will be impressed with me calling them, checking up on Patrick, but if it makes me feel less worried then it will be worth a few seconds of a judgey man thinking I'm a possessive woman.

I try Brandon first but he doesn't pick up, which only fuels my (it turns out, quite pessimistic) imagination. Then I try Evan and every ring feels like it takes a minute. Eventually he answers.

'Hello.'

'Oh, Evan, hi, it's Lola,' I babble. 'I was just a bit worried about Patrick because I tried to call him last night, then this morning, and he's not answering any of his phones and he's not at work.'

I try not to sound overly concerned, which potentially makes me seem more like a crazy girlfriend than just an overly anxious human concerned about another human they care about.

'Oh, that might be my fault, sorry,' he explains. 'I called him up last night, asked him to come over and have a drink with me and then he crashed here. He left not too long ago, to go to work. I'm sure you'll hear from him soon.'

I exhale a tornado of relief. 'Oh, well, that's OK then,' I say. 'Are you doing OK?'

It only feels right, to ask him how he is. It feels polite.

'Yeah, I'm good,' he says. 'But I need to get ready for work.'

'OK, well, thanks for putting my mind at rest,' I reply.

He doesn't waste any time asking me how my leg is – no one from home does. It's strange, isn't it, how I refer to both London and Marram Bay as home? Whichever one I am in, I suppose the other one just feels more like home.

So I suppose now all I need to do is wait for Patrick to get to work, so that he can return my call and I can tell him that I'm late and a bit worried about it.

My phone rings almost immediately, which makes me smile – it's a smile of relief as well as a little laugh at myself for being so ridiculous. Of course he's fine.

It isn't Patrick though, it's Brandon. I suppose he's just returning my call. I suppose I have to answer it and tell him why I called, which is probably only going to make me seem weirder.

'Hello, Brandon,' I answer.

'Hey, Lola, everything OK?' he asks.

'Yes, sorry for calling,' I start. 'I'd tried to call Patrick a couple of times last night and at work this morning, but couldn't get in touch with him . . .'

'Oh, yeah, sorry about that,' he starts.

I'm about to say it's no big deal that he didn't answer my call, and tell him that Evan told me he stayed there last night, but Brandon keeps talking.

'We went out for a few late-night beers and it turned into a bit of a school-night session,' he explains. 'He slept at mine, headed straight to work from here.'

I quickly thank him and hang up.

Men have an interesting relationship with loyalty, don't they? They have a ton of it, or none of it, depending on the circumstances. When it comes to their friends, men are fiercely loyal. I mean, look at Evan and Brandon, both so quick to offer up an alibi for their friend without a second thought. But Patrick, who spent our call yawning and insisting he was going to bed, is obviously not where he said he was going to be. He's clearly lied to me. Zero loyalty to me, but he'd probably die for Evan or Brandon.

Am I really that unimportant to Patrick that the second I am out of the picture he just pretends I don't exist and gets on with his life? I know that he's selfish and a little funny about commitment but I figured we all have our flaws, and if Patrick needed some time to work things out then I was happy to give him that.

Wherever he was last night, he absolutely wasn't at home like he said he was, and I don't care if he was out with one of his mates (and the other lied to cover for him just in case) or if this alleged cleaning lady was the one he was out with. The bottom line is that he's keeping things from me, he doesn't seem to care about the fact I have a broken leg, he had no interest in looking after me – he wheeled me into a doorframe, for crying out loud. I don't need a man like that in my life so balls to him. I'd rather be a single mum than raise a child with a crap dad.

I grab my phone and punch out an angry message to Patrick. I tell him that I know what he's up to, that things are over, and that I never want to hear from him again. A text is all he deserves – well, it sounds like he's moved on without even texting me. Who knows if he hadn't done so before I broke my leg? Maybe he isn't always working, maybe he just says he is. Forget him, I'm better off without him. I feel bizarrely strong and smug, but then I remember my late period and start worrying again.

I need to take a test, obviously. I can't just do nothing, I'll drive myself crazy, wondering, catastrophising, allowing my brain to run every possible scenario before assuming that the worst possible one is the most likely.

I'm not sure how, exactly, I'll manage to take a test. I can't even put my own underwear on at the moment, so I have no idea how I'm going to get to a shop and actually buy one . . .

I rack my brains, searching for a little something left over from my teenage years. Well, when you grow up on an island as small as Hope Island, in a tightknit community like Marram Bay, where everyone knows everything about everyone, it's hard to get away with things. As a teenager I had to be creative, although admittedly most of my tactics were focused around bending the truth. I'm just glad the Marram Bay Facebook group didn't exist when I was a teen, because now it's even easier for everyone to be in everyone else's business, and information spreads even faster than it did by mouth, like in the good old days.

Every time my mum would call me, she would have some gossip for me, courtesy of the Marram Bay Facebook group – so-and-so being shamed for not keeping their lawn at the right length, rumours about Hollywood actors walking around like 'Freddie someone' or 'thingy Hardy' (which was how my mum told it at the time), or even full-blown conspiracies to keep certain businesses out of town if the locals didn't think they were a good fit.

I guess that's what I'll do today, I'll tell a little white lie, to get my mum to take me to a shop so that I can buy one myself. I'll just need to think of a good reason and then find a way to shake my mum off for a couple of minutes . . .

'Morning, love,' my mum says.

'Morning, Mum,' I reply as I gear up to tell my fib. 'I was wondering if we might be able to pop to the shops today. I wanted to get a few things.'

'Oh, love, I can get you anything you need. Don't be dragging yourself out when you're in such agony. Just make me a list, I'll get right to it. I need to pop out anyway.'

Curse my helpful, considerate and loving mother. Just this once, I could do without the comprehensive mum treatment. I suppose there are worse things to have than an amazing mother, but that doesn't help me get a pregnancy test. I am absolutely not asking her to pick one up for me because that comprehensive mum treatment will also include helping me with the test and waiting for the results with me while we discuss honouring grandma Lillian by naming the entirely hypothetical baby after her.

Come on, Lola, get creative. Slip back into your devious teenage mind-set, the one that made sure you never missed any cool parties you had been told you absolutely were not allowed to attend. In hindsight, that makes me sound like a nightmare, but I went to the parties my mum had forbidden me from attending, and I behaved appropriately. I never wound up injured or accidentally pregnant – nope, I've reserved such mistakes for my thirties, obviously.

'Actually, Mum,' I start, pausing for just a split second, hanging in that brief moment where it occurs to me that this plan might not work, that it might somehow backfire. 'I didn't want to worry you, but my leg feels like it's burning up again – worse than the other day. The doctor said I had to go back, if it got any worse, so . . . if you could just drop me off maybe?'

I internally congratulate myself on a flawless plan. I can have my mum drop me at the doctor's but then, while she goes off to do her shopping, I can nip into the pharmacy, buy a pregnancy test – if that doesn't take long, I could maybe see about nipping into the loos, taking the test there so that I don't have to worry about trying to dispose of the packaging at home. Now my plan really is foolproof.

My mum feels my forehead with the back of her hand in the way that mums do.

'Hmm,' she says. 'That is concerning. You'd do right to get it checked out.'

Relief washes over me, as I realise it's going to work.

'But we can't mess around,' she insists. 'I'm going to call Dr Will, ask him to see you as soon as possible. None of this dropping in and waiting to be seen.'

Shit.

'No, Mum, honestly, don't take appointments from anyone else. I'm happy to just drop in, show it to Kim, see what she thinks . . .'

'Nonsense,' my mum replies. 'This is important, Lola, we can't take chances with your health.'

'Mum, really, it's—'

'I'll go call now,' she cuts me off. 'And I'm making sure you get sorted this time.'

Double shit.

Chapter 10

If my mum were to repeat her industry standard back of the hand on the forehead temperature check now, she would diagnose me with *something*, because I am burning up, roasting hot, sweating buckets. It's not because there is anything wrong with me though, nothing other than a bad case of 'how the hell am I going to get myself out of this one?'

My lovely mum has actually brought me into the doctor's waiting room and sat down with me. She is waiting with me. Last time she dropped me off but then popped into the shop next door, but today, concerned parent that she is, she is sitting with me, waiting, reassuring me. The fact that she is so wonderful only makes me feel even worse about lying to her. I guess I was much better at this stuff when I was a teenager.

I rack my brains for a solution. I could make it brief, ask a couple of questions about my leg, or ask for the help he offered me, to make life easier while I'm in plaster . . . just a quick in and out. That way I won't waste any of his time. And, who knows, if Kim is around, maybe I can confide in her, ask her to grab me a test . . . I'd rather not tell anyone, especially not Kim, if I'm being honest. She's my oldest friend, but we aren't all that close anymore, and it was only yesterday I was telling her how amazing my life was, and the tables have very much turned today.

'Lola James,' the receptionist calls out. 'The doctor will see you now.'

She's no sooner said it than Dr Will comes rushing out into the waiting room.

'I momentarily forgot you were in a wheelchair,' he says. 'I thought I'd better come out and help.'

A concerned old lady looks up from her copy of *Yorkshire* magazine.

'Don't worry, Mrs Vickers, I usually have a fantastic memory,' he reassures her.

She seems placated by his words, or perhaps it's his charming demeanour. He seems to boast a far more attractive bedside manner than any doctor I've ever seen before.

'Do you want me to come in with you?' my mum asks.

'No, it's OK,' I reply a little too quickly. 'Thanks, though.'

Dr Will wheels me into his office, parking me up in front of his chair before taking a seat in front of me. He sits forward in his seat, ready to get down to business.

'So, your mum said you were having some DVT symptoms again,' he says, getting straight to the point.

Of course she told him the lie I told her. I swear, if I didn't know better, I'd think she had seen straight through my lie and was trying to teach me a lesson. I suppose this is what you get, when you lie. Consider the lesson learned, whether it was intended or not.

'Erm . . .' I start, but I can't get anything else out. I have no idea what to say.

'Let's take a look,' he says, jumping back to his feet.

As he begins to examine my leg, he looks puzzled. Obviously because there are no signs of anything at all, other than, you know, the bone still being broken.

'Hmm . . .' he says thoughtfully. 'Do you want to tell me about

64

your symptoms?'

'It's actually feeling much better now,' I insist. 'I'm really sorry if I've wasted your time. I'm sure it's fine.'

Will sits back down.

'There's no rush,' he insists. 'There is only one person in the waiting room and she's thirty minutes early. I think she likes to come and read the magazines, chat with the receptionist. She's probably talking your mum's ear off and having a whale of a time.'

I smile at him. 'I think my mum just got the wrong end of the stick,' I tell him. 'And she rushed me down here.'

'I didn't realise you could rush anyone with a broken leg anywhere,' he says with a knowing smile. 'Is there anything you want to talk about? Everything remains between us, obviously.'

I feel like he's looking straight through me. 'I . . . I need to take a pregnancy test,' I admit.

'Oh,' he replies. 'So your leg is fine?'

'Yes,' I admit sheepishly. 'I was just trying to get my mum to drive me here, so that I could buy a test . . . I didn't realise she'd ring you and make me an appointment and tell you what I'd told her. I'm really sorry.'

'Hey, you have nothing to apologise for,' he insists. 'You're in a very difficult position. How about we do a test now?'

'That would be great, thank you,' I reply.

I have no idea what the result will be, but I feel a little better already, just for having someone to talk to, to help me out without judgement.

After taking the test it isn't long before we're back in our seats, waiting for the result.

'Thank you for this,' I say. 'I haven't had anyone else to talk to about it. I, erm, broke up with my boyfriend this morning.'

'Well, that isn't ideal timing, is it?' he replies sympathetically.

'And no need to thank me, I'm just doing my job. Had you been together a long time?'

'Nine months,' I say, laughing to myself. It takes nine months to grow a baby, and nine months to see someone's true colours apparently. 'I thought things were great but, to be honest, it's easy to see how rubbish things were now. I mean, he didn't even want to look after me when I broke my leg – and I don't think he was being honest with me so . . . so . . . balls to him.'

'That's a refreshing attitude to hear,' Will points out. 'A woman walking away from a bad relationship with a good attitude.'

'I guess I have bigger problems,' I reply. 'Any news?'

Will glances at his watch. After what feels like minutes, but is probably only seconds, he looks at the test.

'It's negative,' he says.

'Oh, OK,' I reply. 'Thanks.'

'Is that what you wanted to see?' he asks.

'Well, yes, right? I mean, I'm single . . . so . . . I mean, I know single people have babies all the time, but it's easier to do it with another person, right? And when your leg isn't broken and . . .'

'It's OK, I totally understand. But you have plenty of time to do it in the future, and on your own terms, too.'

'Do I?' I ask, suddenly aware of the fact that, if I'm not pregnant, then my usually like-clockwork period hasn't turned up for some other reason. 'Might something be wrong with me, if I'm late?'

'Have you been having any other issues?' he asks.

I shake my head, a little embarrassed. I really hadn't imagined myself getting into this with him.

'Have you been exercising a lot, dieting, under a lot of stress?'

'Yes,' I reply.

'Which one?'

'All of them,' I say. 'I was a bridesmaid for my bridezilla best friend's wedding. I had a lot to do and a dress to fit into.'

'Well, there you go,' he says. 'Often, things like weight loss and

66

stress can cause you to be a little late. It's nothing to worry about if it doesn't happen often. Was it a wonderful wedding at least?'

I laugh to myself before I reply.

'No, I broke my leg,' I reply.

'Oh,' Will replies, laughing too, but probably only because I am, rather than because he's a doctor who finds injuries hilarious.

'And then she wouldn't look after me either. That's how I ended up leaving London and having to come back home,' I reply. 'I'm a thirty-two-year-old with loads of friends and not one of them wanted to look after me. They were all too busy.'

'Well, that's the good thing about the north,' he replies with a smile. 'None of us have anything going on, which means we have plenty of time for interfering in other people's lives.'

'Yes, it has its pros and cons,' I reply.

'Well, with that in mind, how about I pop over and see you later, and I'll bring you those things I was telling you about, to make your life easier. We've got these things you can put over your cast, so that you can have a shower – best ones you can get.'

'That would be amazing, thank you,' I tell him.

'Back at the lighthouse, yes?'

'Back at the lighthouse,' I reply.

'Well, I might be allowed upstairs this time,' he says. 'To look out the window, I mean, obviously. Hopefully your mum won't kick me out.'

Given all the information I have, I am absolutely certain she wouldn't.

'OK, well, I'll see you later then?' I say.

'Yes, see you later,' he replies. 'Glad I could help.'

As Will wheels me back out to my mum, who is in fact chatting away with Will's next patient, I go over in my head how I feel about my news. It's for the best that I'm not pregnant, even if it is something I want to do eventually, and maybe I am running out of time, but I don't want to do it alone, and I know that Patrick would have run a mile. I'll put it out of my head – Patrick too – and focus on now. At least I have tonight to look forward to, with Will popping over to see me. I know he's just being nice, and that I am on the rebound but, I don't know, there's just something about him now that gives me butterflies in my stomach.

We'll just have to wait and see, won't we?

Chapter 11

You know that horrible feeling when you are absolutely starving, but you have no idea what you want? Well, that's how I feel right now. One of the pros of having parents who employ a chef is always having someone on hand who can make you something amazing. Of course, for a while, the main con has been that that someone is Vince.

Now that Robbie is here though, and we seem to be getting on really well, I finally feel like I have someone who can make all my culinary dreams come true. He's currently preparing me something – a surprise, is what I asked for – in the kitchen, while they are between shifts and Vince is out on his break.

At first Robbie asked me what I wanted, but I couldn't make my mind up. He told me to give him two ingredients that I fancied and, after much mental deliberation, I landed on cheese and tomato.

He asked me if I wanted them in a sandwich – I said no. He asked if I fancied pasta – again, I didn't. I didn't know what I wanted, I just knew what I didn't want . . . so he's making me a surprise.

It's really nice, to have a young, fun person at the B & B, someone I can chat to and hang out with, who I'm not related to, who knows nothing about me.

It's nice to get to know Robbie a bit better too. It turns out he's worked all over the world over the last few years – mostly on cruise ships, but that still counts, especially because they were all five-star cruises.

Eventually he pops a plate down in front of me with small, Cornish-pasty-looking things on it. Well, the shape is similar at least, but the pastry looks completely different.

'What is it?' I ask.

'Your surprise,' he replies with a cheeky grin. 'Don't tell me you've lost your nerve. You said you'd eat anything I made.'

'I did say that, didn't I?' I respond with a laugh. 'I didn't think it would be something so mysterious though. Everything is hidden inside . . . it.'

'Well, why don't you try *it*,' he says encouragingly.

Feeling a little brave, but mostly just being polite, because I did ask for this, I take a bite.

'Oh my gosh,' I say through a mouthful. 'What is this?'

'Do you like it?' he asks nervously.

'I *love* it,' I can't help but stress.

It's like a sealed-up pizza . . . a bit like a calzone, but there's something different about it. The delicious dough, the rich tomato sauce, the melted cheese. I thought the crisp sandwich was good, but this is even better.

'Is that a fried pizza?' Vince asks, horrified, after walking into the kitchen and finding us together, digging into what I can confidently say is my new favourite food.

'It's panzarotti,' Robbie replies.

'It's a fried pizza,' Vince snaps back. 'Get it out of my kitchen please.'

'Yeah, actually, Robbie, if you could wheel me back to the family kitchen,' I say before lowering my voice. 'And pass me the plate, so I can take them with me.'

'Sure,' he replies sheepishly.

'Don't worry,' I reassure him. 'I'll make sure you're not in any

70

trouble with my parents. They did tell me to ask in the kitchen if I wanted anything when they weren't around.'

'Thanks,' he says. 'I don't think I'm Vince's cup of tea.'

'Well, you are absolutely mine,' I reply. I wonder if perhaps that sounds weird. 'Chef-wise.'

Yes, because that doesn't make it sound weird *at all*.

When we finally get to the kitchen, my mum and dad are sitting at the table.

'Look at you, Lady Muck,' my dad jokes. 'Getting chauffeured around by your own personal chef.'

'You have to try what Robbie has made,' I tell them, leaning forwards to place the plate down on the table.

'It looks interesting,' my dad says, straight in there with his hands to try some.

'What is it?' my mum asks.

'Bloody lovely,' my dad says. 'That's what it is.'

'They are panzarotti,' Robbie tells them. 'I learned how to make them in southern Italy – they're really popular over there.'

'Incredible,' my mum tells him. 'You made these?'

Robbie nods. My mum gives him a massive smile and he turns to head back to the B & B kitchen.

'I know we made the right decision, hiring him,' my mum says once Robbie has gone.

'Absolutely. You should have these on the menu,' I say. 'You can't get anything like this anywhere around here, right? You should have a chat with him about maybe modernising the menu. Vince is an amazing chef, without a doubt, but his stuck-up pub grub isn't the most . . . accessible menu. Stuff like this though, it would be loved by everyone. Even kids because, let's face it, Vince's kids' menu isn't very kid-friendly.'

'Do you think?' my dad replies.

'The "fish fingers" are deep-fried whitebait,' I reply. 'Not even I would eat those.'

'We usually stay out of these sorts of things,' my mum says. 'We just hire staff that we trust to do a good job and leave them to it.'

'And Vince absolutely does a good job,' I reply. 'But . . . maybe let Robbie come up with some specials? Maybe give people a taste of recipes he's learned on his travels. The locals who eat here will love trying something a bit different and the tourists who stay here will love it too.'

'That's a great idea,' my dad says cheerily. 'What were we doing without you, eh? If you ever get bored of matchmaking and fancy running a B & B . . .'

'About that,' my mum chimes in. 'Lola, I've offered your services tomorrow evening.'

'Oh?' I reply anxiously. I'm not all that sure my mum knows what my services are, so this could mean anything.

'Yes. So, as you know, the public space here is being used as a stand-in venue for the town hall at the moment,' she reminds me, but I don't need reminding. I still have 'Elvira' playing on a loop in my head thanks to the line dancing troupe.

'Yep.'

'Well, we're hosting a speed dating night here tomorrow, so I said you'd manage it. And no, this isn't a ploy to have you fall in love with a local. I know you have a boyfriend,' she quickly insists. 'But they needed someone to figure out the logistics and, well, that's your job, right?'

Speed dating is a little old-fashioned now, but I see the connection my mum made, and I am happy to help out. Well, she's helping me out so much and I am incredibly bored. It will be nice to have something to do!

I wonder whether now might be the right time to tell her that I broke up with Patrick, but I don't really want to get into the ins and outs of why right now.

'Oh, that's the doorbell,' my mum announces, just in case my dad and I wondered what the ringing sound was – the same chime we've had for as long as I can remember.

'It is indeed,' my dad replies.

'I suppose I'm supposed to go, am I?' she says.

'I mean, I would . . .' I say.

'I don't mean you, Lola, I mean your dad. He's getting so lazy in his . . .' Her voice tapers off.

'In his what?' my dad asks.

'Nothing,' my mum insists. The doorbell chimes again. 'I'd better go get that.'

'She was going to say "old age",' my dad tells me once we're alone. 'She says that now, but when she wants some furniture building or something she'll ask me like I'm twenty-one again.'

'Yeah, you don't seem old to me,' I reply. 'Maybe just lazy.'

I'm kidding, of course.

'Hey, who do you think did most of the painting when we had our makeover?' he quickly insists. 'Now slide me that plate of whatever that is.'

I laugh as I push the plate of panzarotti towards my dad.

'Look who I've found,' my mum interrupts. 'Dr Coleman.'

'Please, call me Will,' Will insists as he is ushered into the kitchen.

He's wearing his usual work attire – a blue shirt with a tie (today's has little French bulldogs all over it). He's also wearing a blue jacket and carrying an Apple Blossom Deli bag.

'Doing house calls, hmm?' my dad says suspiciously. 'What have you got there, lad?'

'Oh, it's not food,' he says quickly. 'Don't let the bag get your hopes up. I was just dropping off some things for Lola, to help with her leg.'

'Got any oxycodone in there?' he asks.

I feel my eyebrows shoot up.

'Paul James,' my mum tells him off with his name before turning to Will. 'So sorry, Doctor. He's been watching a lot of Netflix.'

It's nice to hear he's using that Netflix gift card I bought him for Christmas. I remind myself to ask my dad what box sets he's

73

into because binge-watching TV shows could make this forced life vacation go a lot faster.

'No opioids unfortunately,' Will tells him. 'There's a rather fetching plastic bag you can wear in the shower though.'

'Meh, Lola can have that,' my dad replies with a faux seriousness.

'Thank you so much, Will,' I say. 'My mum has just been wrapping my leg in bin liners.'

'Don't tell the doctor that,' my mum says quickly.

It's so weird how people in small towns – and especially older people – view doctors, isn't it? My mum thinks doctors are rock stars. They're the best kind of people, the most eligible bachelors, heroes without the capes. Jon Bon Jovi himself could check into the B & B – Superman could fly through the door – and she'd probably just remind them what time checkout is. But a doctor is a person to be adored, and you can see how my mum feels about Will by the look in her eye. It's very different to the look she had when we were younger, when she threw him out because she thought he was a horny teenager. I imagine, if she'd known he would grow up to be a doctor, she probably would've lit some candles.

'Doctor, forgive me for asking,' my mum starts, and I instantly worry. 'Are you seeing anyone at the moment?'

I cough and splutter, choking on my own breath. I cannot believe she just asked him that.

'Erm, well, no, I'm not,' he replies.

'Marvellous,' she replies. 'Well, Lola is hosting a speed dating night here tomorrow night. You should come!'

'Speed dating?' Will asks me with a laugh.

'Yep,' I reply. 'I've been railroaded into hosting it by my overly forward mother. But I was thinking of taking part.'

The words have left my lips before I've even thought them through. Why did I say that?

'I thought you said you had a boyfriend,' my mum replies suspiciously over her cup of tea. Well, I have been insisting to her how loved up I am until pretty much right now.

74

'Well, I'm single now,' I tell her.

I look over at Will, who is stifling a giggle.

'Well, double marvellous,' my mum says, still looking a little puzzled. 'I'm sure it's no trouble for a professional like you, to host and participate.'

'Are you a professional speed dater?' Will asks, amused.

'Not exactly,' I reply. 'But I'll tell you tomorrow – I need to save something for our date, don't I?'

My dad, clearly uncomfortable with me flirting in front of him, meaningfully clears his throat.

It's funny isn't it, how mums are always out to find their daughter an eligible bachelor to marry, but dads would be far happier if their little girls stayed single forever.

Wait, am I flirting with Will?! I mean, sure, he's handsome and he has his head screwed on right, but it's too soon to be flirting, right?

Tomorrow is definitely going to be interesting.

Chapter 12

Ding!

'Hello, miss, my name is Toby.'

'Can I give you some helpful advice, just to kick things off, Toby?' I start.

He nods eagerly.

'Don't open with "hello, miss". I feel like I'm a hundred years old now. It would be fine, I guess, if you weren't so young.'

I mean, I'd probably never recommend approaching a woman with 'hello, miss' regardless, but the fact that he looks fresh out of school makes me feel like an old lady.

'How old are you?' I ask.

'I'm eighteen, mi . . .' He catches himself before he does it again. 'I'm eighteen.'

Oh, so he *is* fresh out of school.

'OK, well, don't talk to women like they're your teacher. It will make you seem young,' I suggest.

That is if his baby face doesn't do the trick first. Toby is short and skinny with a round face and an auburn buzz cut. He's got this rabbit-in-the-headlights look in his eyes, like he's terrified, and almost certain the end is near.

'I . . . I didn't realise I was going to be getting feedback on everything . . .' he says. 'I thought after . . .'

'No, sorry, occupational hazard,' I insist. 'I was just trying to help. Let's start again. Hello, I'm Lola.'

'Hello, Lola, I'm Toby.'

'Great to meet you, Toby. I . . .'

Ding!

Toby's eyes widen as he pulls himself to his feet, ready to move on to the next woman.

I know my mum thought this would be right up my street but, I have to say, as a professional matchmaker, I do not advocate speed dating at all. Well, what's the point? A few awkward seconds in front of a bunch of people, all of whom will be judging a bunch of people they've met for a few seconds. That is no way to meet anyone and it certainly isn't enough information to go on, to try and work out if you're into someone. Unless you're just working off face value, but if that's all you care about then you might as well just swipe left and right on a dating app, or approach people in a bar.

This isn't going very well at all, is it? And it doesn't get any better when a heavily tattooed man in a tight T-shirt and a pair of tracksuit bottoms sits down in front of me.

'All right, love, the name's Gaz.'

'Hello, Gaz, I'm Lola,' I reply. 'Nice trackies.'

'Yeah?' he replies as he admires them himself. 'My mum told me not to wear them but you gotta take me as I come, y'know?'

I don't know what expression I pull, but it makes it clear that I don't know because Gaz reacts.

'You don't think I should've come comfortable?'

'Honestly?'

'Hit me straight,' he insists. 'I can take it.'

'Well, one of my legs is in plaster, and I still put a nice skirt on.'

One of my mum's nice skirts, to be more specific. A floaty, floral number that, if memory serves, she wore to my christening – memory of the photo album, I hasten to add. I don't remember what my mum was wearing at my own christening, and even if I did, I probably would've repressed it. Even my mum said it's the ugliest skirt she owns, which is the only reason I'm allowed to wear it. Funnily enough, I didn't pack any going-out clothes when I headed up here.

'Is this a date or a roast?' he asks with a laugh.

'Why can't it be both?' I ask with a smile.

'Well, your nice skirt . . . is not a nice skirt.'

I can't help but laugh. Gaz has this undeniable cheeky charm. He's a little rough around the edges, but he seems friendly enough. Good banter, I think is what the kids would call it.

'Hey, sorry to interrupt,' Robbie interrupts. He leans into my ear to whisper to me. 'Vince has stormed out and we're in the middle of the food for tonight. He wasn't happy making my recipes. We had a bit of a row – I don't know if he's going to come back. I'm terrified to tell your folks.'

'Don't tell them,' I whisper back. 'You got this.'

'Do I?'

'You do,' I say encouragingly. 'So get back in that kitchen and blow everyone away.'

'So, where were we?' I say to Gaz.

Ding!

'Maybe next time,' he says with another laugh.

A thirty-something man with a big, bushy beard sits down in front of me. Not a bad-looking guy, but a total hipster. He's wearing a vintage shirt, a beanie hat and he's placed a pristine Kånken backpack on the floor next to him – you know, the one that all the cool kids carry. I'm sure he's carrying it ironically or sarcastically or maybe, just maybe, because he saw one on Instagram. I wonder to myself why I'm so preoccupied with whatever floats this dude's boat. It's like I'm not even willing to give him a chance, which isn't going to get me anywhere. Just as my attitude begins to shift a little in the right direction, I feel my wheelchair being pulled back slightly.

'What are you doing?' my mum whispers into my ear.

'Speed dating,' I reply pointlessly.

'You're not even trying. You gave that poor young boy a lecture, you made fun of the second man and now, with this gent, I saw the look on your face when he sat down.'

'What look?' I squeak.

'The one you are still doing now,' she tells me. 'All scrunched up and judgey.'

'OK, fine, I'll be less judgey and more datey,' I insist. 'Wheel me back.'

'Erm, hi,' the hipster says when we're finally alone again.

'Hi,' I reply. 'I'm . . .'

Ding!

I puff air from my cheeks. Frustration and regret are just starting to take hold when Dr Will sits down in front of me. Just the cure I need.

'Well, hello there,' he says cheerfully. 'Fancy seeing you here.'

'I know, we have to stop meeting like this,' I joke.

'How's the leg?'

'Still broken.'

'You want to get yourself a better doctor.'

'I'm working on it,' I say, a little light flirtation creeping into my words.

He smiles. 'So, do you think you've met your future husband yet?' he asks.

'I do not,' I reply very matter-of-factly. 'Do you think you'll find a girlfriend?'

'Just the one,' he replies quietly. I feel my heart jump into my mouth. Could he mean . . .? 'My ex, actually.'

'Oh?'

I feel some sort of reaction to this news, deep inside my stomach. It's a sickly, swirly feeling, like I've been shaken about by a waltzer. What do I care, if his ex is here?

'That's her,' he says as he points out a tall, hot blonde, sitting at the next table. She's playfully running a hand through the hipster's beard, paralysing him with a case of the nerves. 'Megan.'

'Oh wow,' I blurt. 'She looks like an influencer.'

'She's actually a primary school teacher,' he informs me, still in hushed tones, but the tables are well spaced out to give the daters privacy. 'She's just moved back here, to start work at Acorn School. They've built an extension!'

There's a faux excitement in his voice, as he tells me about this completely unremarkable development at the local primary school. Wow, now they might have three classrooms instead of two.

'A teacher, that's impressive,' I say. 'I get footballers laid for a living.'

'Hey, it's a tough job, but someone has to do it,' Will jokes. 'I think I'm talking to her next. It will be the first time we've had a proper chat since we split, when she moved away. I only know about her new job from the Facebook group. Have you joined?'

'I haven't,' I reply. 'I didn't think I'd need to, what with me not sticking around for any longer than I have to.'

Will's face falls, and I wonder why I pointed that out.

Ding!

Oh, perfect timing. The one guy here I'm actually romantically interested in and we spent the whole time talking about his ex before I clumsily shot him down. Why, oh why, did I do that? Why did I feel like I needed to do that?

'Well, wish me luck,' he says.

'Good luck,' I call after him as I watch him head over to sit down with his ex.

Megan's eyes light up when Will approaches her. She jumps up from her chair and plants a kiss in that dangerous territory somewhere between the cheek and the lips, the kind you do when you're testing the waters, not wanting to be too friendly, but not too romantic either. It's a move I have made myself many times, and I can spot it a mile off.

It doesn't matter who sits down in front of me now, all I can think about is Will and this girl, this leggy teacher with her ambiguous kisses and her impossibly shiny hair. I can't have a crush on Will already, can I? So soon after Patrick? Sure, we weren't that serious (especially not to him), and it wasn't really going anywhere, but I'm still upset. What am I going to do, rebound myself into the first handsome man I meet?

'Ouch,' I cry out in faux pain. 'Ouch, ouch, ouch!'

Apparently I am.

Dr Will comes rushing over.

'Lola, are you OK?' he asks, wasting no time in looking over my leg. Everyone in the room stops what they are doing and crowds round.

Why did I do that? Why? Why? Am I really so jealous that I'm faking leg pain? I mean, I'm not technically faking leg pain because it really bloody hurts all the bloody time, even on the painkillers I'm taking, but it's more of a background pain than an 'ouch, I need a doctor right now' pain.

'I just . . . I got these shooting pains,' I explain as I notice Megan appear from behind Will. She looks down at me as Will examines me, and if I didn't know better, I'd swear she was looking right through me. I feel like she knows my game.

'Has it stopped?' Will asks.

'It still feels weird, like it might come back,' I say. That can't have sounded at all convincing. 'I think maybe I need to get out of this chair, sit on the sofa with my foot up.'

'Good idea,' Will says. 'I'll take you.'

'What about our catch-up?' Megan pouts.

'We'll arrange something soon,' he says, removing the brake from my wheelchair before taking me back to my living room/bedroom.

'Thanks so much for that,' I say once we're away from the noise. 'It just felt so strange – I've never felt anything like that before.'

Not technically a lie, I've never felt so jealous in my life, and

81

over someone I've only spent a matter of hours with since over a decade ago.

'Perhaps it was all just a bit much,' he says. 'It's an intense experience, to say the least.'

'It is. We didn't even get chance to talk.'

'Well, let's talk now. Let's have a not speedy speed date,' he suggests.

'Yeah?' I smile.

'Yeah, why not.'

'OK,' I say excitedly. 'I'm sorry for taking you from your ex. She seemed like she really wanted to catch up with you.'

'Isn't the first rule of first dates that we don't talk about our exes?' he asks.

'Ordinarily, but you already brought her up,' I point out.

Will laughs as he runs a hand through his dirty blond hair. 'I did. Well, why don't you level the playing field? What really happened with your boyfriend?'

My face falls.

'If you don't mind me asking . . .' Will quickly adds.

'No, it's fine,' I say. 'It's like I said before: I guess we weren't as serious as I thought we were, oh, and I'm pretty sure he was cheating on me. I think I left that part out.'

'You did,' Will says. 'Lola, I'm so sorry. That's horrible. There was, erm, some of that business in my relationship with Megan,' he says. 'That's why we broke up. Horrible memories.'

I knew I didn't like the look of her, the second I laid eyes on her. I guess it wasn't just a jealousy thing.

'Oh, I'm sorry,' I say as I place a hand on his knee. 'This must be the last thing you want to talk about.'

'I just want you to know that I know what it's like.'

'Yeah, it doesn't feel great,' I admit. 'But it also means that I don't feel anything for him anymore. I don't want to talk to him; I certainly don't want to get back with him.'

'Well, you don't have to do any of those things, right?'

'Right,' I reply, although as the word leaves my lips, I realise that I do. I booked us a weekend away in the Lakes – *I* booked it, *I* paid for it, but I used his bloody email address for the confirmation, and I imagine that's the email I'll need for cancelling the damn thing. I didn't take down the booking reference and I'm not even sure which place I ended up booking in the end. I'll need to sort that out ASAP because there's no way I can go, and I'll be damned if I'm going to let him go with someone else.

'You seem like you have a really good attitude towards it all,' he points out.

'I have to,' I reply. 'I can't walk, my mum has to help me shower, I don't have work to keep me busy . . . If I let this get in my head, I'll lose my mind. I just want to move on with my life.'

'That makes sense,' Will says with a knowing nod. 'It's attractive, that you know what you want, that you're not going to let it hold you back in life.'

'Is it?'

'It is,' he says. 'And . . . well, it's a bit embarrassing, but I had such a crush on you, when we were at school together.'

'Really?' I squeak.

'Really. You honestly had no idea?'

'None at all,' I say. I never really looked at young Will that way – he was just my nerdy friend, not the dreamy doctor sitting in front of me here today.

'I figured the feeling wasn't mutual, which is why I never acted on it,' he admits. 'Oh, and also, because I was a huge nerd, and I was terrified of girls. Girls only ever rejected me back then.'

'Well, I'll bet they're kicking themselves now,' I tell him. 'I know I am.'

The words leave my lips before I've thought them through. I was just trying to be comforting, I suppose, but it's come out as more of a declaration. Of course I fancy Will, who wouldn't? But I wasn't flirting with him.

Will places his hand on top of mine. I stare at it, like I can't quite believe it's there. It's all happening so fast, so soon.

As he leans in, as though he's going to kiss me, I feel my entire body grind to a halt. I can't move a muscle. He's only inches away from me when we're disturbed by the sound of my mum flapping in the distance.

'Lola, Lola,' she calls out before appearing in front of us, just as we pull away from each other. She pauses for a split second, obviously realising something was going on, before resuming her panic.

'What's wrong?' I ask her, trying not to seem flustered myself.

'Vince has quit,' she squeaks.

'Quit?'

'Apparently he went out for a cigarette, to try and calm down a bit, you know what he gets like. When he came back in, Robbie had taken charge of the kitchen without him. He was already furious, but then he said that Robbie had orders to cook without him. I said there was no way we'd do that, he's our head chef . . . but then he said it was your call . . . and I said . . . there's no way . . .'

As her sentence goes on, my mum sounds less sure about what she is saying.

'Ah,' I say awkwardly, edging away from Will guiltily. 'About that . . .'

Chapter 13

I shuffle awkwardly in my wheelchair as I play aimlessly with my cereal. I never expected a broken leg to be a walk in the park but I had no idea of the toll it would take on the rest of my body.

First of all, my back is killing me. I don't know if it is from the energy and effort needed to wheel myself around in this chair – I mean, I want to be a good feminist as much as the next strong, independent woman, but my complete lack of upper body strength often sees me asking for the nearest male to open a jar for me – so perhaps that's why I'm so achy . . . or it could be from sleeping on the sofa bed. I'm so used to my gloriously soft yet supportive super king mattress back at home, that this small, springy excuse of a bed feels like a method of torture. If I didn't have the broken leg for perspective, I think I'd be finding sleeping on that thing a lot harder.

I can also see a difference in my hair and my skin. Without all my potions and my strict daily routine, I can see a change already. On the one hand, this is proof that the expensive creams, serums, cleansers et cetera do actually work and are not a waste of money. The bad news is that I didn't pack everything to bring here with me, nor am I able to hover in front of the bathroom mirror for too long, wiping things off and slapping things on.

It's not easy to put much time or effort into my hair or make-up either. There is only so much slap you can apply easily with a small mirror on a table top, and as for my hair, well, washing it is a military operation, with my sergeant major mother, and when it comes to drying and styling, she only knows how to handle her very short hair, or she can pull my damp hair into plaits, just like she did when I was a kid.

Sitting at the table, with my hair in plaits (that my mum did for me), eating Coco Pops (that my mum poured for me), I feel very much like a kid again.

It's after midday now. Today is the first day my mum hasn't woken me up at the crack of dawn, she's been super busy all morning, so it was a while before she helped me out of bed, into my clothes, and wheeled me to the breakfast table for the quickest breakfast I've had since I got here. I'm not complaining, not at all, I love Coco Pops, but my mum's MO is to feed any ailment, so I'm suspicious today. As breakfast goes, a bowl of cereal is very much my mum phoning in her efforts.

The only thing keeping me positive today is what happened with Will last night. We were going to kiss, I'm sure we were, and I know what you're thinking: it's too soon. Believe me I have thought it too, but . . . maybe everything that has happened, has happened for a reason? I know it sounds wild, but think about it: if I hadn't broken my leg I wouldn't have moved back home, Patrick would be doing whatever behind my back (honestly, I rarely saw him and I always thought it was just because we were both so busy and because he worked away a lot) and I never would've reconnected with Will. I know how daft that sounds, about fate, and of course I don't believe it, but what if Will was my one that got away? The more I think about him, the more I wish we had kissed.

My mum enters the kitchen, sits down at the table opposite me and puffs air from her cheeks.

'Lola,' she starts, before pausing to compose her sentence. 'Your dad and I need to tell you something.'

'Oh my God, you're pregnant!' I joke – I always make terrible jokes when I think I'm in trouble.

'Not pregnant,' she replies. 'The one problem child is enough, thank you.'

So I *am* in trouble.

'Uh-oh, what have I done?' I ask. Well, how much can I have done, stuck in this bloody chair?

'You're meddling, Lola,' she explains. 'You're sticking your nose in, and, look, we appreciated your help with the renovation ideas, and it has helped business, but now we have lost our head chef.'

'The thing is, you know what Vince is like,' I start. 'He's hot-headed and he's set in his ways, and Robbie really is a great chef.'

'He is,' she replies. 'He cooked everything alone last night and his food was a big hit with the speed daters, and he's happy to step into Vince's role – we'll just need to get him a new trainee to help out.'

'So, all is well that ends well,' I say with a smile, but my mum doesn't smile back. 'Or not?'

'All was well *this time*,' she points out. 'But we can't have you interfering in the business and causing trouble, just because . . . well, because you're bored. I have more going on than you realise right now – it is extra stress that I don't need.'

For a moment, I overlook my mum's wild accusation that because I am bored, I am interfering with the B & B – I really am only trying to help. Instead, I pick up on the latter half of what she said.

'What else is going on?' I ask her. 'Are you OK? Is Dad OK?'

A look of some kind appears on my mum's face for split second before vanishing without a trace. It's a show of something she doesn't want me to see, like she's hiding something, like maybe something really is going on . . .

'We're both fine, nothing to worry about,' she insists. 'We just worry about the business and can't have you meddling. So, I've done something about it.'

I'm about to try and dig deeper, unconvinced by her backtrack that everything is fine, when I realise something.

'Hang on, you've done something about it?' I ask. 'What have you done?'

My mum's lips purse guiltily. She doesn't say another word; she simply unlocks her mobile phone and slides it across the table to me.

'Oh . . . my . . . God . . .' are the only words I can get out as I take in exactly what my mum has done.

First, I realise I am looking at Facebook, then I realise I'm in the Marram Bay residents' group. Finally, I realise I am looking at something my mum has posted, and it's about me.

'Mum, are you serious?' I ask her.

'Well, why not, hmm?' she replies.

To summarise the lengthy post on the smashed iPhone screen in front of me, my mother has posted something on my behalf – a combination of her own words and the copy from my work website, offering my services to the people of Marram Bay. Everything from our bespoke matchmaking to our coaching sessions to our intensive packages where we take seemingly hopeless individuals and turn them into something someone can fall in love with, because, for whatever reason, it just isn't happening for them. And my mum has offered all of this on Facebook, free of charge, for me to deal with.

'Mum, I think these services are more of a fancy London thing,' I explain, hopefully making her understand that your average Joe just doesn't seek out a service like this. 'It's mostly for people like footballers who want a well-vetted girlfriend who isn't with them for fame, or for young pop stars who want to raise their profile with the right person on their arm.'

'Look at the advice you gave Auntie Val about her roofer,' she reminds me. 'That worked a treat. I haven't heard from her in days!'

'Are you not going to check on her?' I ask through a bemused laugh.

'Oh, no, she'll be fine – you know what she's like. She'll be on top of the world.'

'She might be on top of the roof,' I shriek. 'Anyway, don't change the subject. You need to take this down, Mum, seriously. I can't do this.'

'Ah,' she says simply, removing my soggy cereal from in front of me. 'About that – let me make you something better than this – so, yes, about that . . . It might be too late.'

'Why?'

'You've got a group session, today at 2 p.m.'

'I do?'

'You do,' she informs me. 'There were lots of responses, so I organised a small class, just to keep you busy.'

Suddenly I have a headache to go with my leg pain and my aching back. 'Mum . . .'

'Lola, you can't let them down,' she insists. 'And you are bored.'

I am bored, that is true. 'OK, fine, just one session – I'll give everyone a pep talk and then we'll call it quits, OK?'

'OK,' she replies as the biggest grin consumes her face. 'So proud of you.'

'Don't be proud,' I say. 'Be deleting that post from the Facebook group.'

'I will,' she says excitedly. 'Now let me make you some eggs or something.'

As my mum fusses around me, making me a second breakfast out of pure guilt, I wonder what she's got me into. I suppose it would be nice to help people but, to be honest, the only relationship on my mind is my own, with Will. Oh, and maybe my auntie, who may or may not have run away with a roofer.

Chapter 14

The good news is that there is no line dancing taking place in the B & B function room today.

The bad news is that I am about to have my first meeting with a handful of Marram Bay's most desperate singletons, and I have absolutely no idea what to expect. I only describe them as desperate because surely you would have to be to gather here in this room, ready to take advice from someone only vouched for by their mum.

'Such a good girl,' my mum says to herself as she wheels me into the function room.

Sitting there, in the middle of the room forming a sort of circle, are just four people, and they are a real mixed bag.

My mum wheels me into the space they have left for my wheelchair, pulls on my brake, and leaves us to it. For a few seconds, we sit in silence, as I take stock of my students.

'Erm, OK then,' I start. 'Why don't we go around the room, say our names, a bit about ourselves and why we're here?'

The first person on my left is Kim, local nurse and my best friend from school. I smile at her and she gives me a half wave. It's nice to see a familiar face.

'Hi, everyone, my name is Kim,' she starts nervously. 'Some

of you might recognise me from the surgery. I'm thirty-two, recently had to move back in with my parents to help out and, as you can imagine, my love life has taken a bit of a back seat. So, I thought maybe coming here might be a good way to meet single people, learn a bit more about how to mingle, and get to spend time with my friend, of course.'

'Aww, that's lovely,' I say. 'Who have we got next?'

'My name is Chantelle, but everyone calls me Channy,' a young woman explains. Channy has a very bold look. Her skin is extremely white, but this might be because every bit of make-up apart from her foundation is so dark, and her hair is dyed jet black. She has a septum piercing and a large tattoo stretching right across her chest – a sort of collage of a whole mess of things. I imagine men are intimidated by Channy because not only does she look so confident, she sounds sure of herself too. Self-confidence is absolutely an attractive quality, but sometimes men can find it a little scary.

'Some of you might know me because I work at the deli,' she adds.

'How old are you?' I ask.

'I'm twenty-two,' Channy replies. 'I'm not technically single . . . I'm seeing someone but he messes me around. I need to meet someone new and, well, it's hard to meet people in a small town like this. Everyone my age, I grew up with. There are only maybe fifteen people on Tinder who aren't tourists, and I've tried dating older men, but the one I'm seeing at the moment is older and he's worse than any of the young F-boys around here. So here I am, at the end of my tether. You're my last resort.'

'Great,' I say with faux enthusiasm. No pressure there then.

I'm not sure how I feel about helping someone with a boyfriend meet someone else, but he does sound like a no-good boyfriend. I know all about those.

Next up we have our only male group member – and I recognise him.

'I take it you didn't meet anyone at the speed dating,' I say to him to break the ice. He looks nervous, fidgeting in his seat, nibbling on one of his already quite short fingernails.

'No, miss.'

'Hey, remember what I said last night? I'm not your teach . . . Oh, I suppose I am your teacher now, kind of. Still, please call me Lola.'

'Lola, OK, hello,' he says, still a bag of nerves. 'My name is Toby, I'm eighteen, I've been single for . . .' He pauses, as though he's counting. 'Well, forever, really.'

I decide to put him out of his misery and move on to our final student, and the one I am the most excited to learn about.

'Hello,' I say to the seventy-something lady sitting to my right. 'What brings you here?'

'My name is Doris,' she says. 'Seventy-three years young, my husband is dead and I'm ready to find someone new.'

Everyone's jaw drops – my own included.

'Oh, not recently,' she says. 'My Alan, God rest his soul, left this earth six years ago. Now just feels like the right time to move on, but it's hard, especially at my age.'

'What have you tried?' I ask curiously.

'Well, Channy is right,' she starts, pronouncing her name with a 'ch' rather than a 'sh'. 'Tinder is a wash.'

'Oh, you use Tinder?' I ask, trying to hide my disbelief.

'Oh, yes,' she replies. 'Well, I try, but there's nowt worth catching on there. I'm pretty good with the old iPhone.'

I watch as Doris removes a white iPhone in a lilac flip case from her handbag. She narrows her eyes as she looks at it.

'That reminds me,' she starts. 'What's this club called? I want to check in.'

I can't help but smile. This is so surreal. I thought I'd left my hometown stuck in the late Nineties, well that's where it was when I moved away – in the Noughties, I hasten to add.

'We, erm, we don't have a name,' I say. Well, I didn't even

know we existed – or that we were, in fact, a club until about an hour ago.

'I'd suggest the Undateables, but that name is taken,' Kim jokes.

'Plus, I can get dates,' Channy says. 'If I lower my standards enough. We're more like . . .'

'The Unlovables?' Toby suggests.

'Christ, you're depressing,' Channy blurts out. 'I thought I was supposed to be the goth. No, more like . . .'

'The Unmatchables?' Doris says.

'I like that,' Kim says. 'It sounds . . . less like our fault.'

'Oh, none of you are the reason you are single,' I insist.

'Not even him?' Channy asks, nodding towards Toby.

'No one's fault,' I reiterate. 'You just haven't met the right person yet.'

'The Unmatchables,' Doris says to herself slowly as she taps it into her phone.

I did think to myself, in the hour I had to prepare, that I might be able to match up a few of my singles. No chance of that with this group – there's only one man, for starters, and he's a boy really. Way too young for Doris, too young for Kim – maybe not too young for Channy, but she would chew him up and spit him out.

'I think maybe we should start with some confidence-building techniques,' I suggest. 'Get you in a position where you not only want to approach the people you meet when you're out and about, but also give you the confidence to go up to them and talk to them. How does that sound?'

My group are all happy with my plan of attack. Well, the first step of it anyway . . . The first step is all I have right now – who knows what step will be next? I suppose I'll have to make this up as I go along.

Chapter 15

After a long afternoon session with the Unmatchables, I am exhausted. Physically, from wheeling myself around the function room, but also mentally, from trying to work out how I'll find love for this random bunch, in a town where I don't really know anyone. I don't really know the people anymore, the places – I don't know where people go out for dinner, where teens go to drink cheap cider; I don't know the best walks – I hardly remember the tidal island's incredible history. Tales of ghosts, weird superstitions, notable residents and their scandalous private lives.

I have told the Unmatchables that we can meet again tomorrow lunchtime. Now that we've worked on our confidence together, we're going to try a bit of role-play, run through a few scenarios and see how we get on.

The rich and famous are unusual creatures, with a longer list of requirements when it comes to finding them a partner. Sure, they worry about things that any of us could – like, can I trust this person? – but how many of us need to worry that the person we are with is only with us because we're rich and we can help them get on the front page of *Bacci* magazine? Regular folk don't need to worry about things like that. This is why, for my Unmatchables, I don't think I need to be focusing on finding and vetting potential partners for them, I just need to help them work on the tools to get out there and find their own.

I close my laptop and carefully wiggle down into the sofa, making myself more comfortable – well, as much as I can with a broken leg. It's funny, how the backdrop of my leg makes everything seem so much worse. Every now and then, I'll think about Patrick and I will seethe. It's not that I'm sad about us breaking up, the man was clearly straight trash and I've had a lucky escape, but it's the deceit I can't get over. I can't stop myself wondering what he was getting up to, or how he really felt. He hasn't even made an effort to contact me and smooth things over, so I was obviously just one of a few girls he was seeing.

This reminds me that I need to cancel the trip I booked to the Lakes, but as I reach for my laptop, my phone starts ringing. A tiny, stupid part of me entertains (only for the briefest of moments) the idea that it might be Patrick, but of course it isn't. It's a number I don't recognise.

'Hello,' I answer cautiously. I'm always suspicious of numbers I don't recognise or don't have saved in my contacts, for no real reason whatsoever. I think I watch too many movies.

'Hello, is that Mrs James?' a woman asks.

'Erm, yes,' I reply. Still a miss, but now isn't the time to get into that.

'I hope so,' she replies. 'My name is Faye. I'm calling about your advert.'

My advert?

'On Facebook. About the matchmaking,' she prompts.

Ah, my mum's post.

'Oh, yes, that,' I reply.

So, not only has my mother not removed the post, she's doubled down. My phone number was absolutely not on there when I looked at the post.

'Do I have the right number?' she asks anxiously.

'You do, yes, sorry,' I babble.

'Well, I clicked the link to your website and I was reading about the different services.'

That would be my work website. Nice to see my mother is offering the full range . . .

'I was hoping to purchase the extensive package,' she says.

'Ah,' is about all I can reply, as I think of the best way to tell her I can't do this. 'Well, here's the thing, I'm not really offering anything . . . My mum thought it might be a good distraction for me, to keep doing my job while I'm visiting, but I'm not offering the packages online, and I'm definitely not taking any money off anyone.'

'Oh,' she replies softly.

'But I am running a few workshops. I've got a fun little group together. We're meeting up, working on the different skills you need for playing the dating game – you're welcome to join us.'

'It's not for me,' she explains. 'It's for my brother, Dean. He got divorced a few years ago and since then, he hasn't had a proper relationship. He won't let anyone in. We're all worried sick about him.'

'Oh, OK, well if you want to tell him to come to the workshop, the next one is at 1 p.m. tomorrow, at the Lighthouse B & B.'

'Thanks,' she says. 'I just thought . . . with the extensive package, that guarantees a match at the end of it, or your money back – that's what I need. He just, he got married, they were happy and then . . . they were over, and his life has stalled, and I can't get him back on track.'

There is something in Faye's voice – a panicked desperation . . . something I can't say no to. Well, I have nothing better to do, do I? And she sounds genuinely scared for her brother.

'OK, send him to the group,' I suggest. 'And, any extra advice or help he needs, I'll offer it. I'll do my best to find him someone.'

'Oh, that would be wonderful,' she says. 'How much is it?'

'You don't have to pay me,' I insist. 'I'm happy to help.'

'Oh, my gosh, thank you so much,' she says, and I can tell

96

she really, *really* means it. It makes me wish I'd had a sibling. Someone to look out for me and have my back – maybe an older brother who could put the frighteners on Patrick, make him see the error of his ways so he never messes with another girl again.

'One thing though,' Faye starts. 'I'm going to tell my brother that I paid you for this, just so he feels like he has to give it his all. He can be a bit of a joker and I want him to take this seriously.'

'OK, sure,' I reply. 'Have him come along to the workshop tomorrow. We'll have him head over heels in no time.'

'Promise?'

I was just trying to sound optimistic and reassuring, but it sounds like this really matters to her. I adopt a more serious tone. 'Promise,' I reply.

Well, depending on his age, I have three women from very different age groups in the workshop already, so perhaps I can match up a couple of my singles.

I'm no sooner off the phone and reaching for my laptop when my phone rings again. This time it's Dr Will.

'Hello,' I answer brightly.

'Hello, Lola, it's Dr Will here,' he says seriously. 'I have your test results.'

It's strange, hearing him call himself Dr Will, when I've been calling him that in my head. It's even stranger that he has results for a test I didn't know I'd had. My heart is in my mouth.

'Oh?'

'Yes, it turns out, you need to have dinner with me tonight,' he says, in the same serious doctor tone.

My God, he's smooth.

'Oh do I now?' I ask.

'You do,' he replies. 'I have a very specific treatment plan for you. It's going to take just the right prescription. So, if you'd like to come over to my house for dinner, I can pick you up, feed you, return you home safe . . .'

I hesitate for a moment.

'Trust me, I'm a doctor,' he adds playfully.

'OK, sure,' I reply. 'That would be wonderful.'

Well, it will do me good to get out of the house, and hang out with an adult, and, come on, it's Will. I can't deny that I have a crush on him, a crush that is slowly but surely creeping in.

As soon as I'm off the phone I decide I can put off cancelling my trip until tomorrow, because now I need to get ready for tonight. I've got a hot date with a doctor, and I need to look my best.

Chapter 16

My mum has always had this thing about wearing clean knickers, in case she gets injured and someone needs to call an ambulance. She wouldn't dream of popping out to the shop without clean pants on, just in case she's hit by a car and taken to a hospital where a doctor refuses to save her life, just because it just so happened to be that day when she popped to the shops in her tracksuit without her knickers on. To be honest, I think it's more the embarrassment factor she's worried about, but I always tell her that, in an emergency like that, her knickers will be the last thing she's thinking about. That said, I do remember once, when I was high school age, my dad threw his back out and it was so bad he couldn't get out of his bed. My mum called an ambulance for him, before going on to vacuum the hallway and the bedroom as she waited for the medics to arrive.

Thankfully I had the foresight to know I would be seeing a doctor tonight, and while I highly doubt he'll be seeing my knickers, I did do a lot of prep work. It wasn't my usual prep for dinner with a handsome man – for starters, I don't usually need my mum to give me a shower and wash my hair before helping me into my clothes. I still don't have any smart clothes with me but I was unwilling to wear my mum's impossibly Eighties skirt again. I did bring a T-shirt dress that is kind of smart, so I'm wearing that. Well, it's only dinner at Will's place and, given how much sympathy he has for my situation, I didn't think he'd mind what I was wearing – anything other than the pair of black leggings my mum has cut one leg off is me making an effort under current circumstances.

Just like he said he would, and much to my mum's delight, Will came to the B & B to pick me up. He promised my mum that I wouldn't be back late, but I've taken a key, just in case, because I had a horrible feeling my dad would probably forget I was out, lock the door and the two of them would head up to bed in the lighthouse, where you can't hear anything, and completely forget I was even staying with them.

Will doesn't live on Hope Island; he lives on the mainland. After picking me up and driving me to his cute little Marram Bay cottage, he wheeled me into his living room where he had set the table at his coffee table, in front of the sofa, telling me that he just wanted me to be comfortable. He served me non-alcoholic wine, because unfortunately I can't drink on my painkillers – although I am very, very grateful for them – and the most delicious homemade lasagne I have ever had in my life. It was packed full of salmon, green vegetables and a whole lot of cheese – all ingredients that he assured me were rich in calcium and good for broken bones. I think he was joking, although there is probably some truth in there, unlike my mum, trying to feed me carrots.

We've enjoyed a lovely dinner, an amazing cheesecake for dessert, and we've just been catching up and reminiscing about old times. Now I'm telling him all about my mum's little stunt.

'She must be so proud of you,' Will says as he tops up my glass. 'And she must be so proud of what you do too.'

'I mean, I'm sure she'd much rather I were a doctor,' I reply. 'You save lives; I find boyfriends for girl bands.'

Will throws his head back as he laughs. He looks so good

this evening. His dirty blond locks are neat as ever, his jeans are pristine and his black jumper looks so soft and inviting, I want to run my hands all over it . . . although that might just be because of the person who is wearing it.

'Do you have a good class?' he asks.

'They are an interesting bunch, that's for sure,' I reply. 'I'm not sure if I'm supposed to keep their information confidential – the rules aren't as clear cut in the dating game as they are in medicine. Some are divorced; some are just plain single. Some are definitely complicated. We have one girl who has a boyfriend, sounds like he's messing her around though. I can relate, so I feel so sorry for her. But, yes, it's a very mixed group, ranging from their early twenties to their mid seventies – so if you're after a younger or older woman . . .'

'I don't have much time for younger women,' he says. 'I like a woman who knows who she is, what she wants, how she's going to get it . . . and as for mid seventies, I'm not sure she'd have much time for me.'

My jaw drops.

'Oh, gosh, no, not like that,' he insists. 'What I mean to say is that . . . I get to meet a lot of elderly ladies at work, and they all have such hectic social lives.'

'To be honest, I was kind of amazed that my lady was on the hunt for a man, but good on her. I hope I'm still hungry for love at her age. I think the only thing I'm hungry for now is more cheesecake,' I joke.

'Then I shall get you some,' Will replies with a smile.

He hops to his feet and heads over the kitchen area of his open-plan living space. Will lives in a lovely little cottage on a quiet country lane, not too far from where we went to primary school together, but with the school cloaked by tall trees, the only thing you can see for miles is the ultra trendy Westwood Farm, up on the hill. That's the one thing about Marram Bay I am still in the loop with, because the trendy fruity ciders they make are huge all over the country. Everyone is drinking them in London and I can never quite believe they came from my tiny hometown.

Will's cottage might look traditional on the outside, but inside it's a little more modern. It's minimalist, in that way young, single men appreciate. Sort of pristine and simplistic, not too many soft furnishings, absolutely zero knick-knacks or ornaments. A house doesn't quite look like a home without a woman's touch, does it? It's clean and clinical, like a doctor's surgery, but instead of magazines he just has the one coffee table book. It's called *Anatomy* – I think I'll give it a miss.

'Should a doctor be signing off on second dessert?' I ask.

'Probably not,' he replies. 'But I'm keeping a close eye on you.'

After I take down a second piece of cheesecake, pacing myself enough to make it look like this isn't something I can do with ease, Will clears the table, makes us a couple of coffees and we continue to chat. I can't believe my dorky little friend Will is this grown man sitting in front of me – a grown man who saves lives and makes lasagne. He's an absolute dream.

'Oh, crap,' Will says suddenly, jumping to his feet. 'The causeway, it closed over an hour ago.'

'Oh,' I reply.

It's quite late in the evening now. The plan was to get me home in time for the final crossing, with enough time for Will to make it back over to his side again.

'I just completely lost track of time,' he says, sitting back down next to me. 'It never ceases to amaze me, how people can live with the causeway all their lives, and still mess up crossing the road before the tide comes in. I'm so sorry.'

'I wasn't even looking at the time,' I insist. 'It's easy done.'

'We're looking at, what, maybe two to three hours before it opens up again? It will be the early hours of the morning then . . .'

'Well, I have my key,' I say. 'No one is waiting up for me. Don't worry about it.'

'You could always sleep here,' he suggests.

'Sleep on your sofa instead of mine,' I laugh.

'Actually, I thought maybe you could sleep in my bed,' he suggests. 'With me.'

'Oh,' I reply, a little taken aback. 'It's been a while. Since I slept in a proper bed, I mean.'

Wow, if I were any less smooth right now, the hand Will is stroking my bare knee with would be bleeding.

Will leans towards me slowly and takes my chin between his thumb and index finger before kissing me. It has all the makings of a slow and gentle smooch, but the second Will's lips touch mine it turns frantic, passionate, like he's trying to eat me alive. I suppose this is what happens, when you have a crush on someone for years and they finally reciprocate.

When I was with Patrick I thought that things were great, but then it turned out to be a completely superficial relationship, which I was far more invested in than he was. I'm angry and upset with him but, as far as I'm concerned, good riddance to bad rubbish. Will, on the other hand, takes care of people. I've known him since I was a kid, back when he was chubby and dorky. Will isn't superficial at all – exactly the kind of man a girl should be with. Still, this does feel a little bit fast.

We kiss for a few seconds. Perhaps it's just a case of waiting for it to feel right – it's always weird when you kiss someone for the first time, isn't it?

'Shall we go upstairs?' Will asks after finally coming up for air.

I've never really been a one-night stand kind of girl. Perhaps it is because I've always gone for the wrong guys, but I've always been a romantic with a five-date (minimum) rule, which means I get to know a guy before he breaks my heart.

'Oh . . .'

It's not that I'm not a sexual person because, once I take that leap with someone, I know what I'm good at and I know what I like. It might have taken a few of my younger years filled with awkward encounters to figure it out, but now that I'm into my thirties, I feel like I have my sex life all figured out – when it's active, at least. Perhaps I just feel so awkward because I'm worried it's too soon, and I feel a little vulnerable because of my leg. Well, not only is it still so painful, but my cast is so heavy, it's like having a weight strapped to it, stopping me from moving off the stop without assistance.

Will scoops me up in his arms, carefully but passionately.

The tug of gravity on my leg is excruciating.

'Ow, ow, ow,' I can't help but cry out.

'Oh, sorry,' he says. 'Do you want to lie down?'

'Help me to the sofa,' I say quickly.

Will places me down. I wiggle back a little, quickly trying to find a comfortable spot to ease the pressure building up in my leg.

I look over at Will, who is unbuttoning his shirt.

It isn't just my leg that feels pressure.

'Wait, stop, sorry,' I insist. 'This is just . . . I can't do this, sorry. I think I just need more time, to get my head straight, and obviously I can't get my leg straight. It's really, really hurting me.'

'Well, I could give you some stronger painkillers,' he jokes. 'But they would only make you drowsy, and then we're into something completely different . . .'

I laugh. 'I'm sorry,' I say. 'It's not that I don't like you . . .'

'I know, I know,' he assures me.

He seems understanding, but things feel really awkward now.

'Perhaps I will go home,' I say. 'Soon as the causeway is open.'

'Sure,' he replies. 'We'll probably need to set off soon anyway, by the time we get sorted, get you outside, drive there . . .'

Oh, God, he wants to get rid of me. It takes a while to get me sorted and moved around, but it doesn't take that long. He wants to get rid of me as much as I want to wheel out of here screaming.

'OK, great, thanks,' I say. 'Thanks for dinner.'

'Yeah, no, you're welcome,' he babbles.

We both sit in silence for a second.

'Sorry, I'm going to need you to help back into my wheelchair,' I say.

'Yeah, of course,' he replies.

Will picks me up, only this time it's less like a sexy fireman carrying a damsel in distress out of a burning building, and more like a Mafioso dragging a dead body towards a deep, freshly dug hole.

Maybe I'll be maintaining my five-date rule after all. That is, if Will ever wants to see me again.

Chapter 17

After an awkward goodbye peck with Will, I insist he abandon me outside the lighthouse, so that I can make my own way in. I highly doubt our voices would wake up my mum and dad, who I absolutely don't want to hear me creeping in at nearly 3 a.m., but I also didn't want to prolong the goodbye, which I knew would be awkward.

I wheel myself towards the lighthouse door, which is easy enough, put in my key, quietly open the door, and wheel myself inside. I'm getting a bit better in my chair now. My arms are maybe getting a little stronger, or maybe I just have more of an understanding of spatial awareness. After a little manoeuvring I close the door behind me and, smug in my execution of this mini mission impossible, I go to flick on the lights. Not only has it been a long time since I stayed out too late and needed to sneak back in, but I never had to do it in a wheelchair when I was younger. I feel so proud of myself.

I reverse a little, wheel myself towards the sofa, only to realise someone is sitting on it.

I scream.

'Quiet, quiet, you'll wake your dad,' my mum insists.

'Sorry,' I say breathlessly. 'You scared the sh . . . hell out of me.'

'Sorry, I just, I thought you'd be back by now and I can't sleep, so I thought I'd come for a chat, if you were awake.'

106

My mum helps me out of my chair and onto the sofa.

'I'll grab us some tea,' she says, tightening her dressing down before dashing off to the kitchen.

While she's in there I reach for the face wipes on my bedside table (it's the coffee table) and begin to remove my make-up, and any traces of Will that might still be left on my face. I can still taste him and smell his aftershave on my face and I'm worried that, if my mum notices, she'll be onto me in seconds. The last thing I need is an interrogation right now, and I absolutely don't want to debrief with my mum, on my inability to have sex tonight. Anyway, what's worrying me even more is why my mum can't sleep. Something doesn't seem quite right with her at the moment. She seems even more highly strung than usual, she's interfering more, and now she's not sleeping, which isn't like her at all.

Mum returns with two cups of tea, which she places on the coffee table.

'Shift up,' she demands, squashing her bum onto the sofa with me. 'Look at you, creeping home in the early hours, thinking you can sneak in because you're sleeping down here.' My mother clicks her tongue.

'Mum, I thought you were asleep in your bed. I wasn't going to call and wake you up,' I say in my defence. 'I didn't intend to be this late, but we missed the causeway.'

'Was it a good evening?' she asks me.

'The food was really nice,' I say. 'And we had a good catch-up.'

'I'm sure you did,' my mum says knowingly. 'Will seems lovely, just, you know, don't rush into anything.'

'Oh, God, this is reminding my of my first week of uni when you sent me a Facebook message, asking me if I was on the pill.'

'I care,' my mum insists. 'Is that a crime?'

'It's not criminal, it's just awkward,' I tell her.

'Well, university is no time to wind up knocked up,' she points out. 'And I hope you're on it now.'

I laugh as I reach for my tea.

'Contraception is important. You're currently jobless and living with your father and I – we couldn't afford to keep you and a baby.'

I laugh in disbelief.

'Mum, if I gave you the impression that I was going out with the intention of getting pregnant tonight – or ever – then I think we may have got our wires crossed. And I'm not living here, and I'm only temporarily off work. *And* I have lots to do anyway because you've roped me into enough freelance work . . .'

'I wouldn't be surprised if you focused so much on other people's relationships, that you neglected your own,' she muses.

'Just worry about your own relationship,' I insist. 'Don't worry about mine.'

'Why do you say that?' she asks quickly. 'Do you think I have anything to worry about?'

'What? No,' I insist. 'Of course not, I just mean don't worry about me. Is everything OK? Why can't you sleep?'

I might not be asking her if she's on the pill, but suddenly it's me interrogating my mum.

'What are you two doing up?' my dad interrupts us.

I glance towards the bottom of the stairs where Dad is standing in an impossibly tight pair of boxer shorts, the trendy kind usually only worn by young men.

'Oh, God, Dad,' I say as I bring my hand up in front of me to shield my eyes from his body – specifically his lower half.

'What?' he asks.

'I don't want to see my pensioner dad's underpants,' I say.

At this my dad looks truly offended. I was only teasing him.

'I'm not a bloody pensioner yet,' he insists. 'I still look like a man in his fifties. I'm only fifty-nine.'

My dad points out his age to me, like I don't know.

'You look like my dad in his underpants,' I reply uncomfortably. 'Come on. Sorry, Dad. It's just those pants.'

'I'm in great shape, look,' he insists, tugging on the waistband of his boxers, stretching them out like he's the slimmer of the week at one of the various 'fat clubs' we're hosting here at the moment (well, that's what my mum calls them at least). 'Massive on me. I'm in really good shape, for someone you consider an *OAP*.'

'They're like that because they're too big for him on the hips,' she whispers to me. 'And yet still far too tight.'

'Oh, I'm going back to bed,' he says with a bat of his hand.

'I can't believe you're up,' I say. 'Either of you.'

'I wanted to check my emails,' he replies. 'And I realised your mum was missing. Anyway, goodnight.'

'He says things like that all the time,' my mum tells me once we're alone again. 'Wearing clothes that are too young for him, checking his messages all the time, banging on about how fit he is – he jogged the other day, can you imagine?'

My mum usually complains that my dad doesn't take pride in his appearance and that he isn't active enough. The poor bloke can't win.

'So, why can't you sleep?' I ask.

'Your dad was watching snooker in the bedroom. I couldn't sleep, then he fell asleep and I didn't. I came down looking for you to chat and you weren't here so I thought I'd wait.'

'Well snooker is a notoriously noisy sport.'

My mum pulls an unimpressed face. 'London has made you much cheekier than you were before, and don't think I don't notice that accent you're putting on.'

I am absolutely not putting on an accent. I suppose I've just lost my Yorkshire twang, living away from home for several years, trying to speak clearly so that people could understand me. Up here, people don't think I sound Yorkshire anymore. In London, especially when I first moved there, people found me difficult to understand at times, because of my Yorkshire accent. I didn't *want* to tone it down, I *had* to tone it down so that people could understand me.

'Are we going to talk about what happened?' my mum asks. 'With your fella?'

Oh God, a mother-daughter chat.

'Mum, ideally not ever, but especially not now.'

I sound like a teenager again. It's amazing how much I've regressed since I arrived here.

'It just didn't work out,' I say, softening a little. 'He wasn't who I thought he was.'

'Well, if he had been, I wouldn't have got my daughter back,' my mum says, squeezing me with one arm around my shoulders. 'Even if it is only temporarily.'

For a moment I enjoy a genuine warm moment with my mum. I know that she loves me, even when she's meddling in my life. I feel myself relax into her arms for a moment, but then she opens her mouth again.

'OK, well, you get some sleep,' she insists. 'Terrible black bags under your eyes.'

'Night night, Mum,' I call after her. 'You know where I am if you need to talk.'

'We'll see.' She laughs. 'Night, love.'

I do feel exhausted. I have so much on my mind I decide to just push it all out and let myself fall asleep. I'll work out what's wrong with my mum, I'll figure out what I'm supposed to do about Will, I'll plan my Unmatchables meeting and I'll cancel that bloody trip to the Lakes . . . just . . . tomorrow.

Chapter 18

Messy room, messy mind, that's what my mum says.

For that reason, after climbing the lighthouse stairs backwards, on my bum, where my mum was waiting at the top for me with my wheelchair, I am now in my old room.

I definitely couldn't do this all day, every day, so I've ruled out sleeping up here, but the living room was starting to get pretty full so we agreed we'd put my stuff in my old room, and I fancied a bit of privacy, so I could make some calls without my mum listening. I told her I wanted to spend a bit of time in my old room, which is true. It's an interesting activity, given how well preserved is it. It's like digging up a time capsule.

My mum hung my clothes in my old wardrobe, which, as far as I'm concerned, has sealed the deal that I'm staying here for a while still. Wherever I hang my hat (clothes, shoes and other accessories), that's my home.

She squashed as much in the wardrobe as she could but it's still packed with clothes from my teens. I suppose I could clear it out while I'm here, take them to one of the charity shops in town perhaps – or open a branch of Tammy Girl, because I have enough stock for it. There are lots of clothes in here that I didn't wear for a long time before I moved out.

I wonder if any of it might still fit me, but I'm not sure how much use I have for combat pants and fishnet tops – an ensemble sixteen-year-old me would have loved.

I wheel myself over to my desk. I admire my CD rack, which boasts everything from Savage Garden to Slipknot. I went through many phases. If you look around the room, you can map out these phases from a pink-and-pop-loving girly girl child, to football-loving tomboy as I hit double digits. After that short-lived sporty phase I transitioned to a rock chick. The CDs make so much sense once you have this knowledge. Poppy me would've been horrified at Slipknot, and rock chick me would've rather died than admit Savage Garden were great. These days I feel much more comfortable liking a bit of everything but when you're young, you forge these strong identities and live your entire life by them.

I've brought my laptop up with me (well, my mum carried it up for me) so that I can cancel this trip to the Lakes. I was going to call Patrick, have him forward me the email, or get him to cancel it, but I cannot bring myself to call him – in fact, I don't want to contact him at all. I don't want to hear his stupid voice but, most of all, the fact he hasn't called me speaks volumes. I don't want to be the first one to make contact. Petty? Perhaps, but if it makes me feel better then I think I'm allowed a bit of pettiness.

I open my laptop, type in Patrick's email address and rack my brains for his password. He's definitely told me his email password before, and I was sure it was W35tHam87. It doesn't seem to be working though. I try a few different combinations but none of them seem to be working, so I try a few things he might've changed it to. I'd say I feel like a hacker, but I have no idea what I'm doing.

Wait, did I just click to have my password reset via my phone? Oh God, it's not going to tell him the location his emails are being accessed from, is it? Because I doubt he knows many people living on a tiny tidal island in Yorkshire.

And now my battery is dying. Brilliant. I grab my charger from my bag and reach down under my desk to plug it in. It's maybe just an inch of two out of my reach, but with one big stretch . . .

I fall out of my chair and hit the floor with a loud thud. My God, that hurt. Not just my broken leg, but every other bone in my body, which I hope and pray are not now broken too.

I fight off the inevitable tears as I try to pull myself up but I can't do it. Without both legs, I don't have the strength the pull myself up from the floor.

'Help,' I call out. 'Help, Mum, please, help.'

A few seconds later, a man appears at my bedroom door.

'Oh, thank God,' I say. 'Can you help me up please?'

'Yeah, of course,' he replies.

The stranger scoops me up from the floor with a gentle ease and places me down on my bed.

'Are you OK?' he asks. 'Are you hurt?'

'I don't think so,' I say, looking myself up and down. 'Just achy.'

'Oh no,' he says seriously.

'What?' I ask, looking myself up and down for wounds or protruding bones I might've missed.

'I think you've broken your leg,' he jokes.

I laugh.

The stranger looks like he's in his late thirties maybe, early forties max. He's got very dark hair that is blown backwards, and a short, neat dark beard. He's got a bit of that super sexy salt and pepper colour going on, mostly in his beard and then just the tiniest bit in his sideburns, creeping up into his hair. He's wearing dark blue jeans and a black leather jacket. He looks like a bit of a bad boy, but the fun kind, with good looks and cheeky charm.

'Thanks for your help,' I say. 'I was just trying to hack my ex-boyfriend's email account and it went a bit wrong. My laptop needed plugging in, and then I just fell.'

'You were trying to hack your ex-boyfriend's emails?' he repeats back to me.

I can't tell if he's impressed or offended.

'Yeah,' I reply. 'What are you going to do, call the police?' I laugh.

'I am the police,' he points out, suddenly very straight-faced.

I stop laughing. 'What?'

'I am the police,' he says. 'DC Dean Gardner.'

'Wha . . . Are you here to arrest me, Detective?' I ask sarcastically. 'For failing to hack into an email account I have forgotten the password for?'

'Relax,' he insists, as a smile erupts across his face. 'If anyone's going to need a pair of handcuffs slapping on them, it's going to be me. My sister has roped me into your sad singles club.'

My eyes widen with horror. 'You're Faye's brother?'

'I am indeed,' he replies. 'And you're the one taking money off her to try and sort out my love life?'

There's this real mocking tone in his voice that I don't appreciate. But I did promise his sister I wouldn't tell him I wasn't charging her for this.

I raise my eyebrows.

'No judgement,' he says, with, actually, quite a lot of judgement. 'It's just . . . not sure I want someone sorting out my love life when their own is clearly a car crash.'

'OK, well, you need to leave my bedroom,' I insist, snapping into formal mode, ignoring everything he just said. 'Go wait in the function room, please, with the other . . . the other . . .'

'The other sad singles?' he asks with a devastatingly handsome grin. 'OK, sure. You need help getting back into your chair?'

'No, I . . . Oh, erm, could you get my mum for me please?' I ask pathetically.

'She just nipped out,' he replies. 'She seemed like she was in a bit of a hurry, so she let me in and rushed out with your dad.'

Well that's weird.

'Oh . . .'

'You need help getting downstairs?' he asks.

'No,' I reply insistently, but I absolutely do, or I'll be stuck in this teenager's bedroom all day. 'Actually . . . yes, please. I can find a way to get to the top of the stairs and go down on my bum; I just can't get the chair to the bottom.'

'I'll take the chair first, come back for you?' he asks.

'If you could take the chair to the bottom of the stairs, please,' I say. 'But you don't have to come back.'

'Back in a sec,' he says, ignoring me.

I feel a little rattled if I'm being honest. Who does Dean think he is? Waltzing into my bedroom, making me feel like a criminal?

With no other options I grab my phone from on top of my bed and punch a quick message to Patrick, telling him to cancel the mini break. With a bit of luck he'll do it, and he won't text me back.

Dean walks back into the room, still smiling widely, like he's reading my mind. He knows he's rattled me.

He removes his jacket to reveal a grey T-shirt that clings to his biceps in a way that makes me sit up and take notice – much to my own annoyance.

'Are you making yourself at home?' I ask.

'As warm and welcoming as you are,' he starts sarcastically, 'no, it's just easier to carry you downstairs without this heavy jacket on.'

'You don't have to carry me, honestly,' I insist. 'I can scoot down on my bum.'

'As funny as that would be to watch . . .'

We're interrupted by my phone ringing.

'Ergh, it's my ex,' I blurt out. 'I just texted him and asked him to cancel a holiday I booked in his name, but I don't ever want to talk to him again . . . which is why I was trying to get into his emails.'

Before I realise what is happening, Dean takes my phone from me and answers it. My jaw drops.

'DC Gardner,' he says before giving the other person a chance to speak. 'Hello?'

He has a thoughtful look on his face as the person on the other end of the line talks.

115

'No, this is Lola's phone,' Dean explains. 'Sorry, they just get so easily mixed up on the bedroom table when you have the same phone, you know? Imagine if she accidentally took my calls – violent assaults, gruesome murders . . . Anyway, pal, while I've got you, I think Lola was just after you cancelling that trip she booked. Looks like the two of us are going to be jetting off somewhere on those dates, is that OK . . .? Super, thanks . . . Bye.'

Dean hangs up and hands my phone back to me.

'I don't think he'll call back,' he says with a triumphant grin. 'Can I carry you downstairs now so we can get this weird workshop out of the way, please?'

I nod. Dean scoops me up and, of all the people who have carried me in recent weeks, I have never felt so safe. Usually, I feel on edge, like I'm going to be dropped, but I slot into Dean's arms just right, like the space was made for me.

'You're a regular superhero, aren't you?' I tease.

'All part of the job, ma'am,' he replies.

Chapter 19

Two things are very different at today's Unmatchables meeting. First of all, we have an extra person, because Dean is here. Second of all, unlike during our first session where everyone was attentively watching me and hanging off my every word, today, so far, no one is paying much attention to me at all. Everyone is staring at Dean.

As far as the ladies go, I get it. Dean is undeniably handsome, and he's definitely up there with Will on the list of Marram Bay's most eligible bachelors (even though, so far, they seem like complete opposites). Dean is clearly Kim, Channy *and* Doris's type. What I don't understand is why Toby can't take his eyes off him, although now that I'm looking more closely, I can see a harmless aggression in his eyes. I suppose he feels threatened.

'Do you have handcuffs?' Channy asks Dean, after he finishes telling us a bit about himself.

Dean – a local detective – was born and raised in Marram Bay. He looks and sounds like a real man's man, from his manly good looks to his passion for rugby league. He mostly talked about his hobbies and his job, only briefly mentioning that he is divorced. It doesn't sound like he wants to talk about that.

'I do have handcuffs,' he says with a chuckle. That cheeky

glimmer in his eye sparkles.

'Do you actually use them?' I ask. 'Is there any real crime in Marram Bay?'

'Well, I cover a larger area than Marram Bay,' he explains. 'And if there isn't any crime, then I'm obviously doing a good job.'

'Anyway,' I start, changing the subject. 'Today we're going to work on how to talk to members of the opposite sex. Build our confidence, work on our conversational skills . . . Toby, do you want to help me out?'

'Oh, no, I couldn't,' he says. 'I'm not ready yet.'

'You don't really need to do anything,' I tell him. 'It's just to give an example to everyone.'

'I can't,' he insists.

'OK, no worries,' I tell him.

For a moment, the function room is in complete silence. We're all sitting in the middle of the big empty room again, in a circle on what is usually the dance floor area.

'I'll do it with you,' Dean offers.

'It's OK,' I start. 'I'm sure I can do it alone.'

'Well, that isn't the spirit of this club, is it?' he says. 'We're not here so we can keep doing things alone, we're here so we can do things with other people.'

I can't help but feel like he's taking the piss out of me.

'God, do it with him,' Channy insists with a sigh. 'Before I do.'

'Young lady, he is far too old for you,' I insist firmly. Where the hell did that come from?

'Ah, so I'm old,' Dean muses. 'That's why I'm single?'

'I didn't say you were too old,' I reply, getting a little flustered. 'I said you were too old for a twenty-two-year-old. Anyway, conversation.'

I take a few seconds to compose myself. Yesterday went so well and now, with Dean here, I can't seem to get anything right.

'OK, well, before I demonstrate how to talk to the opposite sex, it's worth noting that, before you can get to know someone else, you need to know yourself.'

Dean scoffs. I shoot him daggers.

'I know that it sounds cliché, but it's a lot harder to be happier with another person if you're not happy with yourself. And that's not to say you need to change yourself, but you do need to know who you are, what you want – and you need to believe in yourself. Know your worth. If you know how amazing you are, how can anyone else possibly miss it?'

'That makes sense,' Kim says.

'So, talking to people – and these rules can apply to anyone, really, male, female, just to chat, or if you want to make friends. These aren't strictly romance rules. Dean, say you walk into a coffee shop and I'm standing there, what would you say to me?'

'You have the right to remain silent . . .' he jokes. The room roars. Everyone finds him so funny and so charming – everyone but me.

'Assume you're not there to arrest me,' I point out. 'How might you strike up a conversation with me?'

'Well, I wouldn't,' he says. 'You don't look like the kind of woman who would appreciate a man cracking on to her while she's just trying to buy a coffee, and even if you did, I can't know that for sure.'

I massage my temples. This isn't even sincere; he's just doing it to screw with me because he doesn't want to be here.

'Am I annoying you?' he asks.

'No,' I lie.

'I'm a detective, remember, I can tell if you're lying.'

'You're a Marram Bay detective,' I remind him. 'The only thing you investigate is which goat ate the flowers in the school garden.'

'Probably Phillip,' he replies, as though I'm just supposed to know the local goats.

'Oh, that Phillip,' Doris says with a knowing laugh. 'Did you know he's from France? You have to speak to him in French.'

119

'*Je sais ça*,' Dean replies.

'Wait, sorry,' I start, going off course. I can't let this pass me by. 'Phillip is a goat and he's from France?'

'Yes. Alfie Barton, the farmer up at Westwood Farm, bought him on the internet,' Doris explains. 'He's a pygmy goat, so only small, but he's mischievous.'

I can't help but stare for a moment.

'I used to be his cleaner – Alfie's not Phillips's,' she says.

'Alfie is my mate,' Dean tells me. 'He runs the farm, makes posh fruity ciders. We go to the rugby together – his lad loves it. You'll be amazed how much random French you can learn from a man constantly screaming at his goat.'

I just don't know what to say. I feel completely lost.

'Ah, Alfie Barton, there's a man I wish was single,' Kim says with a sigh.

'Oi,' Channy says angrily. 'That's my boss's fella you're talking about.'

'I know, I know,' Kim insists. 'Lily is lovely. But still . . .'

'OK, I feel like we're way off track,' I say loudly.

'You'd like Lily,' Dean tells me. 'She's a cockney too.'

'OK, I'm clearly not a cockney,' I point out. 'I was born here.'

'Sorry,' Dean says with a cheeky smile. 'I just thought you sounded like a Londoner.'

'To talk to people in public,' I say loudly, hopefully overriding everybody else's voice. 'Start by making normal conversation – ask them if they've eaten here before, what drink do they recommend. Compliment them on something – nothing weird, nothing sexual. Just, you know, I like your watch; that's a cool phone case – something like that.'

I look over at Dean, waiting for him to say something mocking. He doesn't say anything. He just grins.

Everything, from his outfit to his attitude to his bad-boy good looks remind me of Jeffrey Dean Morgan's character in *The Walking Dead*. The only thing he's missing is the baseball bat.

'Once you're chatting to people, you have to give them your undivided attention,' I continue. 'It's important to—'

'Lola,' I hear my mum call out from a different room. 'Lola.'

'Just one second,' I tell the group before wheeling myself over to the door.

'What's up?' I ask her quietly.

'I need to talk to you,' she says. 'It's important. It's about your dad.'

'Oh God, what's wrong?'

'We'll talk when you're done here,' she says. 'I didn't realise you were still going.'

'Mum, you can't do that – I'm worried sick now.'

'Just finish up,' she says. 'I'll make us some lunch and we can chat.'

'Is Dad OK?'

'He's fine,' she reassures me. 'Talk soon.'

As I wheel myself back over to the gang, I can't stop worrying about what she's going to tell me. Is something wrong with my dad? Is he ill? Is this why he's on a health kick? Oh my God, is that why he's lost weight, because he's ill?

'You OK?' Kim asks me.

'Yeah, sorry,' I say, trying to get back on track. 'Where was I?'

'Something about how, when you're talking to someone, you need to give them your undivided attention,' Dean reminds me smugly.

I think I'm supposed to find that funny, but I don't. All I can think about is what is going on with my parents. The sooner I get the session over with, the sooner I'll know. I don't know if that makes me want to hurry up or slow it down.

Chapter 20

In the kitchen my mum has laid the table and covered it with finger sandwiches, crisps, scones and little cakes. There's a large pot of tea and two cups, which she begins to pour the second I wheel into the room.

'OK, it must be something bad,' I say. 'Because, if this is my lunch, there isn't a carrot in sight.'

'There's carrot chutney on the cheese sandwiches, but I take your point,' she says. 'Sit down. Or, rather, wheel up, I suppose. Take a sandwich.'

'I can't eat until you tell me what's wrong,' I say.

'There's no easy way to tell you this,' she starts. 'Your dad is having an affair.'

I burst out laughing. 'As if,' I practically cackle. 'No offence, Mum, but even you struggle to tolerate Dad. No other woman would put up with the excessive snooker watching and those weird little undies he's wearing.'

'It's not a woman,' my mum corrects me, 'it's a girl – one of the girls from the tourist centre. She's nineteen.'

My dad is a volunteer for the tourist board, working out of a little hut on the beach a couple of times a week. He's one of a few people who work there. It's mostly retired people or young people looking for something to put on the CV. I considered it myself, in the summer before I went to uni.

I stare at my mum. I'm speechless.

'I realise this is a lot for you to take in,' my mum tells me calmly.

'How can a nineteen-year-old girl find a man my dad's age attractive?' I ask in astonishment.

'Oh, I don't know,' she says. 'Maybe she thinks he has money because we own this place. Hah! Someone wants to tell her how much we spend on little bars of soap – it's more than you'd think.'

'How do you know he's having an affair?' I ask.

'He's been volunteering much more. I've seen calls to the tart on his phone – he wipes his text messages.'

'Yeah, because he's scared of identity theft. He's deleted every text and email he's ever received,' I say with a laugh. 'And I take it her name isn't "the tart"?'

'It's Karla.' My mother snorts and rolls her eyes. 'With a K.'

'That tart,' I joke.

'You don't believe me and that's fine. He's your dad and you think the best of him, but do me a favour, Lola, just keep an eye on him, you'll soon pick up on it.'

It's easy to make jokes and write my dad off as too old to bag young chicks but my mum really does seem worried about this, and while she's always assumed I'm up to something (usually for no reason), she has always trusted my dad implicitly. It really worries me that something has been able to rattle her.

'Mum, if you're really worried about it, let me look into it. I'll get to the bottom of it,' I promise her, leaning over in my chair to hug her, careful not to fall out this time.

'Thank you,' she says, preening my hair for me. 'Don't eat too many crisps, OK?'

'OK, Mum,' I say with a laugh.

'So, enough about me,' she says. 'How are the sessions going?'

'Yesterday was great, but I really struggled with today's.'

'I saw that dreamy new fella who started today,' she says. 'I let him in earlier, told him you were in your bedroom.'

I laugh. 'Unbelievable,' I say to myself.

'What is?' my mum asks, sipping her tea innocently.

'You told me I had a lifetime ban on boys in my bedroom,' I remind her. 'And today, you just sent a random man up.'

'So I sent a client up to your bedroom,' she says, unaware of how dodgy that sounds. 'Plus, it's not like you can get up to no good with that thing on your leg, is it?'

Don't I know it.

'Well, the new guy is very annoying,' I say. 'His sister arranged this for him, she made out like he's a hopeless case – she might be right. He was acting the class clown the whole time, refusing to take things seriously.'

'Well, did you ever think that might be some sort of front, for some sort of insecurity?' my mum asks curiously.

'It did cross my mind that there might be some reason he doesn't want to meet someone, yes, but it could also be that he doesn't want my help,' I reply.

'Give him the benefit of the doubt, hey?' my mum suggests.

'Like you're doing with Dad?'

'Well, I am now, because you told me to,' she replies.

I think for a moment. 'Maybe I'll give him a few one-on-one sessions, see if I can get through to him when he isn't playing the clown.'

'Is he a comedian?' my mum asks.

'He's a policeman,' I reply. 'A detective.'

'Wow, that's a respectable job,' my mum says. 'Not quite a doctor, but it's up there. Speaking of doctors, have you heard from Will today?'

'Nope,' I reply.

Don't think this hasn't been at the back of my mind all day – I feel like I've really blown it with him. Things just got so awkward last night – but it's hardly my fault, is it? I mean, I know it was my broken leg that, erm, halted proceedings, but I didn't ask for a broken leg. I gave it my best shot.

'What do we have here?' my dad asks as he walks into the kitchen.

'Paul,' my mum says nervously, like she's the one who has been caught with her pants down. I suppose she feels disloyal just suspecting him. 'What are you doing here? I thought you were volunteering all day?'

'Thought I'd pop home for lunch with my girls,' he says. 'And what a lunch it is.'

'I thought Lola deserved spoiling,' she says. I notice her relax a little. She must feel relieved that he's come home to have lunch with her. If he were having an affair, would this not be the prime time to do it in?

'So how's it going today?' I ask my dad. 'And can you pass me the cream please.'

'It's going great,' he replies. 'You know the Valentine's Day Festival is coming up? Well there's talk of having it outside, on the island, at the abbey.'

'Erm, the abbey haunted by a jilted bride?' I ask. 'Cream please.'

'It's a proper romantic spot – lots of couples go there,' my dad insists. 'Lots of proposals there.'

'Pass me the cream,' I say slowly. 'And, go on, give me the tourist bit about the abbey. I don't quite remember how the story goes.'

'Hope Abbey, an eighth-century building that has been in ruins since the eighteenth century. Rumour has it there's a secret tunnel network underneath the island, which the monks who lived in the abbey used as an escape route in times of trouble,' my dad says, reeling off the tale like I'm sure he does all the time. 'It's a popular spot for lovers, with hundreds of marriage proposals happening there each year. This is in spite of the rumours that it is haunted.'

It's nice to see my dad light up like this, nerding-out over the history of the island.

'Paul, are you going deaf in your old age?' my mum teases. 'Lola asked you to pass her the cream.'

Instead of laughing it off like he usually would and passing me the cream before continuing with his story, my dad pushes his chair back in temper and yells at my mum at the top of his voice. 'I am *not* getting old!'

My mum looks like she wants to cry but she doesn't and that must take strength because I've got a lump in my throat just watching. This is completely out of character for my dad. I don't think I've ever heard him raise his voice like that before, not even at a snooker foul.

Affair or not, there is certainly something weird going on with my dad. I just need to work out how I can get to the bottom of it.

Chapter 21

It's been a few years since I visited the Hopeful Ghost pub – I think it might have been Christmas three years ago. I come home every year to spend Christmas with my family, but I always head back to London to spend New Year with friends.

This pub is one of the few things in Marram Bay that moves with the times. Everywhere else prides itself on being classic, which is what the tourists want. When it comes to the pub though, no one seems to want a little old bloke pub full of guys with flat caps and their elderly dogs. Instead, the Ghost is a super modern gastro pub, with shabby chic, intentionally mismatched furnishings, uber cool folk bands and weird and wonderful drinks – more than your average pub. Being the home of Westwood Farm, the Ghost has the widest variety of their fruity booze I have seen – fruit ciders, fruit-infused spirits, fruity wines.

I'm sitting by the lovely warm fire (the harsh January weather feels even harsher up here, by the sea) sipping on an alcohol-free elderflower cider, waiting for Dean to arrive. He's been working this evening, but we absolutely need to talk about what he wants to get out of our sessions, so I agreed to meet him here when he finishes. My mum dropped me off, wheeled me in, and told me to message Will to make sure he knew nothing funny was going on, that it was strictly work. I didn't have the heart to tell her that I haven't heard from him – I suppose he's busy at work. That, or last night was just so embarrassing he doesn't want to see me.

I notice Dean walk in. He glances around the room and gives me a thumbs-up before heading to the bar to grab a drink.

'How's it going?' he asks, sitting down at the table next to me.

'Not bad,' I say, shuffling in my wheelchair.

'Can't we get you some crutches?' Dean says.

I can't help but pull a puzzled face at his use of 'we'.

'I have a check-up soon. I'm going to ask,' I reply. 'They said I have to keep my weight off it, and the cast is so heavy, my boyfriend negotiated to get me a chair. I think he was worried he'd have to help me if I had crutches.'

Dean looks at me for a second.

'Ex-boyfriend,' I correct myself. That must be what gave him pause.

'So it's a recent break-up?' he asks.

'Yes,' I reply. 'But, in hindsight, it was always going to happen. We casually dated for too long, made it official but still didn't see each other much. He had work and . . . things.'

'Ah, *things*,' he repeats back to me. 'I understand *things*.'

'Well, we're not here to talk about my love life, we're here to talk about yours,' I remind him. 'Have . . . *things* ever got in the way of your relationships?'

Finally, things make sense. If Dean's wife cheated on him, it's no wonder he's struggling to get back into a relationship. He'll have a hard time trusting.

'Nope,' he replies. 'Never been cheated on but you don't need to be, to recognise that it's a crap thing to go through.'

I nod in agreement. Damn, I really thought I'd had him figured out then. I can tell that he doesn't want to talk about what went wrong with his marriage, not yet at least, so I'll leave it for now.

'How's the drink?' he asks me, changing the subject.

'Great,' I reply. 'These booze-free ones are so good, you actually don't care that they're not alcoholic.'

'My buddy makes them,' he tells me.

'Ah, yeah, you said earlier,' I reply. 'That's really cool.'

'Yeah, it's great for me, when I go to his house. Cider on tap – literally,' he jokes.

As he has a little chuckle at his own gag, I get lost looking at him. Little creases frame his eyes and his cheeks pull into that huge grin of his. It's a contagious one. You can't help but smile too (unless he's ruining your dating classes or catching you hacking your ex's emails that is).

'Look, there's a reason I asked to meet with you,' I start.

'Uh-oh,' he replies. 'Someone's in trouble . . .'

'OK, see, this is the problem: you don't take things seriously,' I point out. 'I know that you don't want my help and you think that this is all just a big joke, but what you need to remember is that your sister set this up for you because she loves you, because she's worried about you, because all she wants is for you to be happy.'

Dean's face falls into something more serious. 'I know,' he admits. 'I know that. Her heart is in the right place I just . . . I don't want this. I don't need this.'

'I'm sure you don't,' I reply. 'You're a good-looking bloke, you've got a good job, great friends. You seem like you're happy. But, you know, what's the harm in humouring me? It's something to do, it keeps me busy – don't you feel sorry for me?'

I smile and bat my eyelashes, deciding that maybe a little playful humour of my own might be what's needed to get through to him, but that's not what he picks up on at all.

'You think I'm good-looking?' he asks.

'What? No! I . . .' I'm babbling. 'I'm just saying, you're not *bad*-looking.'

'Not *bad*-looking *is good*-looking though, right?'

Perhaps this is why he's single.

'You are just incapable of taking things seriously,' I tell him.

'And you might think it's cute, and other people might think it's cute, but I don't. I'm just trying to do my job and I've got enough on my plate and enough of my own stupid shit with my wanker ex-boyfriend and my parents are driving me mad and I've got all these responsibilities, and Will isn't texting me, and I just want to go to the bloody toilet on my own, without any help, and shower myself, and not need my mum to help me and . . .'

Ah crap, I've unravelled. I need to try and pull it back.

'Sorry,' I say.

'Don't apologise,' he insists. 'Listen, I'm sorry about your ex, but if I know him, and I think I do after our conversation – cockney, scares easy, doesn't know a good thing when he has it – then I think we can both agree, you're well rid. I'm sorry about your leg, but you're on the mend. I'm sure your parents are doing their best. And I don't know who Will is, but he's an idiot if he doesn't text you.'

I smile. 'You're actually pretty charming when you want to be,' I point out. 'Will is someone I went on a sort of date with. It was a bit awkward and I haven't heard from him since.'

'Do you think maybe you're moving on a bit quickly?' he asks. His eyes narrow and his brow furrows, like he's genuinely concerned for me.

'Do you think maybe you're moving on a bit slowly?' I reason.

'Touché,' he replies with a chuckle. 'Just, you know . . . Ahh, forget it. OK, you've convinced me. I will give this a go, for my sister, because I love her.'

'Thank you,' I reply. 'I promise you, it isn't going to be as bad as you think it is.'

'I'll be the judge of that,' he says. 'So, what do we do first?'

'I worked with this guy once – he was the frontman of a popular rock band. He'd spent years partying, drinking too much, having loads of casual sex.'

'Oh, OK, maybe this isn't going to be as bad as I thought,' he says with a wink.

I roll my eyes, amused.

'Anyway, when he finally met someone that he liked, he'd forgotten what it was like to have a girlfriend. He didn't know how to compromise or do things with someone else. So, why don't we try and practise a little compromise? Is there something you like that you might not think a woman would enjoy?'

I watch the cogs turning in Dean's head as that little glimmer appears in his eyes. He pinches his tongue between his pursed lips as he formulates a plan.

'Actually, there is,' he eventually says.

'OK, so why don't you find something for us to do that you think I won't like, and I'll find something for you to do after that I'll probably be more into than you?'

'OK,' he says. 'Tomorrow. I am going to text you an address in the morning; you're going to meet me there.'

'Erm, OK,' I say. 'And what happens there?'

'We compromise.'

Dean has the look on his face of a man who has something very specific in mind. Is it weird that I'm looking forward to it?

Chapter 22

'Oh . . . my . . . God . . .' I moan. 'Oh my God!'

'Do you like that?'

'I love it,' I practically squeal. 'It's so good.'

'Not too hard?'

'Not at all!' I insist.

'Everything OK in here?' my dad asks as he enters the kitchen.

'Everything is great,' I enthuse. 'Robbie has just made me some brunch and . . . oh my God! Seriously, he's the best thing that has ever happened to this place.'

Since Vince flounced out of the kitchen and Robbie took over as head chef, he has really come into his own. He's trying new recipes left, right and centre, and they are all absolute winners.

Today, for brunch, he has made me . . . well, I don't know what to call it, but what it is, is a soft-boiled egg stuffed inside an avocado, which is covered in crispy breadcrumbs. It's a millennial's dream – if it doesn't have a name, he should absolutely call it that.

'Please, try one,' Robbie says to my dad.

My dad examines it suspiciously before taking a bite. As the perfectly cooked yolk runs out, I feel like I'm in an M&S advert.

'Bloody good, that is,' my dad tells him. 'Good work, lad.'

Robbie looks so pleased with his work. I'm so happy for him.

He probably would've been here for years, working under Vince, being underappreciated.

We make small talk as we eat before my dad finally asks me if I'm ready to go. He's giving me a lift, to meet Dean, *somewhere*.

My mum got me up and dressed before I ate, so I'm all ready to go. As she helped me into my clothes and pulled my long blonde hair into French plaits for me, just like she used to do when I was a kid, she told me to keep an eye on my dad for her, to sound him out in the car, to try and work out if *something* is wrong. So far though, he just seems like my usual, quiet, straight-talking dad.

'So, this lad I'm taking you to see,' my dad starts as soon as we've set off.

I laugh. 'He's not really a lad, he's a man – a police detective, in fact. A proper grown-up.'

'Is this not a date then?'

'No, no, no,' I insist. 'It's work. I'm trying to help him find love. His sister asked me to help him. He's divorced. She just wants him to find someone.'

'Divorced?' my dad says, looking away from the road to glance at me for a second. 'How old is he?'

'Oh, he's not old,' I say. 'Maybe forty, tops.'

'How old do you think I look?' my dad asks, seemingly out of nowhere.

'Erm, I don't know,' I say.

'Come on,' he prompts. 'I don't look my age, do I?'

'Well, no,' I reply. 'You look great.'

My dad nods, more than satisfied with my answer. He's quiet for a few seconds before the latest Dua Lipa track comes on the radio.

'Ah, I love this one,' he says, turning it up. 'The girls play it at the hut all the time.'

I suppose the girls at the hut are the younger volunteers at the tourist information centre. Weirder than my dad seemingly hanging out with them, listening to Dua Lipa, is just how odd he seems right now. My mum is right: he does seem different. My dad doesn't care about pop music or if he looks young for his age!

I feel immediately uncomfortable and turn the music down.

'Get any good scores on *Pointless* last night?' I ask him. If there is one thing my dad loves, it's quiz shows.

'I didn't watch it.'

'What?' I gasp. 'I don't think you've missed an episode since the show started . . .'

'I just didn't fancy it, and, well, it's not very cool, is it?'

My jaw drops at the idea of my dad living his life based on what is and isn't cool. He's in his fifties. Aren't you supposed to be happy enough in your own skin to live your life how you want to by that age?

'Well, here we are,' my dad says as we pull up on a residential street. 'I'm going out tonight, so let me know if you need a lift home later.'

'But you never go out,' I point out.

'Lola, what is wrong with you today? Why do you care so much about what I'm doing? We don't see you for months at a time and now you're back and you're bloody interfering,' my dad rants, instantly shutting me up.

'Sorry,' I say weakly.

My dad helps me out of the car and into my chair. He asks me if I want him to wait with me until Dean appears but I tell him no thank you. I feel awkward around him. He's definitely up to something, I'm just not sure what. I still don't believe he'd ever cheat on my mum, but something isn't right . . .

I'm snapped from my thoughts by my phone ringing. It's Dean.

'Hey, you close yet?' he asks.

'Erm, I'm here,' I tell him. 'I'm outside a random house?'

'Great, I'll be there in two seconds,' he says. 'Are you excited to spend a couple of hours doing what I want to do?'

'I am,' I tell him. 'Are you looking forward to what I have planned for us after?'

'I am indeed,' he replies. 'Oh, I see you.'

Dean hangs up and hurries over to me.

'So, just so you know, one of my friends is here with me, and I haven't told him that my sister hired you to find me a bird because, you know, that's so embarrassing. So as far as he knows, we're friends. OK?'

'Yeah, sure,' I reply. 'But where are we? Are we at your friend's house?'

'Nope,' he replies. 'I said I'd meet you here to throw you off. Where we're actually going is around the corner.'

'Oh, OK . . .'

Dean wheels me along the street and around the corner where, tucked away, surrounded by houses, is a stadium. It's not the biggest stadium I've ever seen, not a patch on Wembley, but it's big enough.

Dean wheels me over to a tall man in a rugby shirt who is waiting excitedly to greet us.

'Lola, this is my buddy Alfie, Alfie this is Lola,' Dean introduces us.

Alfie leans forward and hugs me in my chair. 'Nice to meet you,' he says.

'Nice to meet you too,' I reply. 'Big fan of your booze.'

'Oh yeah?'

'Yeah,' I reply. 'How do you think I ended up in this chair?'

I'm not sure whether or not Alfie knows I'm kidding, but as Dean laughs, he laughs too.

'So, Lola, Alfie's lad has gone to Blackpool with his friend for the weekend, so we have a spare ticket,' Dean tells me.

I smile to myself, at the thought of Marram Bay locals going to Blackpool for a weekend. From one tourist town to another. I suppose the tone is totally different though.

'Oh wow,' I blurt out. 'I've never even watched rugby before.'

'Well, just think of it this way, if you had a boyfriend, and he liked rugby, you'd have to get used to going all the time – I think they call it compromise.'

Alfie is oblivious but I know just what Dean is getting at.

'OK,' I say, as a huge smile pulls across my face. I guess I am excited. 'Let's do it.'

Alfie gives me my ticket – well, his son Frankie's season ticket – and we head towards the gates that are currently welcoming a big crowd of fans.

'Where and how am I going to sit?' I ask.

'Well, there is a bit for wheelchairs,' Dean says. 'But, I've had a word, and there's somewhere we can store your wheelchair, if you want carrying to your seat?'

'Erm . . .'

'I'll carry you,' he offers. 'I've done it before, I know what I'm getting myself into.'

'OK, yes, let's do it,' I say excitedly. 'Pick me up. Let's score some goals . . . Are they goals?'

Dean laughs. 'We'll get to that soon enough,' he tells me.

'How old is your son?' I ask Alfie.

'He's ten going on fifteen,' he replies. 'He's my stepson. Only been in his life a couple of years but last year he decided he loved rugby so I find myself here every time there's a game on. I've never really been that into sport, but even I love it now. I think you'll enjoy it.'

Once my wheelchair is stored, Dean carefully lifts me up and carries me to my seat.

'Is that OK?' he asks.

'Great,' I reply.

I think he was referring to his grip but, I don't know, it just feels good being in his strong arms.

We have to hover for a few seconds, at the bottom of the steps that lead into the stands, so Dean readjusts his grip. As he does so, he accidentally grabs my bum.

'Eee,' is the awkward, involuntary sound that comes out of my mouth.

'Are you OK?' he asks me. I don't think he's realised what

he's done.

'Yeah, all good,' I reply.

'Don't be so nervous,' he tells me. 'You're gonna love it, I promise.'

Chapter 23

The Pingley Pirates are playing the Cholton Cobras. The Pirates are our team – I say our, because that's how you have to talk. They're not the Pirates, we're all the Pirates, and what you might not know is that, as fans, it is apparently super important for you to bellow instructions at the players. Everything from shrieks of 'what the hell are you doing?' to technical instructions such as 'get it out wide' to impossibly violent and hopefully not literal demands like 'break his neck'.

'What do you think so far?' Dean asks me.

'It's good . . .' I say hesitantly. 'It seems like there's a lot going on. I just . . . have no idea what it is.'

'Basically, if you've got the ball, all you have to do is put it down over the other team's try line. While you're doing that, the other team are going to throw themselves at you, to try and stop you. You can pass the ball to your teammates, but you're only allowed to throw it backwards, see.'

I watch as one of the Pirates throws the ball to a teammate, before no less than four Cobras launch their gigantic frames at him, all piling up together on the ground.

'Oosh,' I wince. 'That was violent.'

'It's pretty much always like that,' Alfie tells me. 'Apart from when it's *even more* brutal. Took me a while to get used to it.'

I like Alfie. He seems like a sweetheart. He's not your typical farmer-looking kind of guy. He has soft features and kind eyes. Sure, he looks strong enough, but he seems like a modern man – I mean, come on, he fell into rugby league because his stepson was into it.

The crowd of rugby goers aren't quite what I expected. I've only been to a few football games in my life (which I didn't really enjoy, to be honest) and it wasn't like this at all. Things here seem so laid-back. The last time I went to watch football, I felt like I was surrounded by young laddish men but here, I'm surrounded by families, excited little kids wearing pirate hats and eye patches, and old people who look like they've been coming here their entire lives. Everyone is so full of passion, chilling out, drinking, eating pies and hotdogs.

There's a band, somewhere – I haven't been able to spot them yet – with wind instruments and a big drum, belting out chants and popular songs with lyric changes to apply to the players, which everyone but me seems to know the words to. The last one I heard was about a Pirates player called Billy John, sung to the tune of Michael Jackson's 'Billie Jean'. I don't feel like I know enough about the players to understand the in jokes, but it's amusing nonetheless.

Dean isn't singing along. Nor is he chanting along with the 'you don't know what you're doing's' and 'the referee's a wanker's'. I don't know if that's because I'm here, or because he's a bit too cool, but you can tell that he loves it. Surrounded by all this family-friendly positive energy, I don't blame him. It's hard not to feel happy and excited here, like you're part of a big family.

By halftime the score is 16–10 to the Pirates.

'Do the teams ever draw?' I ask.

'With so many ways to score points, and different things being worth different points, it's really rare that teams draw. This is a pretty important final, for the Yorkshire derby, so you can't end on a draw. Are you enjoying it?'

'I am,' I admit. I can hardly believe it myself, but I am.

Halftime is a party all of its own, with impossibly small children from local primary schools coming onto the pitch to play mini games in little squares of the pitch set out with colourful cones. There's a kicking competition, where a couple of people from the audience kick the ball from three different places on the pitch to win a variety of prizes and there's even a dance troupe, fronted by the Pirates mascot himself, Pauley the Pirate, who can bust some incredible moves for a man in a massive pirate costume.

As we get back into the second half, and the Cobras start closing in on us, the crowd somehow comes alive even more. Their cheers and chants roar around the stadium, the band is in full swing and Pauley the Pirate is excitedly dabbing on the sidelines. I might not know about rugby league, but even I can tell that this game must be important.

As one of the Cobra players kicks a goal to equalise, 22–22, Dean hangs his head in his hands.

'I swear, draws hardly ever happen,' he insists with a bemused chuckle.

'What happens now?' I ask.

'We just need to hope we do something in the final . . .' Dean looks at the clock '. . . two minutes.'

If I could move an inch, I'd be on the edge of my seat. Can they do it in this amount of time? I don't even know but, for some bizarre reason, I believe in them and in an even more surprising turn of events, I actually really, *really* want them to win.

From where we are sitting, behind the try line, we can see the Pirates trying their best to make it in our direction. Two minutes left to battle past the Cobras soon turns into one, which quickly turns into thirty seconds.

A big, buff player called Gamble gets the ball. You can see him thinking, it must only be for a split second, about what to do. With a wall of Cobras in front of him, he kicks the ball. Time stands still. The stadium falls silent. The ball flies through the posts and comes hurtling towards us. I lift my hands to my face to stop it from smashing into me. Dean also reaches out to protect me, which sort of ends up in us both catching it.

Everyone goes crazy.

'Oh my God, we won,' Dean says excitedly.

'We did?'

'Yeah, that drop goal gave us one point.'

Everyone is screaming, chanting, celebrating – myself included. I'm so happy and I don't even know why. I guess it's just hard not to get caught up in it.

A few people around us start chanting 'put it up your jumper' at us.

'They're telling us to keep the ball,' Dean tells me. 'The winning ball, no less.'

'You can put it up your jumper,' I laugh. 'It looks pretty dirty.'

'I can't believe we won in the last few seconds – now that's rare. Maybe you're a lucky charm.'

'Maybe I am,' I reply, smiling back at him. He looks so happy.

'Why don't you guys come over for dinner this evening?' Alfie suggests. 'I'll cook, Lola can meet Lily, we can hang out – celebrate the win.'

There's a hint of optimism in his invitation. I do wonder to myself, why he's so keen to continue hanging out, until it suddenly becomes blaringly obvious: he thinks Dean and I are on a date, and he thinks it's going well.

'Well, we're going somewhere after this,' Dean says tactfully. 'Somewhere that I don't know about because it's a surprise.'

'You'll find out soon enough,' I tease.

I suppose this is my chance, to say that whatever we're doing will end late and we can't make it, but . . . it might be helpful, to see Dean around his friends? This might be a good lesson for him?

'I'd love to come over after, if Dean is free,' I say.

'Yeah?' Dean says to me. He sounds surprised. 'Yeah, me too.

141

Count us in.'

'That's great,' Alfie says. 'I'll tell Lily. Just give us a bell when you know what time you'll be done.'

'Well, you've survived your first rugby match,' Dean says as he helps me to his car. 'And you enjoyed it.'

'I did,' I reply. 'I'm more surprised than you.'

Dean helps me into the passenger's seat and fastens my seatbelt before putting my wheelchair in the boot and joining me.

I eyeball the police radio in his car. It's weird, to think of him as a policeman. Obviously I know that he is one, I just can't imagine it, and I don't know how wide his jurisdiction is but I find it even harder to imagine any real crime happening here in Marram Bay.

'So, where to, miss?' Dean asks, doing his best impression of a chauffeur.

'To the Seafront Cinema, please,' I instruct in a similar high society tone.

'Ooh, the cinema,' he replies. 'And what's on at the cinema today?'

'Well, you took me to watch sports so, sorry, but I'm taking you to see a chick flick. And before you complain about not liking girly movies, that's what this is all about, OK? Compromise.'

'You didn't complain about the rugby, you loved it,' he reminds me. 'What makes you think I'm not going to enjoy a chick flick?'

'Hmm, I don't know, maybe the manly attitude, the hard-man job, the love of sports.'

It's obvious really.

'OK, so what lame girly movie are you forcing me to sit through?' he asks.

'*When Harry Met Sally*,' I tell him. 'Don't worry, it's really good. Even you might enjoy parts of it.'

The Seafront Cinema sits in the touristy beach part of Marram Bay. It's a Grade II listed building, which you could probably guess, even if you didn't know, because it's impossibly gorgeous.

They just don't make them like this anymore.

Built in the early 1900s, it has always been a cinema, and has maintained a lot of the authentic, early charm of what it was like when it was first built.

The Seafront Cinema is one of the only remaining gaslit cinemas in the country. It also has an external box office, looking out to sea, where you can purchase your tickets before you even step foot inside. Any modernisation over the years, such as installing new seats and a more modern concessions stand, have been so subtle, you'd never tell. With its classic-looking screen, its fuzzy red chairs and the retro lamps on the walls, it feels like stepping back in time.

Not quite jumping all the way back to the old days when it opened, but time travelling just a little, the cinema screens movies from all different decades. Today we're heading back to the late Eighties with *When Harry Met Sally*.

I can't imagine Dean being all that fond of the movie – I imagine he'd much prefer something with lots of weapons and violent action – but compromise is all about doing things that you might not want to do all that much. Plus, I really lucked out with the movie that they are showing today because *When Harry Met Sally* is all about where we find love – sometimes it's right under our noses. That might be an avenue to look into with Dean; perhaps the love of his life is a part of his life already . . .

I order a large cherry coke and a huge bucket of sweet and salted popcorn. What can I say? I'm a hungry girl and I like to snack when I'm watching movies.

'What are you getting?' I ask Dean.

'That's not to share?' he says with a laugh.

'Erm . . .'

'I'm just kidding,' he insists, before turning to the girl working at the concessions stand. 'I'll have what she's having.'

The hairs on the back of my neck stand on end. That's a line from the movie. What are the chances, that I bring him to see a movie and he quotes a line from it? I'm sure it's just coincidence and not a sign of any sort, but even so.

Dean loads my lap with our snacks and drinks before wheeling me to our seats.

'If you give it a fair shot and you hate it, we can leave,' I tell him.

Well, we *can* leave, but if we do I'll be sure to give him a lecture on compromise and falling at first hurdles.

'You're so sure I'm going to hate it, aren't you?' he replies. 'You really think I'm going to walk out?'

'Look, I'm just trying to help you,' I remind him. 'This stuff might seem dumb but it's going to get us to the bottom of why you don't want to be in love.'

'I've been thinking about it, and I think I've figured it out,' he starts.

'Oh yeah?'

'Yeah, see . . . I've been having this dream since I was twelve, where a faceless guy rips off my clothes.'

Oh, there it is, that cheeky glimmer in his eye.

'You bastard,' I laugh. 'I knew you were trolling me. You've seen this movie before, haven't you?'

'Of course I have,' he replies. 'You think because I'm a copper who likes rugby league, I haven't seen *When Harry Met Sally*?'

'Well, yeah,' I reply, shovelling a handful of popcorn into my mouth. I suppose I like to eat when I feel awkward too. Maybe I just like to eat . . .

'Rest assured, I have seen it, I love it, I am willing to sit through it now and be perfectly behaved.'

'Did your sister make you watch it? Or your . . .'

Why have I brought up his ex?

'I like romcoms,' he says with a casual shrug. 'It's OK to like romcoms.'

As the title card for the movie appears, Dean shushes me before I can say anything else.

'OK, quiet, it's starting,' he says.

Just when I think I am starting to figure this man out, he completely pulls the rug from under me. This is going to be a harder case to crack than I thought . . .

Chapter 24

Westwood Farm isn't very much like a farm at all. I grew up around farms, spending time in farmhouses, and this is not a farmhouse.

Alfie and Lily live in an ultra-contemporary mansion. Pretty much the entire place is made of glass, and with floor-to-ceiling windows on all sides, the place has a panoramic view of the countryside that I am so jealous of. With the rooms being mostly glass, there isn't much room for paint or wallpaper, but what this means is that the view, and the room, changes with the seasons. Right now it has a dark and wintry outside, offset by the warm glow of the fire inside. In spring, I imagine the pink glow of blossom trees and the yellow bursts of daffodils will be the wallpaper, before the miles of green that come with summer. I'll bet autumn is the best, with all its warm, cosy colours beaming in from all angles.

It's fully dark now, so my imagination is running away with me.

Lily is just as lovely as Alfie – such a sweetheart. She's from London herself, and she used to work in the city too, so we have a lot in common. We're a similar age, similar type – the main difference is that she's a mum. I think Alfie said their son was ten years old, but I can't believe she's a mum to a ten-year-old. She doesn't seem old enough.

The pair of them made dinner for us. Pork with all the trimmings, including the boozy cider applesauce Westwood Farms will soon be selling. Apparently, we were one of the first few people to try it. Of course, it was amazing.

Since then we've just sat by the fire, chatting. We're having coffee and biscotti that Lily brought from the deli she works in. I've been getting to know Lily better while Dean and Alfie chat, but I've still been keeping my eye on him, seeing what he's like around his friends, trying to work out how comfortable he is around proper couples.

'What are you grinning at?' I hear Alfie ask Dean, which catches my attention.

'Doesn't he always do that?' I ask, barging my way into their conversation.

'Only under certain circumstances,' Alfie tells me as he sips his coffee suspiciously. 'Usually when he thinks he's right about something . . .'

'Hmm, that's probably true,' Dean admits. 'But I *am* right about something.'

'Go on,' Alfie prompts.

'I'd rather not,' Dean replies smugly.

'Go on.'

'I don't think you'd want me to.'

'Come on, Dean, spit it out,' Lily demands. Even she wants to know now.

'You're pregnant,' he tells her.

I cringe. Never point out that a woman is pregnant, not when she has a bit of a bump, not when you see her buying a pram or walking out of an antenatal class, not when she has a huge bump and looks like she's about to pop – not even when she is giving birth. Not ever. And even if it were OK to point it out at blaringly obvious signs, Lily doesn't look pregnant at all. Not even a bit. She isn't even bloated after her dinner, whereas I feel like I need to roll my leggings down.

'What?' Alfie replies. His eyebrows shoot up and his jaw falls down.

'How do you know that?' Lily asks. 'How could you possibly know that?'

Dean just shrugs.

Lily turns to her husband suspiciously. 'Did you tell him?'

'Of course I didn't,' he says. 'I don't know how he knows.'

'What kind of detective would I be, if I didn't notice everything?' Dean asks. 'Sorry, I didn't want to find out before you wanted to tell me . . . I'm burdened with obsessive observation.'

I wonder to myself what else Dean picks up on. I feel like he can see right through me now.

'But how?' Lily asks.

'You weren't drinking this evening,' he tells her.

'Neither was Lola,' she replies.

'Yes, but Lola has a broken leg and she took painkillers after she ate,' he replies. 'Not only do you pretty much always usually have a drink with dinner but there was this guilt in your eyes as you poured my drink, like you were holding something back.'

'Mate.' Alfie laughs. 'You should be solving murders somewhere where they actually have murders. You're wasted here.'

'I'm pretty busy with a case at the moment,' Dean insists.

'Oh yeah, your tractor thing,' Alfie chuckles.

'That sounds too boring for me to even want to know a bit of what you're talking about,' Lily says. 'But, yes, we are pregnant. The doctor confirmed it today.'

'Congratulations,' I say. 'I don't even know you, and I'm so happy for you.'

'Yeah, congratulations guys,' Dean says.

'Thank you,' Lily replies. 'It's been a decade since I was pregnant with Frankie. I'd forgotten what it was like. The only part I really remember was the birth and that's only because it was on the tube.'

She says this to me, like we're in some sort of London club.

I try to imagine someone giving birth on the tube and it makes my blood run cold. Most of the time, I can't even get a seat.

'The doctor says all is well though.' Lily pauses thoughtfully. 'First time I've seen the doctor here – interesting guy.'

'How so?' I ask. I try not to sound too curious, but I'm pretty sure it's Will she's talking about. Will who still hasn't contacted me.

'You know, I thought he was flirting with me . . . but he either wasn't, or changed his tune when he realised I was knocked up.'

She laughs. I bite my lip anxiously.

'Oh, it's OK,' she reassures me. 'I don't think he was. He had a bird waiting for him, I think. Some dolly bird. I was his last appointment, so I guess they were going somewhere after.'

My breath feels heavy in my chest. Is that Will she's talking about? It has to be. Who else could it be? I don't even know what other doctors work there and I've left it too late to ask her his name now, I mean, why would I be asking *now*?

'You OK?' Dean asks me.

And now I know Detective Dean can see straight through me. He knows everything I'm thinking, everything I've done, everything I'll ever do.

'I'm fine,' I lie. 'Just my leg, I think I've done too much today. It's really starting to hurt.'

'Oh no, let's get you home,' Dean says.

'We don't have to rush,' I insist.

'It's OK, I've got an early start anyway.' He turns to Alfie and Lily. 'Guys, thank you so much for an amazing dinner, and congratulations again. I'm made up for you.'

The car door has no sooner closed when Dean starts interrogating me. 'OK, what's really wrong?' he asks.

'What? Nothing . . . I . . . ergh, I'm wasting my breath lying, aren't I?'

'What kind of detective would I be—'

'OK, OK,' I interrupt him. 'Will, the guy I mentioned, he's the only doctor I know around here. I went on a sort of date with

149

him. I haven't heard from him since and I'm guessing that's who Lily was talking about . . .'

'Ah,' he says simply.

I look out of the window as we drive through Marram Bay, heading for the causeway, which thankfully is open for a few hours still. Sometimes it's easy to get it right, other times it's a nightmare. If time had been on my side the other night, I wouldn't have stayed with Will long enough to make things awkward.

'We've been friends since we were kids but then I moved away. I know I'm only here now while my leg heals, but . . . I don't know what I thought was going to happen. He reconnected with an old girlfriend a few nights ago,' I admit. 'I guess my timing has just always been off with him.'

'So you're going back to London when you're better? You haven't got a taste for the sea air?' Dean asks.

'Nah, fumes and sweaty commuters all the way for me,' I joke, trying to perk up a bit.

'OK, I can't handle this,' Dean blurts out. 'If he's going to ghost you for another girl, he's clearly not worth it. I can't let you be sad about him, so, go on, do your worst, try to fix me – you like trying to fix me.'

I laugh. 'Thanks,' I say. 'I don't know what I'm more surprised about – that you're letting me fix you or the fact you know what ghosting is.'

'I'm surprising you a lot today, aren't I?'

'I guess you are. OK . . . hmm . . . well, now that I know that I know you're an expert on *When Harry Met Sally*, what can we take away from it?'

'That men and women can't be friends,' he says.

I frown. 'Well, I'm not sure how true that is, but what I take from it is that sometimes the person for you is right under your nose. So, are there any women in your life who you might not have considered romantically?'

Dean thinks for a moment. 'There's a prostitute informant I

frequently work with in Leeds,' he offers.

'Work, that's a good place,' I say, ignoring his joke. 'Anyone at work?'

'There's a DC called Karen I work with a lot. We get lunch together sometimes, but . . . I don't know, we don't have anything between us, in either direction.'

'Hmm, let me think on it,' I tell him.

At least if I figure out Dean's problems I'll stop worrying about my own. Why hasn't Will called me? Why do I care so much? I just need to let it go or pluck up the courage to call him . . .

However, despite knowing that I should practise what I preach, I've never been all that great at doing either.

Chapter 25

In ten minutes' time I have another meeting with the Unmatchables. That gives me ten minutes to call Will. I'm going to do it. I'm just going to do it and see what he says. I will say 'hello' and 'how are you?' and then I will let him do the talking, see what he has to say for himself.

'Lola, hello,' he says brightly as he answers the phone. 'How are you?'

'I'm good, thanks. How are you?' I reply. It's like no time has passed since we last spoke at all.

'I'm good, thanks. Things have just been so busy here. Sorry I've gone a little quiet on you; know that it wasn't intentional.'

Phew! So he's just been busy, and it was probably a different doctor that Lily saw. It's a huge relief. It's being in this wheelchair. I've got like a *Rear Window* thing going on where I'm looking at everything through a telescopic lens, just because I'm stuck in this chair and have nothing better to do.

'Oh, don't worry about it,' I insist. 'Do you want to go for dinner tonight?'

'Erm, sure,' he replies. 'Just checking the diary but it's clear.'

'Oh, OK, awesome,' I reply. 'Well, maybe you can pick where

we go. I feel so out of touch with what restaurants are around these days.'

'Sure thing,' he replies. 'I've got a patient to see so I'll look into it and let you know.'

'Wonderful,' I say. 'Well, have a good day and I'll see you later.'

'Yeah, you too,' he replies.

I sigh my biggest sigh of relief before wheeling myself into the function room where Kim, Doris, Channy, Toby and Dean are waiting for me.

'My mum informs me that she has put the heating back on, you'll all be pleased to hear,' I tell them. Everyone is sitting there in their coats. 'Apparently they turn it off when the line dancers are in because it gets a bit sweaty.'

'Billy Ray Cyrus will have that effect on you,' Dean reasons.

I smile at him. I'm starting to appreciate his constant joking around a bit more now – perhaps because I'm in a better mood, or because we had such a good day together yesterday. Maybe the two go hand in hand.

'So, before we get going, has anyone had any developments in their love lives since the last time we met up?'

'I've finally dumped the guy I'm seeing,' Channy announces.

'I mean, that's like the opposite of progress,' I point out with a laugh.

'I know but . . . man was trash,' she says casually. 'Promises me he'll stop messing around with other girls, I go over to see him and what do I find? A long blonde hair in his bed, and I'm not blonde, am I?'

'Sounds like you've got him banged to rights,' Dean says. 'Impressive detective work.'

'Cheers,' she says. 'If I hadn't just sworn off older men, I'd be trying on your handcuffs for size.'

'OK,' I say loudly. 'Today we are going to be talking about *When Harry Met Sally*. I watched it yesterday and it made me realise that, sometimes, the person we're supposed to be with is

153

already in our lives. They're not someone we're going to bump into down the bread aisle or match with on Tinder or Matcher or Grindr or whichever dating app you prefer.'

'Tinder,' Doris confirms with a nod. 'Not tried Grindr . . .'

'I don't think you'd like it,' I insist as she reaches into her handbag for her iPhone. 'So, think about the people you spend time with, think about the people you see every day, the people you know who are also single and looking for love . . .'

I'm laying it on really thick as a big old hint for Dean that maybe he should have a chat with the woman from work who he goes for lunch with, and just see where it goes. I'm not saying he should ask her on a date or try to kiss her or anything like that – God no – just chat to her, see if she's single, if she's looking . . . look at her in a different light and see if there's anything there he's been overlooking.

'Can men and women be friends?' Channy asks.

'Of course they can,' I reply.

'But can they?' she persists. 'Doesn't someone always want to bang someone?'

'I have plenty of male friends I don't want to bang,' I tell her, borrowing her phrase.

'Ah, but do they feel the same?' Dean asks. 'Or do *they* want to bang you?'

'OK, we all need to stop saying "bang",' I insist uncomfortably. Having Doris in the room sometimes feels like hanging out with my gran and I'm not sure we should be saying 'bang' in front of her. Then again, she has been on Tinder.

'I do love the movie but the question of whether men and woman can be friends is a pointless one,' I start. 'If a woman wants to be friends and a man wants more, that still equals friendship. If a man wants to be friends with a woman who wants to be more than friends, that still doesn't equal anything more than friendship. It's all about being what you are comfortable being.

154

Perhaps it is harder, to be friends with someone who you fancy, but that's on you. Don't punish your friend for not being sexually attracted to you.'

'Yeah, that's fair enough,' Dean agrees.

'I always seem to develop crushes on my female friends,' Toby says. 'But sometimes I think it's just because they talk to me. They never fancy me though.'

'You could still have already met the person who is right for you,' I tell him. 'You keep your eyes open; they could be right under your nose.'

I feel my phone vibrating in my pocket. I take it out and see that I have a message from Will saying that it had slipped his mind when we spoke earlier, but that he said he'd go visit his auntie tonight. He needs to take a rain check on our dinner date.

I glare at my phone suspiciously, as though it were the phone that just bailed on me.

'Can I borrow you?' Dean asks me. 'Just for a few minutes. I have a personal question.'

'Oh, OK, sure,' I say.

Dean wheels me away from the group and into the small storage room attached to the function room. The door has been left open, since someone set our chairs out for us.

'What's wrong?' I ask.

'What's wrong with me? What's wrong with you?' he replies.

Oh, for God's sake, I'd forgotten about his sixth sense.

'What?'

'You saw something on your phone and your brow furrowed, your face fell, and I can tell by your body language you wanted to throw your phone across the room,' he says. 'Now, I've wanted to throw a few phones in my time, but only when something has been up.'

I let out the breath I've been holding in for God knows how long.

'I called Will, asked him to dinner . . . He said yes on the phone but now that I think about it, he didn't sound all that enthusiastic. Now he's texted back and given me some excuse about seeing his auntie tonight.'

'Do you believe him?' Dean asks.

'I would be inclined to say no but . . . is this just because my ex cheated on me? Am I being overly sensitive?'

'You could ask him.'

'Ah, but if he's telling the truth I'll think he's lying, and if he's lying he'll be, well, y'know, lying, so . . .'

'OK, there's only one thing for it,' Dean says. 'Stakeout. Tonight.'

'What?'

'We'll watch him, follow him, see if he goes to see his auntie. If he does then you've got to stop worrying about it and get on with your life. If he doesn't, well, at least you'll know.'

'You'd do that for me?' I ask.

'What, sort out your love life? It's only what you're doing for me,' he replies. 'Someone has to sort out of the love life of the person who sorts out people's love lives.'

I laugh.

'Anyway, you were right with what you said before. Men and women can be friends.'

'Thank you,' I reply.

I feel like a crazy person, needing to know the answer, but my trust has been knocked and I don't know how to fix it. I just need to learn to trust people, but I need people to be trustworthy too, and that's on them.

If Will doesn't go to see his auntie then at least I'll know and I can stop wasting my time on him. Either way, I'm sort of looking forward to going on a stakeout with a real policeman, even if it's just to catch a cheater rather than a serial killer.

Chapter 26

Have you ever watched a slasher movie? Most often a beautiful, scantily clad, blonde bimbo will hear a bump in the night when she's home alone and instead of doing the smart thing and calling the cops she will go downstairs in the dark to check it out, and it's a movie, so it is almost certainly going to be something grisly. In situations like that the smart thing to do is stay where it's safe rather than risk walking in on something nasty . . .

Well, I have called the cops, but rather than sit pretty and hope everything is OK, I'm out here in the dark, in Dean's car, hoping there's nothing grisly waiting for me around the corner.

'We need to talk about what you think police stakeouts are like,' Dean says.

'Why?' I ask curiously.

'Let's just say movies have a lot to answer for.'

OK, so maybe I had my mum make us up two thermos flasks of coffee, and I brought sandwiches and doughnuts, but it's winter and I figured we'd be hungry.

'Oh, the doughnuts aren't a police-based dig,' I point out. 'They just go well with the coffee. And the sandwiches are from my mum. I told her we were going on an evening winter picnic. I made up something about how I was testing your endurance as a boyfriend.'

'I think that would be a different test,' he replies.

'I do too, but my leg is broken,' I joke.

The surgery is open until 7 p.m. today, for people who commute to jobs outside of the village and can't make appointments during work hours. So we're parked across the street from the car park, waiting for Dr Will to emerge so that we can follow him – hopefully to his auntie's house, where I will kick myself (at least I would if I could) and remind myself to trust people. Just because a man hurt me, doesn't mean all men are going to turn on me. Then again, if you're always stubbing your toe on the bed, you're going to be a little wary of beds.

'Oh, damn, I meant to ask you to bring your Savage Garden for the trip,' he says sarcastically.

'Oh, you clocked that, did you?'

'I did,' he says. 'I'm very observant.'

'Not that I feel like I need to justify my taste to a man who is wearing double denim,' I start. 'But not only was that a CD I got when I was probably about twelve, they're actually a decent pop band. One of the best.'

'Doubling down, I like your confidence,' he says. 'What's in that bag?'

'Oh, just the twenty-seven bags of crisps my mum sent for our fake picnic,' I reply.

'Twenty-seven?'

'There are actually five, I think. She sent flavour options.'

'I love crisps,' Dean says. 'I bet you I can identify all five flavours.'

I laugh. 'Really?'

'Yeah, really,' he says. 'Come on, try me.'

I smile at him. I get the feeling he's only doing this to distract me. It is torture, sitting here, waiting to see if the guy I like is lying to me. I might as well play his game.

'OK, sure,' I reply. 'But they're from my mum so they're just going to be your standard flavours, no berry and Prosecco or lamb and mint sauce.'

'Hit me,' he demands.

I reach into the Bag for Life between my feet, carefully open a packet of crisps and remove just one. Dean opens his mouth and gestures for me to pop one in. I do, weird as it is to be feeding him.

'Prawn cocktail,' he says confidently.

'I feel like this is too easy,' I admit as I riffle through the bags. But then I see one that might just catch him out. 'Ooh, OK, try this one.'

'I'm tasting onion,' he says through a mouthful of crisps. 'But not cheese and onion, not spring onion . . . pickled onion.'

'My God,' I blurt out in amazement. 'You are actually good at this.'

'I told you I was,' he says. 'I . . .'

As his voice trails off I follow his gaze through the windscreen that has steamed up a little. I can still see Will though, making his way from the surgery into his car.

'What happens now?' I ask.

'We follow him,' Dean says. 'If you still want to . . . We could always just sit here and keep playing the crisp game.'

I appreciate him giving me the opportunity to bow out, but I have to know. I need to put my mind at rest or I'll drive myself crazy.

'Nah, let's stick with the plan,' I say. 'When we realise that everything is fine, I'll feed you every last crisp in this bag.'

'As you wish,' Dean says as he starts his engine.

'How do you go about not being seen?' I ask as I attempt to lower myself into my seat.

'Well, normally when I'm following someone, I've learned a little of their routine, so I know if we're heading to their home or their work,' he explains. 'You stay a few car distances away, avoid driving directly behind them, try not to copy their route

159

exactly, change lanes if you can, give way to people. If people aren't expecting to be followed, which I doubt your doctor will be, they're not really looking for someone on their tail. I don't drive a flash car; this one just kind of blends in. If it's work, I'll make use of the surveillance equipment, park in the opposite direction, use my mirrors – I don't think any of that will be necessary tonight though. We're just seeing where he's going, right?'

'Right,' I say. 'We'll just see if he arrives at his auntie's house and whether he does or he doesn't, it will be easy to tell. I don't exactly need to make a Kodak moment out of it.'

'Right,' Dean echoes. 'And whatever we see, we'll deal with.'

I bite my lip. He's got me worried now. Does he think Will is lying to me? How could he know? He hasn't met him, so it's not like he's done his creepy detective analysis of his body language and the tone of his voice.

'Looks like he's slowing down,' Dean says. He pulls up across the road from the little cottage Will has stopped outside. 'That's Sunflower B & B.'

'Chances his auntie lives in a B & B?' I ask softly.

'You do,' he points out.

'Hmm.'

He messes around in his car for a few seconds before getting out and approaching the door. He's only halfway up the garden path when the door opens and a woman emerges. She hurries over to Will, wraps her arms around his neck and kisses him passionately. I want to look away; every fibre of my being wants to look away. I feel like I'm staring at an eclipse. I know I shouldn't be looking. It's detrimental to my health to be looking. Still, I can't make myself look away.

'So, chances that's his auntie?' I ask pointlessly.

'It's looking pretty slim,' Dean replies.

As Will ushers the woman into his car I recognise her. It's his ex-girlfriend. She just had to come back into his life right now, at the same time as me. I don't suppose I stood a chance. Don't get me wrong, I'm not blaming her at all. She probably doesn't even remember me. Will should have been honest with me. I don't know if he was ever going to have dinner with me but then got a better offer, or if he was always going to call and bail on me. I suppose either way, he would have broken it to me eventually.

'You want me to follow them?' Dean asks as they drive away, starting up his car and putting it into gear.

'Nah,' I reply. 'I don't really need to see any more. That was pretty clear.'

Dean shuffles in his seat. I don't think it's the chair that is uncomfortable though, I think it's the situation.

'Lola, I'm so sorry,' he says placing a hand on my shoulder. He gives it a squeeze.

'Meh,' I reply. I don't want to cry in front of him. 'It's just men, isn't it? Well, some men. Always on the lookout for something better or unable to turn it down, blah blah blah.'

'You've just got to know that we're not all like that,' he says. 'I, for example, completely leave women alone.'

A half laugh slips out. 'I should probably go home,' I say. 'We've got an early group meeting tomorrow.'

I feel like I've been punched in the stomach. I somehow feel even worse than I did when I found out about Patrick . . . I suppose it's because I told Will what I'd just been through and he was so sympathetic. Excellent bedside manner, but it was all an act. I just feel like such an idiot. I knew it was too soon to be moving on but I did it anyway. I suppose I thought it would distract me, and I had this stupid, romantic notion that we were meant to be together and, you know, in the words of *When Harry Met Sally*, when you find that person you want to spend the rest of your life with, you want the rest of your life to start straight away.

'Yeah, of course,' Dean says. 'I'll take you home now.'

'Thanks.'

As we drive along the causeway in the pitch black, I look out to sea. There's nothing there though, just dark, empty space. It doesn't feel like a world to be explored or a dangerous freezing cold sea, it's just black. The end of the movie.

'I really am sorry,' Dean says. 'At least you have our group of misfits to keep you busy, eh?'

'Yeah,' I reply. 'Thanks.'

I suppose he's right but the last thing I want to do is help other people find love now. Well, what's the point? Doesn't it always end in tears?

Chapter 27

I woke up feeling blissfully happy. It only lasted for a moment before reality kicked in, a matter of seconds, but it felt wonderful. For those first few seconds I was awake, I thought I was back in London and that nothing had changed. Then I tried to roll over and it felt like my leg was stuck in a bear trap. I'm not in my lovely flat, working my dream job, with my handsome boyfriend and army of fabulous friends. I'm here, in agony, with absolutely nothing going for me. My friends aren't my friends anymore – if they ever even were. With my job and my money and my boyfriend, I just fit into the bullshit lifestyle they all live for. As soon as the things that made me fit in with their way of life started to vanish, no one wanted me around anymore. Patrick wanted someone on his arm (and absolutely not in a wheelchair). My friends wanted someone to look sexy in their Instagram snaps. I can see them all online, across various social media accounts, living their best lives, and it's like they've forgotten I exist. No one has even sent me a message to see if I'm OK.

What a life I had. I thought I had everything but it was all superficial bullshit. And now, when I'm better, what do I do? Do I go back and resume my role? How can I? I want friends I can rely on, not friends who will drop me as soon as I can't go clubbing anymore.

Everything is getting to me today. I appreciate my mum dressing me but, my God, today it felt even more demoralising than ever. I feel like such a stupid, pointless baby. How is this my life? How am I even an adult? People my age have houses and husbands and kids and pets and responsibilities and what do I have? My mum dressing me, my friends bailing on me, men treating my life like trash.

'You OK?' Kim asks me.

'What?' I reply, snapping out of my little bubble of doom.

'Are you OK?' she asks again. 'You've just sat there in silence for about five minutes.'

I glance around the room dopily, taking in my surroundings. 'Yes, sorry, I was just thinking . . .'

I fall silent again. How on earth am I supposed to find these people love when I'm questioning if it even exists right now. You think people feel something for you, whether it's your partner or your friends, and then you realise it was nothing. A pure fabrication. Maybe even a projection on my part – I thought everyone loved me for me.

'Do we think she needs to see a doctor?' Doris asks.

'Maybe,' Channy replies. 'Just make sure it's not Will bloody Coleman.'

My eyes dart in Dean's direction. I shoot him an angry look. I can't believe he's been gossiping about me. I'm about to say something when he gives me a subtle shrug, as if to tell me he hasn't said a word.

'Why wouldn't we call Will?' Kim asks. She works with him, after all. 'Today is his day off, anyway.'

'Because he's a dick,' Channy says. 'I don't want to ruin the good doctor for anyone, but he's the older guy I was seeing. The one who was messing me around, cheating on me, treating me like crap. I'm so much happier for dumping him.'

'Will was the guy you were with?' I ask.

'Yeah.'

'Didn't you only break up with him like two days ago?'

'Yeah,' she replies. 'When I found a blonde hair in his bed, I knew he must still be at it.'

'Probably just need a painkiller, don't you?' Dean suggests. 'I'll take you for one, and you'll need to eat, right? I should make you a sandwich. Is everyone free for a while? Why don't we reconvene in an hour? After lunch?'

I assume everyone is happy with this, but I don't pay attention. The cogs are turning in my head and my mood is shifting from one of self-pity to something a little more vengeful.

'Well, that's a plot twist,' Dean says once we're in the privacy of the kitchen. 'What are you going to do?'

'I'm going to call Will,' I say. 'Invite him over, have a chat.'

'I'm not telling you how to get away with murder,' Deans insists.

'You won't need to,' I reply. 'I've got a much worse torture in mind for Dr Love.'

Like the difference between Liam Neeson in *Love Actually* and Liam Neeson in *Taken*, my attitude has completely shifted. I don't feel like a victim, I don't feel hard done by, I feel like I want to make him sorry, and unlike Liam I *do* know who he is, I *do* know where he is, and I *will* make him sorry he ever messed with me and my new friends.

Chapter 28

'I'm sorry about before,' I explain to the group. 'I think the pain was making me a bit funny.'

'No worries, my love,' Doris assures me. 'We're glad you're feeling better.'

'Today we're talking about behaviour in relationships. What's the worst thing you've done in a relationship?'

'Not had one,' Toby says very matter-of-factly.

'I was quite stuffy with my husband,' Doris says. 'He was a joker, a bit like this one.'

She nods towards Dean who flashes her a smile. She must see a little of her late husband in him because this visibly warms her.

'He never took anything seriously and it used to annoy me. Now I realise that he was the light in my life and now that it's gone out . . . well . . . I'm not sure there's a bulb in the world that can replace him. I wish I'd spent less time complaining about him being silly, not tidying up after himself, leaving his dirty gardening boots in the conservatory . . . None of it seems important now.'

Oh boy, do I have a lump in my throat. I thought I was depressed before but this has tipped me over the edge. For a moment, everyone just stares at her. Kim wipes a tear from her face as quickly and as subtly as she can get away with.

'None of that, my love, I'm OK,' Doris reassures her.

'Shall I go next?' Dean asks, moving things along. It's funny because I know that he hates this stuff and that he thinks it's stupid, and yet he's doing it anyway. I know he was only attending because he thought his sister had paid for it, but now I feel like he's participating, and it kind of feels like he's doing it for me.

'In my marriage I perhaps wasn't as vocal as I could've been, about what made me happy and what I wanted,' he says. 'I should've spoken up more.'

Intriguing . . .

'My biggest relationship mistake is this bloody idiot,' Channy announces as Will walks into the room.

'Oh, hello,' I say brightly, turning round in my chair to greet him. 'This is our newest member, Will. Come in, sit down, take a seat.'

Will looks confused. He ought to. I told him there was an emergency and he needed to come over immediately.

'Sit down, Will,' I say firmly.

There's this look in his eye, like he knows I know everything. Well, with Channy sitting here mouthing off about him, he must know I know that much, at least. I'm pretty sure I told him about Channy, in anonymous terms, when we had dinner. As everything falls into place in his head, he grabs a chair and sits down with us.

'Will, I can't believe you're here,' Kim says. I don't think she knew anything was going on between us. I never told her I was going for dinner with him. I suppose she's just surprised because he's a handsome doctor who shouldn't have any trouble finding women, which he clearly doesn't. His problem is obviously that he finds too many women.

'We broke up like two days ago – I can't believe you're here,' Channy adds.

'Weren't you already here?' he asks her defensively.

'Yeah, for advice about you and the way you treat me.'

'Are you not a very good boyfriend, Will?' I ask. 'We were just talking about what our worst behaviours in relationships were. Would you like to tell us yours?'

'A wandering eye,' Doris suggests.

'It's a different part of his anatomy that wanders,' Channy says.

'Is there a cure for that, Doc?' Dean asks him.

Oh, poor Will. Poor, sweaty Will, melting in the function room central heating that everyone else is enjoying. His guilty conscience is burning its way out of him, turning his face red, allowing beads of sweat to hurry down his cheeks. He almost looks like he's crying, but I don't imagine he feels guilty enough for that. Just embarrassed and perhaps a little frustrated at being caught out.

'I'm sorry,' he tells me.

'Don't apologise to me, apologise to Channy,' I insist.

'Sorry, Chan. Sorry, everyone.'

'You know what, I'm not sure you should be here,' I say. 'I think it's completely inappropriate, turning up here, thinking it will just be another way to meet women, like when you came to the speed dating night.'

'He was at the speed dating night?' Channy squeaks. 'He told me he was visiting his auntie.'

For Will, 'visiting auntie' is clearly a completely disgusting euphemism.

'I think you should get out,' I tell him. 'Before anyone says anything else.'

A blatant but silent threat that if he doesn't get out of my sight right now, I will tell everyone everything. He might not care about women, but I'm sure he cares about his reputation in the village. Oh my God, I bet it *was* him who was flirting with Lily, before learning she was pregnant. What a pig.

'Lola, wait, can we chat in private?' he begs.

'Absolutely not,' I reply. 'You mess with my friends, you mess with me.'

'I really think—' he starts, but Dean doesn't let him finish.

168

'OK, I think you need showing the door,' Dean says, jumping to his feet, taking Will by the arm with one hand, the other gripping grimly on Will's shoulder.

'Oh yeah, what are you, a bouncer?' Will asks as he tries to struggle free.

'Worse, I'm a police officer,' Dean replies.

'Phwoar,' Doris shouts. 'Put your handcuffs on him.'

Dean frogmarches Will to the door, gently nudges him through it and closes it behind him.

'I think that's the last we'll see of him,' Dean announces, dusting off his hands theatrically. 'Unless, you know, we get ill . . . but there are other doctors – ones with cleaner hands.'

'I can't believe you did that for me,' Channy says. 'It was like you all had my back.'

I could tell her about me and Will, but what would be the point? It would only upset her, and we're both rid of him now.

'You're going to meet someone who doesn't think it's OK to treat you the way Will treated you,' I tell her.

'I know,' she replies. 'I think I already have.'

Oh God, I hope she's not talking about Dean. What is it about the mention of handcuffs that makes women go nuts? Myself included, if I'm being honest. There was definitely something pretty sexy about watching Dean manhandle Will like that . . .

Chapter 29

Robbie has given me food for thought today. Quite literally, he's trying to cheer me up with cakes.

Not content with revamping the food menu, now he's working his magic on the dessert menu and, believe me, it is magic.

After observing that I 'looked like I needed cheering up', Robbie signed me up for taste testing, so I'm in the kitchen, waiting for him to feed me better – a trick straight out of the Linda James playbook, although I don't think she's put him up to it today. I guess I've championed him since day one so he probably feels brave enough to run things by me first.

'So, what's on the menu, chef?' I ask with as much enthusiasm as I can muster. I don't have much enthusiasm for anything right now, especially not the Unmatchables' meeting that's planned for after. I keep suggesting we space them out a little more, but everyone is raring to go. Every few days, everyone finds a spare forty-five minutes. They just keep asking me to arrange another one, and I don't really have an excuse not to help them; I'm just sat on my arse all day. It all seems so stupid and all I can think about is how to nip it in the bud. I don't think I'm the right person to help anyone anymore – at least not while I'm feeling like this.

'First up we have two different types of profiteroles: chocolate and salted caramel. But here's the twist,' he says excitedly. 'They're filled with ice cream instead of cream.'

'Oh, damn, that does sound good,' I admit. At least being miserable hasn't taken its toll on my appetite, although that might be dangerous for my thighs while I'm unable to move.

'You can try either,' he starts.

'I'll try both,' I quickly insist.

'Or you can try both.' He laughs.

Oh, wow. Profiteroles stuffed with ice cream are a dream come true for me – a dream I didn't even know I had.

'Yep, they're incredible,' I tell him. 'My dad will *love* them.'

'Really?' he asks, his eyes wide with optimism.

I thought chefs were supposed to be egotistical, angry, sweary types – like Vince. Robbie isn't like that at all; he's kind of nervous, terrified people won't like his food. Someone once told Vince their steak wasn't medium rare so he stormed into the dining room, snatched it up, marched outside with it and threw it into the sea. The customer had no idea; she thought he'd just taken it to the kitchen to make her another one. My mum told me the full story later.

'Really,' I insist. 'So, so good. Can you even top that?'

Robbie pushes a small glass dish across the table to me.

'Strawberry and elderflower trifle,' he announces before biting his lip anxiously.

I can't help but raise my eyebrows. 'Interesting,' I say. 'Let's give it a go.'

I take a reasonably sized spoonful, making sure to get a little bit of each layer before popping it down the hatch.

'Oh my *God*,' I gasp. 'Robbie, oh my God.'

'Yeah?'

'Yeah! What kind of sponge is that, is that lemon?'

'Yeah, lemon drizzle.'

'Wow. You are just so incredibly talented. Seriously, my mum and dad are lucky to have you.'

'Thanks,' he replies.

'Do you have a girlfriend?' I ask curiously.

'Nah,' he says with a laugh. 'Between travelling for work and being a bit of a dork, I never really seem to hit it off with people.'

'There's nothing wrong with being a dork,' I reply. 'What do you think makes you a dork?'

He reaches into his trouser pocket and pulls out a set of keys. He dangles them in front of my face.

'See this key ring?' he asks.

'The little silver hammer?' I reply. 'Yeah . . .'

'It isn't a little silver hammer, it's Mjölnir.'

'Me-what now?' I ask with a laugh.

'Mjölnir,' he says again, as if hearing it a second time will make sense to me. 'It's Thor's hammer. I'm a Marvel nerd.'

'Ohhh,' I reply. 'OK, yes, you are kind of a dork, but there are plenty of dorks out there.'

'Yeah but sadly we're all introverts,' he laughs.

'Lola,' my mum squeals angrily as she enters the kitchen. 'Oh, Lola, come with me, come see what you've done.'

'I don't actually think I've done anything,' I insist as she wheels me through the B & B.

As we pass the reception room, Dean, Kim and Doris are waiting. Kim is helping Doris take her coat off. Dean is reading one of the tourist leaflets from the stand in the doorway. My mum's huffing and puffing catches their attention.

'You lot can come see this too,' she announces. 'Come on, follow me.'

As instructed they all follow me and my mum into the function room. She wheels me up to the storage cupboard before whipping open the sliding door. Inside there, on a pile of yoga mats on the floor, Channy and Toby are kissing. Like, really kissing. My mum opening the door only just breaks them from their passion. Toby looks like a rabbit in the headlights as he jumps up to his feet.

172

Channy just sits up. I can't say that she looks as if something like this hasn't happened to her before.

'Oh, God, guys, no, what are you doing?' I ask.

'Only what you told us to,' Channy says.

I hear my mum gasp behind me. 'Lola James, I thought you found people love, not . . . forbidden fumbles.'

I hear Dean echo the words 'forbidden fumbles' but my mum doesn't pick up on it.

'You've turned this place into a knocking shop,' she tells me.

'Come on, Mum, they were only kissing. And I certainly didn't tell them to,' I insist.

'You did,' Channy replies. 'You gave us that talk on how the right person for us was right under our noses, and you were like really, really stressing it to us. We realised you meant within the group and, well, we didn't really fancy each other but we gave it a go and turns out we do.'

'We might be in love,' Toby says sheepishly.

'Well, *maybe*,' Channy says. 'We'll see.'

'Erm,' is about all I can say. I smack my lips together as I rack my brain for the right words. I lightly chew on my lip until something comes to me. 'Yeah, OK, that's not what I meant though.'

'Oh,' she replies. 'Well, it worked, so . . .'

'Yeah, I guess all is well that ends well,' I reply, still cringing at the whole thing. 'Weird kind of yoga though . . .'

'Lola, this isn't funny,' my mum snaps. 'That's it, I'm pulling the plug on this whole thing. You're not doing this here anymore. What if a guest had seen? Or one of my line dancing old ladies?'

'I'm an "old lady" and I didn't mind it,' Doris says, a little offended that my mum is trying to make out like her generation aren't raging deviants who want to watch a young goth chick and a nerdy teenager kissing in a cupboard. I look over at her and notice she's got her glasses on now, which she didn't when I first spotted her in reception.

'Well then I'm glad I'm kicking you all out,' my mum says. She raises her hand as though she's going to run it through her hair, but that would make it messy so she retreats. My mum likes to keep a tidy head of hair.

'But, where are we going to go?' Doris asks. 'This group is the highlight of my social calendar.'

'I'm sorry but I'm not having this debauchery going on in my B & B,' my mum tells me. 'I've got enough on my plate, Lola. This is my business.'

'Yeah, OK, fine, class dismissed; everyone needs to go home,' I say.

If I'm being honest, I'm not that upset about this at all. I don't want to do this anymore. I'm not in the mood for it. I am bitter and grumpy. I just want to wallow.

'I need to get back to work. Please disperse,' my mum instructs.

'Well, at least Channy and Toby found . . . something before my mum pulled the plug,' I say with a shrug of my shoulders.

'What about us?' Doris asks. 'What are we supposed to do?'

'I don't know,' I say. 'I . . .'

I'm about to say that I don't think we can have the classes anymore when Dean chimes in.

'Why don't we all go for a day out on the beach?' he asks. 'Is everyone free? I know it's not exactly the weather for it, but there's plenty to do indoors as well.'

'Oh, I don't know,' I say. 'I'm sure everyone is busy.'

'I'm sure we're not, right, guys? What about it? Going out into the field trying to find love?'

I'm sure Dean thinks he's doing the right thing by everyone; keeping the group together and finding us somewhere else to go. I just want to give up now.

'Oh, yes, that would be lovely,' Doris says.

'Yeah, today is my day off,' Kim adds. 'I'm all for it.'

'Can we come?' Channy asks. 'I kind of feel like we're a part of the gang, even if we're loved up.'

'Of course you can,' Dean says. 'You're like my weird little sister. Toby is like my weird little brother . . . and yet somehow I don't consider the two of you related. I must make that clear.'

'Dope,' she replies.

'I actually have a couple of days off, so I'm wide open,' he says. 'Anyone else have a car?'

'I do,' Kim says helpfully.

'Perfect,' he replies. 'We'll split into two groups and all head over to the bay.'

Reluctantly I go along with the plan. I suppose it will do me good to get out of the house, especially with my mum on the warpath. Does she really think I'd convince two youngsters to hook up in a cupboard? I can honestly say, in all my years doing this job, I've never done anything remotely like that.

I suppose it's my fault. I *was* laying it on so thick, trying to convince Dean that he should get to know his colleague a little better. No wonder they thought I was hinting that they should get it on. They seem like they like each other though . . . I never would have called that. They are such opposites. Channy is a wild child and Toby is a nervous teenager. I guess opposites do attract.

Dean loads me into his car before running around to get the door for Doris.

'My lady,' he says playfully.

Doris giggles like a schoolgirl.

'If I were thirty years younger,' she tells him.

'If you were thirty years younger, you'd still be in school,' he replies.

Where oh where has that grumpy, mick-taking cynic gone who marched straight into my bedroom and near-threatened to arrest me? This guy isn't that guy; this guy is kind of happy and smiley and fun. He's charming – more charming than he was when he was playing the bad boy. Now he's just regular charming. I think I like being around him. I'm kind of glad he's signed us all up for a beach day. At least it's not all doom and gloom, at least I have someone to cheer me up, even if it is just the guy I'm trying to find a girlfriend for.

Chapter 30

Our trip to the bay started out pretty civilised. We went for afternoon tea at the cute little café on the seafront, tucking into sandwiches, scones and cakes, washed down with pots and pots of tea. It was nice, although the sweet treats didn't have anything on what Robbie made me earlier.

We sat at a table by the window and chatted as we looked out to sea. It's was as cute and touristy as you could get. We didn't talk much about love and relationships, but that's just the way I wanted it to be today. I suppose it has been a nice distraction.

The bad news is that I forgot to bring my painkillers with me, and I haven't actually taken one today so I'm really starting to feel my leg aching. The good news is that after our afternoon tea we decided to take a walk on the beach, but because it was far too cold we ended up going into Treasure Island, the amusement arcade.

I know what you're thinking: Lola James, why are you, a woman in her thirties, excited about a seafront amusement arcade? Do you just really like penny machines? It turns out that Treasure Island has changed a lot since the last time I visited, which is probably when I was a teenager.

When you walk through the doors it still looks the same, with the same retro arcade games, from penny machines to those horse-racing ones to rows and rows of various slot machines, all lighting up in different colours and bursting with different noises to entice people to play with them. What has changed is the big burly bouncers who stand at the back and, no, it's not a sad sign of the times; the bouncers stand in front of a hidden door that leads to the speakeasy upstairs.

So, in a fortunate turn of events, I have wound up not only temporarily off painkillers, but in a bar. A real, well-stocked bar, with an extensive, fancy cocktails menu. It might not be drinkies with my London girlies but it's something even better. Just a bunch of weird, mismatched friends and a couple of horny kids hanging out in a bar together.

'I don't know why he keeps ID-ing me,' Toby complains as he places a round down on the table in front of us. 'You'd think once would be enough, but he asks to see it every time – even though he knows that I am, he says he refuses to believe I'm eighteen, or that I carry my passport around as ID.'

'I think you look eighteen, babe,' Channy reassures him.

'Thanks, babe,' he replies.

There is only a split second before they launch at each other, face first. It's been like this pretty much all day with the two of them snogging. I suppose it's cute. As they really get into it, Channy clumsily swipes Doris's drink off the table but she's too engrossed in her kiss to even realise.

'I, erm, I'll go get another one,' she says as she gets out of their way.

'I'll come with you,' I tell her. 'Keep you company.'

What I actually want is a break from the peep show. I'm happy for them, obviously, but I feel really, really single right now. Watching them so into each other is making me feel strangely lonely.

'Can we get another sea breeze, please?' Doris asks the barman.

'Already?' an elderly man sitting at the bar chimes in.

'What's it to you?' Doris asks.

'Nothing to me,' the man replies. 'I thought that young man just brought you one.'

'His girlfriend knocked it over,' I reply.

'And who are you to care?' Doris asks him.

She's a sassy bird, when she wants to be.

'I'm the owner,' he says. 'Technically.'

'Technically?' Doris replies. She seems very interested in talking to him.

'You see that stressed-out fella over there, hunched over a laptop, looks like a cross between a lumberjack Salvador Dalí and Steve Jobs?'

His description is actually spot on.

'He's my son. We own this place together. I used to run it, when it was just an arcade but he's come in and modernised it and he's making a really good go of it. I'm kind of surplus to requirements now and, since my wife died . . .'

'Oh no, your wife died?' Doris asks. 'My husband died.'

'I hope this isn't too forward, and I hope you don't think it's because our significant others are dead, but I'd really like to buy that drink for you, and I'd love to have a natter if you fancy it?'

Doris, God love her, looks at me for permission.

'I wouldn't want to ditch my friends,' she says.

'Your friends do not mind,' I assure her. 'If you want to have a chat, go for it.'

'The name is Sylvester,' he says. 'And I promise to take good care of your friend.'

'You'd better,' I tell him. 'You think I look injured? You should see the other guy.'

Sylvester just laughs.

I'm about to wheel myself back over to the others when I decide to check my phone quick, see if I have anything from my mum welcoming me back into the family home. I do hope she isn't still mad at me.

My phone opens up on Facebook and at the top of my newsfeed is a picture of my friends – my ex friends. They're all there with their partners but there's one girl I don't know. I notice her first, which is funny considering it is Patrick who has his arm around her waist. He's already got a new bird, and our friendship group are completely accepting of her. Lola who, eh?

'Do you have shots?' I ask the barman.

He has to lean over the bar to see me.

'Sorry, I just . . . I thought you might be a kid,' he says with a laugh. 'Thought I'd better check. We've got Kapop Shots . . . bubble gum or blueberry?'

'Oh God,' I can't help but blurt out. 'Blueberry, I suppose.'

'One blueberry, coming right up.'

'Make that two,' I tell him.

'Lola James, is that you?' I hear a female voice ask.

'Unfortunately,' I reply when I see who it is. It's Erica Salmon, the girl who used to bully me at school.

'Oh my God, it's been years,' she says. 'I'm just here with the kids and my husband. I popped up for a lemonade. You look no different.'

Erica doesn't look much different either, other than being pregnant. She's still tall and skinny with a brunette bob that is so perfect it could pass for a wig. I don't know how to describe her face other than cute, but in the most small, piggy, obnoxious way. Did I mention she used to bully me at school? She made my PE years hell. It's hard not to be bitter about it, especially when I'm in such a bad mood.

'And look at your leg,' she says. 'Remember how much bigger your legs were than everyone else's at school? We'd call you Steam-Lola. Remember?'

I spent years listening to this crap. I wonder what it would be like to stand up to her now that I'm not an embarrassed little kid who wants to cut her own legs off.

'You know that only hurt my feelings when I was a child,' I

tell her. 'Now you're just some mean bird closing in on middle age. It's not very becoming of a woman in her thirties.'

As I knock back both my shots, her jaw drops.

'Neither is getting drunk in the middle of the day,' she says, nodding towards my shots.

'Another shot please, Mr Barman,' I say. I'm only really doing it to annoy her. I probably won't drink it. But who does she think she is, walking over here like I would ever be pleased to see her, as though we were friends, when she's the reason I spent my childhood thinking I was too fat even though I wasn't.

'I think she's had enough,' Erica tells the barman. 'Lola, do you think you might have a drink problem?'

'Yeah, my problem is that I don't have a drink,' I reply.

'I mean a problem with your drinking,' Erica insists.

I roll my eyes. 'It sounds like you're the one who has a problem with my drinking, love.'

The barman happily pours me another. He seems amused by our bickering, but this is an argument that has been on the tip of my tongue since my GCSEs. I was always just too scared to have it.

'Well, you are just horrible now,' Erica exclaims. 'You used to be such a sweet girl.'

'I used to be a pushover,' I point out. 'Well not anymore – no one is treating me badly ever again.'

As my voice rises a little, I suddenly realise this little outburst is about more than just this girl being the reason everyone in our PE class called me Steam-Lola for four years. It's just the icing on the cake. I mean, come on, it's the fact that it's the first thing she brought up upon seeing me again! I've never understood why school bullies are always so naff. Steam-Lola, really? Steamrollers don't have fat legs; they don't have legs at all. They should've called me Swo-la – not that I'm helping. I just think that, if you're going to do something, at least do it right.

Erica takes her lemonade and walks off in a huff.

Soon after, Dean sits down on a stool next to me.

'Hey,' he says. 'You OK? You never came back, and I noticed that Doris has pulled.'

'Hey,' I reply. 'Have you ever seen desperate housewives?'

'That's not really my kind of TV show,' he replies.

'I wasn't talking about the TV show,' I reply as I watch Erica leave.

'You OK?' he asks me.

'Yeah, I'm fine,' I reply. 'Just . . . annoyed at a lot of things and a lot of people.'

'And, on top of all that, you have a blue tongue,' he tells me. 'I hope you don't need to see a doctor.'

'Har-har,' I reply. 'It's from my pity drinks. Would you like one?'

'Sure,' he says before knocking it back. 'But only because you probably shouldn't.'

'I can't even reach the bar properly, never mind prop it up and get smashed to drown my sorrows.'

Kim comes over to the bar. 'Guys, Toby and Channy have asked me for a lift home,' she says. 'It's probably for the best. They're about two buttons off a public indecency charge. I might call it a day too. Thanks for a lovely time though.'

'Yeah, thanks for coming,' I reply.

'See,' Dean says. 'You helped them find love. And love over there – Doris is having a great time.'

'Yeah, go Doris,' Kim chirps. 'You've just got me and Dean to sort out now and your work here is done.'

She smiles optimistically. I'm glad she isn't feeling defeated. I, on the other hand, just feel . . . meh. I have three people to sort, in reality: Kim, Dean and myself, but honestly, what's the point?

'See you guys later,' Dean calls after them as they head for the door.

'Bye,' Kim calls back. Channy and Toby are kissing as they walk. Toby actually clips his shoulder on the doorframe. It jolts his body but he doesn't even notice. Oh to be young and in lust . . .

As Dean looks into my eyes he narrows his own. His eyes are

the darkest shade of brown I've ever seen. So brown that you can't make out any of the usual details people have in their iris. I can tell that he's trying to get inside my head by the way he's looking at me, but, with those dark eyes, it is impossible to see inside his. I can feel him creeping in through the little flecks of blue in my green eyes, finding a route to my deepest, darkest thoughts.

'Do you ever feel like you're in a mess?' I ask.

'Are you kidding me? Divorced in my thirties, remember,' he tells me.

'At least you're not living with your parents.'

'Nope, I live alone with my dog.'

'You have a dog?' I ask, perking up a little.

'I do, Rufus, a chocolate Labrador. My ex-wife and I got him before we got married. When we split, she didn't even fight to keep him, can you imagine? When she said I could keep him and that she wasn't bothered about seeing him, I knew then that I'd rather spend the rest of my life with him than her. He's the cutest thing. Because I work unusual and sometimes long hours, my sister goes over to take him for walks. If you leave the door open long enough, he'll take himself for a walk. He'll just pick up his lead in his mouth and stroll off; it doesn't even need to be fastened to his collar. He's a good boy though and if he can't find his lead, he won't be off without it.'

'My God, that's impossibly cute.'

'Yes and, most importantly, proof that love exists, and that I am capable of it.'

I laugh, but my smile doesn't last long.

'I know what you need,' Dean says.

He removes a £10 note from his pocket and uses it to point to a sign behind the bar as he addresses the barman.

'Can you turn this into pennies, please,' he asks referring to the sign about getting change for the arcade games. 'We're going to go and feed coins to your penny machines until we win . . . well, more pennies I guess.'

The barman laughs and obliges, giving Dean a little plastic tray full of pennies.

'I'm not sure if this is more or less than I expected,' he says looking down at his coin haul. He thinks for a second. 'I suppose there's one thousand there.'

'You expect me to feed one thousand pennies into a machine?'

'I expect you to feed one thousand pennies into multiple machines and I expect you to smile while you're doing it, OK?'

I laugh. 'OK, sure, if I can reach in this chair.'

'I didn't think of that, but we'll find a way.'

'I actually have an appointment at the hospital tomorrow, to check how my leg's doing. I'm hoping they'll give me crutches. I just need to see if my mum is still speaking to me, to see if she'll give me a lift.'

'Which hospital is it?' he asks.

'The one I was at in London arranged for me to visit a hospital in Leeds while I'm here,' I tell him. 'So not too far, but too far to wheel myself.'

'I'll take you,' he suggests.

'What?'

'Yeah, I'm working the night shift tomorrow, which means I'm free all day. I'd love to take you. It will teach me responsibility or something. That's how I talked my ex into getting a dog.'

'Are you comparing me to a dog?'

'No, you're much harder work,' he tells me with a smile.

Suddenly it feels more like Dean is trying to fix me, rather than me trying to fix him, which was always the plan. It's kind of nice.

Chapter 31

It's a miracle, I can walk!

Well, I can hop. Aided by crutches. But I am out of that stupid wheelchair with its dumb squeaky wheel and its uncomfortable seat. Even better news is that this is because my leg is healing perfectly. No more wheelchair, no operation on the horizon. A few more weeks on crutches and they'll give me a brace to wear and I cannot wait. I'll be back to wearing short skirts and sky-high heels in no time – well, after I spend a few hours shaving my leg. I dread to think what it's going to be like in there.

As promised, Dean picked me up and drove me all the way to Leeds. He was helpful and attentive – everything Patrick wasn't when he took me to hospital. Dean hasn't walked me into any walls because he was too busy texting, nor has he left me to fend for myself.

After my appointment we went for a short walk in Leeds city centre, just to try out my crutches. We went to one of the fancy bars in Millennium Square for a late lunch – I bet it would be so lovely to sit outside there, when the weather is right. Dean, who tells me that he works in Leeds quite often, says that he likes to go there at different times of year because they always have events on. He says that Marram Bay might have things on all year round, but it's the same stuff he's been going to since he was born, so he likes to visit Millennium Square for the summer music festivals and the annual Christmas market.

Now we're on the way back to Marram Bay, but if you thought my excitement for the day was over, you would be wrong. Tonight Dean is doing surveillance and he's asked me if I'd like to join him. It's just sitting in the car, watching, but to be on a real police stakeout rather than just stalking the guy I'm kind of dating is exciting to me.

'So, what's the crime we're investigating?' I ask.

'Tractor advert fraud,' he replies.

Oh. Oh, OK. I take it all back, maybe this is going to be boring.

'Wha . . . what's that?' I ask, hoping it's way more exciting than it sounds.

'So, basically, there is a gang working out of Marram Bay who are selling tractors to farmers, but then taking their money and not giving them the goods.'

'Christ that's a dull crime,' I blurt out.

'Would you rather Marram Bay have a serial killer?' he asks straight-faced.

'For the purposes of this stakeout, yes,' I admit. 'But just, you know, without people we know dying. Maybe a potential serial killer that we can arrest before he gets going. I reckon Will has form.'

'I reckon so too,' he laughs. 'Would you like me to arrest him?'

'Yes please,' I reply.

'OK, sure, I'll get right on it,' he jokes. 'But for now . . . I know you think it's an uncool crime – although in my line of work we think all crime is uncool – but there's a lot of money being stolen. Unsuspecting farmers are buying them – the last guy paid £12,000. He saw an ad on Facebook, assumed it was a local farmer, checked the tractor out. It looked good, it had low mileage – he thought he'd snapped up a bargain. They gave him a phoney PayPal link to pay for it, acted like the money hadn't gone through, said they'd drop the tractor off the next day when it was paid for. You know what folk are like around here: they're too trusting, they don't lock their doors. They have Facebook pages for connecting with their kids who have moved away. They're not savvy about cyber crime.'

'That's awful,' I admit. 'Boring, but awful. It must be devastating, to part with that kind of money in a scam.'

'And the worst thing is, not only are they out of their hard-earned cash but they feel foolish too.'

'I'll bet,' I reply. 'So you're going to bring them down?'

'I am,' Dean says as we pull up across the road from an old farm building. 'We think they're working out of here now. They have to move around the area a lot, and change the tractor they're selling so people don't make the connection. A tractor has just been leased to this address. We think they're going to try and sell it.'

'So how long do you have to sit here?' I ask.

'The tractor should be arriving in the next hour,' he says. 'I'm just here to watch them receive it, get a look at the guys, get a look at the tractor. If it's our guys, an ad will go up tomorrow and if it follows the pattern of the other fake adverts we'll send one of our guys in to try and buy it. I've been trying to crack this case open for months and I'm finally on the verge of a breakthrough.'

'Wow, really?'

'Maybe,' he says. 'Maybe not. Not sure how much I should be telling you.'

I laugh. 'Well, don't worry,' I insist. 'It's not interesting enough to tell anyone about.'

We make small talk, listening to the radio, laughing together, all while Dean keeps an eye on the farm. It's getting dark out now. You know what it's like in winter – you feel like you've only just had your lunch when the night creeps in early. At first it's slow, as the sky turns to a miserable dark blue. Then, all at once, pitch black, and it's only 6 p.m. It's never bothered me much, living in the city, especially one like London that never really seems to

187

go to sleep, no matter what time it is or how dark it gets. Here though, in a small town surrounded by the sea on one side and fields on all others, when the night-time hits, the lights from inside are all that we have. They barely illuminate more than a few metres outside the town. We're just outside town, right where the darkness starts. Hiding here in Dean's car, with the engine off, it's pitch black. It's starting to get chilly too.

'Sorry, are you cold?' he says.

'I'm not so bad,' I reply. I'm lying though; I'm freezing.

Dean reaches into the back of the car and grabs a tartan blanket from the back seat.

'Here,' he says as he wraps it around me. Once the blanket is cloaking my shoulders, for extra warmth, Dean places an arm around me too. He lightly rubs on my shoulder. 'Better?'

'Much better,' I say.

I'm still a bit on the cold side but I do feel better. Now that I have crutches it will be easier to get around and, spending time with Dean is proving to be a great distraction.

While he stares at the farm, I stare at him. As far as I can tell, and unless he's lied to me (which, let's face it, men seem to be doing a lot recently), there doesn't seem to be anything wrong with him. He's gorgeous, charming, attentive, caring, gorgeous – wait, I already said that one. He seems like the whole package, so why is he single? Is it by choice? I might be on a bit of a downer at the moment, and I might struggle to trust the next person I'm involved with, but why wouldn't he want to be loved? I can't understand why anyone wouldn't want to be loved. It's the easiest thing in the world to love someone and have them love you too – on face value, at least. It does get harder when people get greedy – greedy for attention or sex or whatever it is that makes people cheat.

Dean catches me staring.

'What?' he asks.

'Nothing,' I say, looking away. 'Nothing.'

'What, do I have something on my face?' He laughs. 'There won't be tractors over here; over there is where you should be looking, Detective James.'

Dean is so, so impossibly charming. I look into his eyes as he stares back at me.

'What?' he asks with a chuckle. 'What's going on in that head?'

Right now, at this very moment in time, I don't think Dean can read me. The reason for that is because I can't read myself right now. What am I thinking? What's going on? Is Dean's face moving closer to mine?

Lights appear behind Dean's head, lighting him up like an angel. It isn't a sign from a higher power though, it's a tractor.

'It's here,' I say, pulling away, pointing out of the window.

'Oh, thanks,' Dean says.

As he gets on with his work I'm left alone with my thoughts. What the hell was happening there?

Chapter 32

Getting around the B & B is so much easier now that I'm on crutches. At the hospital they taught me how to go up and down stairs on them, so I'm sleeping in my old bedroom now, at the top of the lighthouse. It does take a while, to go all the way up and down the stairs, but I'm only doing it once when I get up and once when I go to bed, so it's not so bad.

I've just woken up after my first night sleeping in a proper bed and I feel glorious. I guess the blinds were closed when I popped up here the other day so I didn't get to appreciate the view. Being a converted lighthouse, and with my room sitting at the top of it, I have a panoramic view of the island and the sea. I pull on the string next to my bed, which opens all of the blinds at once. It's quite a bright day, for a February morning. There's enough sunshine to glisten on the water. I hop around my room, looking out of each window, taking in the vastly different view I get from each one. There is no way I appreciated this properly when I was growing up – what a dream.

I hear my phone vibrating on my bedside table and I hop over to it. It's Kim.

'Hey, Kim!'

'Hi, Lola, how are you?'

'I'm doing good thanks. I have crutches,' I tell her excitedly.

'Oh, good for you,' she replies. 'You'll be back to normal in no time. When are you thinking of heading back to London?'

'Maybe next week,' I say. 'Got a few loose ends to tie up here first, before it's back to reality.'

'About that,' she starts, pausing for a second to gather her words. 'I've been thinking and, well, I guess you're right about love being under our noses . . .'

'Oh God, not Will,' I blurt.

'God, no, I've seen his true colours,' she says. 'I can hardly look him in the eye at work. No, I was thinking about Dean.'

Her words weaken me for some reason. I've been making the most of being vertical, but I sit down when I hear this.

'Dean?'

'Yeah,' she replies. 'He seems like a great guy – I can't understand why he's single. I was hoping you'd put in a good word for me? Maybe set us up on a date? I don't mind if it's under the pretence of practising, now that the Unmatchables have been forced to disband.'

'Oh, Kim . . . I . . . I just don't think that's a good idea,' I say.

Why would I say that? They're my only two singles left. If she's interested in Dean, and Dean is starting to soften, why wouldn't they be perfect for each other?

'Oh?' she says curiously.

'Yeah, he's just . . . I've been spending a lot of time with him and . . . he's just . . . he's really damaged.'

I'm not sure that's true. Yes, there is something that is holding him back, but he's certainly not damaged.

'Oh, well, I'm happy to take my chances,' she says. 'Anything is worth a shot, right? Look, I've got to get back to work, but think about it.'

'OK, bye,' I say.

I bite my lip as I glance out to sea. Why did I do that? Why wouldn't I want them to find love together? Channy and Toby, despite their differences and a complete lack of sexual attraction for Toby on Channy's part, are great together and I'm so happy for them. Why can't I bring myself to set my other friends up too?

I hop into my clothes, put on a little make-up and pull my hair into a bun. I don't have anywhere to go today so I might as well be comfortable. On my way downstairs I hear my mum in her bedroom so I pop my head through the door.

'Mum? Are you OK?' I ask, when I spot her kneeling on the floor with her head in her hands. She's crying her eyes out.

'Lola, sorry,' she says as she jumps to her feet. 'Sorry, I forget you can move now. There was a level of privacy that came with you being stuck in that chair.'

Oh wow.

'I just, erm, need a second to compose myself,' she says, sitting down on the bed, wiping her eyes.

'Take your time,' I insist as I sit down next to her. 'Where's Dad?'

'Ha,' she replies. 'There's some sort of *emergency* at the *tourist centre*.'

You can hear the disbelief in the way she says the words.

'I don't know what kind of emergency they could possibly have, other than running out of leaflets for the hot air balloon festival or something. He's had to rush in.'

'Oh.'

'Oh indeed.'

'Mum, are you OK?' I ask seriously. She doesn't seem like herself at all. My mum never gets upset over big things like this; she gets upset over improperly ironed valances and missing hand soap.

'My life is out of control,' she replies with a sob.

'So is your hair, Mum,' I can't help but blurt out. I've never seen my mum with a hair out of place. Even in the photos taken immediately after she gave birth to me, she looked like she'd just walked out of a salon.

At this, my mother breaks down in tears.

'Oh, no, I was just kidding,' I say as I grab her for a hug.

'I gave him enough time to get to work before calling the office – they said he isn't in at all today. He told me he's working this morning and tonight. Working late. At the tourist centre. I know you don't believe me,' she sobs, 'but your father is having an affair. I know it must be hard for you to understand. He's your dad, but he is having an affair. He's lying to me, sneaking around, pretending to work – I'm not an idiot.'

'I know,' I tell her.

'We've been having marriage counselling,' my mum confesses. 'He's turned into a grumpy old man and I thought it might help us.'

'Marriage counselling is a positive step,' I tell her, trying to put out of my head that the couple in question is my mum and dad.

'Except he isn't taking it seriously,' she says. 'I've tried to tell him that things aren't what they used to be, that it isn't fun or exciting anymore, and now I suppose it's because he's finding those things elsewhere.'

I may not be one hundred per cent certain about this but my mum needs someone on her side right now.

'What can I do?' I ask.

'I want to spy on him tonight, when he's supposedly working late. The only problem is that he'll have our car, and you don't have a car . . .'

'I can get us a car,' I tell her. 'I can get us a car and the best damn detective in Marram Bay, if it will help?'

'Oh, Lola, can you ask him? That would be amazing,' she says. 'I just need to know, for my sanity . . . I'm going mad . . .'

I hug her again. 'Of course I'll ask him,' I tell her. 'Just don't worry about it for the rest of today, OK?'

'OK, I'll try,' she says. 'Lots to do around the B & B anyway. I feel like I'm running it single-handedly at the moment.'

'I'm going to help you,' I tell her.

'You're a good girl, Lola James,' she says, and I know she means it.

'I'll take care of you, Mum. We can start with your hair.' I chuckle.

'Now now, Lola,' she says, looking at my hair. 'We don't want to make things worse.'

As she disappears into her bathroom to sort herself out, I take my phone from my pocket and punch Dean a text, asking him for a favour. I'm sure he'll be asleep but he calls me straight away.

'Hey, Lola, what can I do for you?' he asks.

'Hey,' I say, keeping my voice as quiet as possible. 'It's my mum. She's convinced my dad is having an affair. She wants to follow him and she's asked for my help. I'm worried about what she'll do if I don't – she's so upset.'

'Oh, Lola, I'm so sorry,' he says. 'That must be awful for you.'

'Well, I'm not convinced that he is cheating,' I insist. 'But he's definitely lying about something. I'm worried he's ill or something . . .'

'I mean that it must be awful for you being caught in the middle of this, no matter what the reason is,' he says. 'Of course I'll help you. When does she want to do it?'

'Are you free tonight?' I ask.

'I can be,' he says.

'Are you sure? Please, if you're busy, we can do it another time.'

'Free as a bird,' he insists. 'Don't worry, we'll get to the bottom of it.'

'Thank you so much,' I say. 'I'd be lost without you at the moment.'

'It's nothing,' he says. 'Just being a cool customer.'

As soon as I hang up I remember that I was supposed to ask him if he fancied a date with Kim. Actually, no, that's not true – it was on my mind pretty much throughout the whole call but I just couldn't bring myself to do it.

Well, he's helping me out tonight. I need him. After that, that's when I'll ask him. I suppose I'll be gone soon, but I just can't imagine spending my last week here without him around, and if he gets a new girlfriend, he'll get lost in that first flush of romance . . . I'll probably never see him again.

Chapter 33

I really lucked out, making friends with a policeman. It means that we can effortlessly follow my dad without him having a clue. I almost feel sorry for him, going about his business while we spy on him. It feels like a betrayal, even though I know he is lying about something.

My poor mum, who hasn't slept properly in days, has fallen asleep in the back of Dean's car. She has come dressed from head to toe in black. I told her that it wasn't necessary but I think she's terrified of him seeing her, just in case she's wrong. I'm happy she's getting some sleep; she's been looking so tired. I guess, with me and Dean in the car, she feels like she can take her eye off the ball for a moment.

'How are the Unmatchables doing?' he asks. 'Since we, erm, disbanded.'

'Fine, I think.'

Tell him that Kim wants to go on a date with him. Tell him, Lola.

'That's good,' he says. 'I was worried they'd be lost without us. It kind of felt like we were their mummy and daddy.'

'It did, didn't it? And what a dysfunctional family.'

'We're dysfunctional but we love each other,' he reminds me.

'Oh, shit, there's my dad,' I say.

'What? Where?' my mum babbles as she wakes up. I guess she wasn't sleeping that deeply after all.

She hurries on a pair of oversized black sunglasses. 'Oh, you're incognito now, Mamma,' I tease to lighten the mood, but she shushes me.

He emerges from the tourist centre, where he's been for about thirty minutes, and hovers outside. After a couple of minutes a young girl walks out to join him.

'That's Karla,' my mum says, her voice barely audible. I think she's in shock. Perhaps she wasn't as convinced something was going on as she thought she was. Not until right now, at least.

Karla stands next to my dad as he locks up. The pair of them are laughing and joking together and I can hear my poor mum sobbing behind me. Just as I am thinking that this doesn't mean anything the pair of them get in my dad's car and drive off together.

'Quick,' my mum says, 'follow them.'

'On it,' Dean says.

He tails my dad with all the care and attention he would give a lead in his big tractor case.

I'd say it was exciting, but this is my dad we're following; my mum's husband of nearly forty years. I can't even imagine what she must be going through right now.

'Maybe he's just giving her a lift home,' I reason as we follow them.

'Yeah, but he said he was working late,' she reminds me through her tears.

My dad parks down one of the backstreets of town, gets out of his car and runs around to open the door for Karla. Oh, what a gentleman. We watch from Dean's car as the two of them walk just a few feet down the road and head into Bounty – the only nightclub Marram Bay has to offer, usually favoured by the young and the rowdy.

'Lola, have you ever known your snooker-loving dad to

frequent nightclubs with young women on an evening?'

'I haven't,' I admit.

'Well, that's that,' my mum says quietly. 'Let's go home.'

Chapter 34

Peering down into my cast as best I can, I can see hair, dry skin, dust that I imagine is made of me, which is completely grossing me out. It is an intimidating mess that I have no idea how I'm going to tackle.

Speaking of messes, after catching my dad heading out on the town with his young lady friend, my mum seems to have shut down emotionally. She doesn't want to confront him about it yet and I know that it isn't really any of my business. It's up to her how she wants to handle it and I'll stand by her whatever she decides. One thing is for sure, she is a stronger woman than me because at breakfast this morning when my dad cranked up the radio and started bobbing his head to a Chainsmokers tune I wanted to hit him over the head with a frying pan; but my mum, the amazing lady that she is, cooked him breakfast in the same pan I was planning my assault with.

She is acting as though everything is normal, just biding her time as she works out what she's going to do. I am amazed by her strength. The second I realised both Patrick and Will might not be being completely honest with me I didn't take a moment to think things through. I kicked them to the kerb.

After breakfast my dad went out 'to work' for a couple of hours so I parked myself on the sofa, ready to try and relax and watch a bit of TV. I must've fallen asleep for a while. I don't know how long for.

I awake with a fright as my mum charges through the room with her Dyson. She's wearing her usual purple apron, a pair of pink marigolds and, in the hand that is not controlling the vacuum cleaner, she's holding a feather duster. As she moves around the room at a dizzying pace, vacuuming and dusting like Kim and Aggie on speed, a ridiculous smile remains plastered across her face.

'Mum.' I try to get her attention, but it doesn't work. 'Mum,' I try again, shouting this time. Still nothing. 'Linda,' I yell at the top of my voice.

My mum stops suddenly and stares at me, the vacuum cleaner still running.

'What is going on?' I ask.

'Nothing is going on,' she replies. 'Just cleaning up, then I need to make your dad's tea. He'll be home from work before we know it.'

'Let that lying bastard make his own tea for once,' I can't help but snap. I immediately feel bad.

'Lola James,' my mum starts, but her bottom lip starts trembling. She turns off the vacuum cleaner, turns away from me and dusts nothing in particular.

'Mum, don't try and tell me that nothing is wrong, you're acting like a malfunctioning Stepford wife.'

'It's tomorrow,' she says calmly.

'What's tomorrow?' I ask. 'It's the . . . oh.'

It suddenly occurs to me exactly what tomorrow is – my mum and dad's fortieth wedding anniversary.

'I don't know how I'm going to get through it, darling,' my mum says weakly as the feather duster falls from her hand.

Suddenly I feel terrible for being so hard on her. It might be frustrating for me to see what's going on, but she's living it. I pull myself up onto my crutches and hop over to give her a hug.

'I'll be here all day tomorrow. I'll help you through it,' I promise her.

'Thank you. You are a good girl, Lola. I don't always tell you, but I'm proud of you.'

We continue to hug and cry together for a minute or two until my dad walks through the door. Those couple of hours have gone by really quickly – well they have for me, but I guess I took a long nap. I'll bet my mum has felt every agonising second of it, wondering where he is, what he's getting up to.

'Hello, family,' he says in an uncharacteristically happy manner. My dad has always been on the verge of grumpy old man territory so this chirpy version of him sticks out like a sore thumb. He spots that we are crying and wraps his arms around us both.

'What's wrong with my two favourite girls?' he asks.

'Oh, it's just all this business with Lola's leg,' Mum lies. 'She's so worried she's not going to be able to look after herself when she goes back to London.'

'Lola,' my dad starts as he slips off his jacket and sits down in front of the TV, 'don't upset your mum.'

My mum shoots me a look, warning me not to say anything. For her sake I will bite my tongue but you've got to love the nerve of the man, telling me not to upset my mum and doing exactly that himself.

I know a lot has been going on, but I can't believe I forgot it was my parents' wedding anniversary tomorrow. I can't help but worry about how tomorrow will play out. Will Dad even remember? Will Mum be able to keep a lid on things or will she choose tomorrow to confront him? Will she ever confront him? There's no way she could run the B & B without him, unless I moved back home . . .

It's certainly given me a lot to worry about and now I'm terrified.

Chapter 35

Another day, another awkward James family breakfast. Today is my mum and dad's fortieth wedding anniversary, and as if it isn't bad enough that my dad is probably cheating on my mum, he has also forgotten that it is their anniversary. I didn't think things could get worse, or that my dad could look like any more of a dick than he does now, but he has proved me wrong. Good work, Dad.

Dad breaks from his newspaper crossword puzzle only to sip his coffee. It isn't unusual for my dad to sit at the breakfast table in silence (apart from those weird acid reflux sounds that come out of his mouth after he eats toast), but today all it's doing is making my mum furious. I know that she was dreading having to pretend everything was fine today but she was prepared to try. Now it turns out my dad has forgotten, my poor mum looks like she's about to lose it with him.

My dad scratches his head in puzzlement. 'Four-letter word, the clue is "a stupid person" ends in the letter L,' my dad tells no one in particular.

'Paul,' my mum helpfully suggests.

'Very funny,' my dad replies without looking up. He clearly thinks she's joking.

'Fool,' I tell him. How very, very apt.

'Cheers, Lola,' my dad replies, offering me a thumbs-up. 'Right, just off to the loo.'

Dad has no sooner left than Auntie Val walks in.

'Look what the cat dragged in,' I announce. 'We haven't seen you in a while.'

'You're lucky I can still walk,' she announces. Far too much information.

'Nice,' I say sarcastically.

She takes one look at my mum, who is sitting with her head in her hands, and her face falls.

'What's wrong with her?' she asks. 'Is it related to "The Change"?'

My Auntie Val mouths the words 'The Change' rather than saying them out loud, like it's some kind of curse.

'Really?' I ask in disbelief.

'What?' she asks. 'The women in our family transition at a very late age – I could still have a baby.'

'You couldn't if you transitioned,' I point out. 'That's definitely not what you mean.'

'So, what's up?'

'Dad has forgotten their wedding anniversary. Their *fortieth* wedding anniversary,' I remind her quietly.

'Oh!' she whispers. 'Why didn't you remind me?'

'I didn't remember either, I've had a lot on.'

'I feel like I've been in bed for days.' She laughs. 'Come here, sis. No need to be upset. You know what men are like, they forget everything.'

'Thanks,' my mum sobs. 'I'll be fine, just being silly.'

'How about we teach him a lesson,' Val suggests. 'Let's go out tonight, somewhere he'll never expect. Let's go the pub or the club or something.'

'I really don't think that's a good idea,' I insist, knowing full well that my mum isn't one for hanging out in places like that.

'No, it's a great idea,' my mum says excitedly.

'What?' I can't help but say.

'Your dad can go on a night out, why can't I?'

I shoot her a look that says, "We both know the only reason Dad goes out at night," but she's not interested. Her mind is made up.

'Brilliant,' Val says with a clap of her hands. 'I'll pick you up after work; make sure you're ready. You can come too, Lola, if you can get dressed up with that thing.'

'Oh, bring Dean,' my mum says. 'Val, you will love Dean. He's a policeman.'

'Oh, well, he can definitely come but he doesn't need to dress up – he can dress down, dress in uniform, undress . . .'

'Cheers, Val, I'll pass that along,' I say sarcastically.

'I'm actually looking forward to it,' my mum says, but she's still got that crazy look in her eye.

The last thing I need is a night on the town with my heart-broken mum and my cougar auntie. I think I will ask Dean along because, if the shit hits the fan, he might have a Taser or something.

Chapter 36

'Do you think I'm still young enough to pull?' my mum asks as Val drives us into town.

I can't help but squeak in horror.

'I know he forgot your anniversary, but copping off with a man in a bar is a bit extreme, sis,' she insists.

'I didn't say I was going to,' my mum insists. 'I just wondered.'

Tonight my mum looks absolutely beautiful. She's really made the effort. Her beautiful dark hair is as perfect as ever and she's wearing a lovely black dress with her black pearl necklace and earrings. My mum looks great for her age, so no doubt I'll be taking after my dad – yet another reason for me to be mad at him.

'Here we are,' Val says as we park up in town.

My mum hops out of the car with a real spring in her step, clearly excited about her night on the town with her sister and her daughter.

It is only as I get out of the car that I notice where we are. 'Val, is there a reason you've parked outside Bounty?'

'I thought Linda might like to get straight to the nightlife.'

'I'm all for it,' my mum says, rushing inside before I have chance to stop her. It is only as I glance over at Auntie Val to ask her if this is a good idea that I spot my dad's car parked not too far from where we are standing. It was Bounty where we followed him to with Karla – if they're in here together and my mum catches them, I can't even imagine what will happen. I have to do something to stop it.

'Auntie Val, you have to stop her going in there. My dad is here,' I say as I struggle on my crutches to chase after my mum.

'I know, come on – let's go inside.'

'Wait, you knew that my dad was going to be here?' I ask.

'Of course, I just didn't know that you did. Hurry up, we're going to miss it,' she insists as we walk through the door to the club.

'Miss it? Val, did you not think there might be a better way to confront my dad about cheating on Mum? A way that might not upset her so much?'

Val stops dead. 'Lola, what on earth are you talking about?'

'Wait, so you don't know? Mum told me a while ago that she suspected Dad was cheating on her. I noticed he was being sneaky too so we followed him one night and he came here with a girl from work. He's in here now, probably with her.'

Val laughs as she manoeuvres me into the main room at Bounty, a matter of seconds behind my mum.

I watch as my mother's jaw drops.

Well, this is a surprise . . .

Chapter 37

'Surprise,' everyone in the club calls out at my mum.

My dad immediately rushes over to her with a glass of champagne and plants a big kiss on her lips. My mum is definitely surprised, that's for sure.

'Auntie Val,' I say slowly. 'Explain.'

My auntie laughs at me. 'You thought your dad was having an affair? That's hilarious. Why would you think that?'

'Because my mum told me that he was. He was being suspicious and sneaking around, going to clubs with young women.'

'Oh Lola,' she chuckles. 'He's been planning a surprise party. That girl you saw him with, her dad owns the club and she's been doing party planning for him. Your dad has no idea about throwing parties – that's why she's been helping him.'

'I could have helped him. Why didn't he tell me about this?'

'Because you can't keep a secret,' Val insists. 'There's no way you wouldn't have let slip to your mum. Did you see my incredible acting skills this morning? This was always going to be a role for me.'

I'm sure one day I will find this absolutely hilarious, but right now all I feel is incredibly guilty. I can't believe I thought my dad was having an affair. I should have known he would never do that to my mum, but the signs just seemed so obvious. I feel bad because the reason he was sneaking around was so he could throw my mum this incredible anniversary party. As I glance around the beautifully decorated room I can see our entire family and all of my mum and dad's friends – even the ones who don't live locally. I notice their friends Judy and Peter are here and they live in Australia. My dad has clearly put a lot of thought into this.

'Is your policeman here?' Val asks.

'No,' I reply simply. I did invite him on the weird night out though. He said he'd meet up with us when he finished work if I let him know where we were and it wasn't too late.

'*C'est la vie*,' she says with a big sigh.

'*La vie*,' I reply.

'The good news is that there's someone here I'd like you to meet,' she says. 'My roofer's younger brother. He's only twenty-six, but what he lacks in age he makes up for in . . . I don't know, other things. I told him you were single. He said he'd love to meet you. So, here you go, a blind date.'

She points to a man standing at the bar who is blatantly chatting up one of the waitresses, not that it looks like he's having much luck.

'Blind as in that's what you were when you picked him out for me? Look at him, he's a player.'

'Be grateful, Lola,' my auntie snaps. 'I'm just trying to return the favour. He's sound as a pound, is Gary.'

Oh God, Gary! I don't know about sound as a pound, but he's as cheesy as a bag of Wotsits.

Gary is wearing red trainers, purple chinos and a T-shirt that is about two sizes too small. If it isn't bad enough that looks like a member of One Direction's reflection in a fun house mirror (he's quite short and rounded) his bright orange hair is looking pretty greasy.

'Beauty is in the eye of the beholder,' Val reminds me. 'Come on, let's go say hello.'

'Gary, hello,' she says, just as he strikes out with the waitress. 'This is Lola.'

'*I'll* get your coat,' he says loudly the second he claps eyes on me. 'You've pulled a gentleman.'

Val laughs wildly, completely charmed by this. It just makes me cringe.

'Well, I'll leave you two alone,' Val says with a wink.

'So this is your parents' party?' Gary asks.

'Yep,' I reply, not keen to make conversation but too polite to walk off. 'They've been married for forty years.'

'Amazing,' he replies.

'I know, it's an achievement if couples last forty months these days.'

'Not that,' he replies, 'the fact they even bothered. Marriage is a pointless institution. We weren't made for monogamy; we were made to shag as many people as possible.'

'You realise you're at an anniversary party, right?' I check. 'The whole point is to celebrate marriage.'

'Well I'm here because Val told me you were looking for action,' he informs me. 'Did you know ginger men are the best in bed?'

'Are they really?' I say, clearly uninterested. A couple more seconds of this and I can hop away without feeling too rude.

'I don't know,' he tells me with a laugh. 'I haven't shagged any.'

'Right. Well, I'm going to go,' I tell him, making a move to hop away.

'Wait,' Gary says, grabbing me by the arm. 'I don't know how that leg is treating you, but you don't want to have sex in the disabled toilets do you?'

'No, no thank you,' I reply.

'It doesn't hurt to ask, does it?' Gary says, his grip on my arm still quite tight.

'It might if you don't get your hands off my daughter,' my dad interrupts.

Gary looks absolutely terrified by my intimidatingly large dad

210

and releases my arm, tenderly pats me on the shoulder and then dashes off at the speed of light.

'Who was that?' my dad asks me.

'Someone Val was trying to set me up with,' I say.

'She really did set you up – he's a pillock.'

My dad looks so sweet in this blue suit, which he must have taken to the dry cleaners himself – probably a first for him.

'It was very sweet of you to do all this for Mum,' I tell him, still feeling guilty about the whole affair thing.

'What's sweet was the way you stood by your mum recently. She told me what's been going on.'

'Dad, I'm . . . I'm so sorry—'

'Don't apologise,' he says, before I have chance to explain myself. A tear manages to escape from my cheek. I quickly wipe it away.

'You did the right thing. As crazy as she drives me sometimes, I love your mum to pieces. I'd never do anything to hurt her. I've been doing all sorts to try and throw her off the party scent. I didn't realise it would backfire. And party planning aside, if I've been acting weird it's because I'm getting old and it scares me. I can't eat toast without taking medication, for crying out loud.'

I laugh and give my dad a hug.

'You're not getting old, Daddy. But even when you do get old, I'll still love you.'

'I love you too,' he says. 'Right, time for me to go and give a speech. Then I can cut all this soppy rubbish out.'

There's my dad.

'Your friends are all here somewhere,' he says. 'Oh, and Robbie.'

'My friends?'

'Yeah, four of them – I spotted them leaving the B & B a little while back. An older lady, one about your age and a couple of kids.'

I laugh. I suppose they are my friends now.

I glance around the room for them and spot Doris sitting at a table with Sylvester, Kim is chatting with a woman I don't recognise, and Channy has Toby pinned against the wall. They are so intense. It's nice to see everyone so happy. Everyone but Kim . . . I feel awful for not asking Dean out for her.

'If that guy comes back, what will you do?' he asks.

'Not have sex in the disabled toilets,' I reply with a cheeky grin.

'That's my girl,' he says proudly.

Chapter 38

Sitting alone in the corner of Bounty, I watch my mum and dad as they slow dance to 'Careless Whisper' by George Michael which, given the circumstances, is that not an awful choice of song?

It's nice to see them happy. It might have only been for a few days, but I honestly thought they were going to break up and that would have been awful. Not because they're my parents and it would have sucked for me, but they have been married for forty years. Imagine if those forty years had been for nothing; if they weren't meant to be, or if one of them gave it up because they thought they could find something better elsewhere.

I was so stressed out, thinking about them having a messy divorce, the lighthouse being sold, trying to visit them both separately at Christmas, and all with a backdrop of both Patrick and Will's betrayals (of varying severity).

At first I was like, do you know what, I don't ever want to put myself out there, I don't want to give anyone the chance to hurt me. But here, tonight, seeing my mum and dad dance together, so madly in love after all this time . . . That's what I want, and not every man I meet is going to lie to me or cheat on me.

There are a few couples on the dance floor with them. No sign of Gary sadly, so no one for me to dance with (in the disabled toilets or otherwise).

I'm sitting in a dark corner on my own, sipping on my virgin cocktail. I've had to swear off the alcohol again because since I got my crutches, the pressure I'm feeling in my leg is horrible.

'Hey,' Dean says.

'Oh, gosh, you snuck up on me,' I say. 'Sorry, I was miles away. Hello.'

'One thousand pennies for your thoughts,' he jokes.

'So, I know I was kind of vague in my message but this is the surprise anniversary party my dad has been planning for my mum – *this* is what he's been up to all this time. I feel awful.'

'Lola, I'm a detective – a pretty good one – and even I thought he was guilty. Sometimes you've got to wait for all the evidence.'

'That reminds me, what's going on with your tractor stuff?'

'Oh, we got them last night,' he says.

'Oh, cool,' I reply. 'Wait, last night you were with me.'

'Yeah, you needed my help,' he says. 'It's no big deal.'

'But wasn't that your big bust?'

'Lola, it's no big deal.' He takes a seat next to me.

'You're amazing,' I tell him, resting my head on his shoulder. 'The party is nearly over – you didn't need to come.'

'I know, but I said I would,' he says. 'Also . . . I need you to return the favour.'

I sit up again. 'Oh, really?'

'Yeah, my cousin is getting married this weekend,' he says. 'My sister asked me if I had a date for the wedding and I didn't want her to think she'd wasted her money on you so I said yes. I was going to make up some excuse, like my date was ill . . . but then I remembered that she hasn't met you in person, right? She told me she spoke to you on the phone?'

'That's true . . .'

'And she refers to you as Linda.'

214

'Yeah, my mum posted the advert on Facebook that she responded to.'

'So . . .' Dean stands up before getting down on one knee in front of me. 'Will you be my date to this wedding? You won't even need to use a fake name, if she thinks you're called Linda.'

'It would be my pleasure to be your fake wedding date,' I reply.

Dean jumps up and grabs me for a hug, as though I'd just said yes to marrying him. With our faces just inches apart, we stare into each other's eyes for a moment. I feel my breathing quicken as a knot forms in my stomach.

'Lola, listen,' Dean starts.

'Oh, sorry,' I hear Kim say. 'Are you two . . .'

'I'll go get a drink,' Dean says.

As Kim sits down next to me, I feel so guilty. I feel like she's just caught me . . . but caught me doing what? Nothing. Then why do I feel so awful?

'I've been thinking,' she says when it's just us two. 'I don't think Dean and I would work. You were right, I was just doing a Channy and taking your words too literally.'

'Really?' I ask.

'Yeah, I don't think he's my type,' she insists.

I wonder whether she's only saying this because she just walked over to find us having a bit of a . . . of a what?! A moment? Was that a moment? I don't know if she thinks she's stepping aside so that I can move in, but I wish I could help her find someone. The perfect person for her.

Seeing how kind and generous Kim can be only goes to show how superficial my friendships in London are. Here she is, stepping aside for me. Gia only stepped aside so they could get my broken body off her dance floor.

As Kim pulls her phone out of her bag, I notice her green phone case. There's something on the back, something I recognise . . .

I reach out and twist her phone in her hand so I can see the back of it.

'Is that the Hulk?' I ask, noting the large green man on the back.

'Oh, erm, yeah,' she says, sounding embarrassed. 'Since I moved back home I've had a lot of time just sitting around in front of the TV, watching it with my dad while my mum is out. I know it's not very cool but I've got super into Marvel movies. Avengers, Thor, Iron Man . . .'

'Are you kidding?' I ask.

'OK, look, I know it's not cool, but it could be worse,' she says awkwardly.

'No, I'm not making fun of you,' I insist. 'It's great that you like Marvel because . . . One question: do you know what Thor's hammer is called?'

'Mjölnir,' she says cautiously. 'Why?'

'OK, I have someone you need to meet,' I tell her. 'Come with me.'

I struggle to my feet and hop across the room to find Robbie. Perhaps I *can* return the favour with Kim. Maybe she's just the nerd Robbie is looking for . . .

Chapter 39

My mum, having found a new lease of life on her post-party high, has really stepped up for me today. It's Saturday, the day of Dean's cousin's wedding, and I have agreed to be his date.

I haven't been feeling my usual, fabulous self, thanks to the big ugly cast on my leg and my inability to keep on top of my usual beauty regime, so my mum – or my fairy godmother as we're calling her today – has solved all my problems. She's done my hair for me. She actually curled it with hair straighteners after watching how-to videos on YouTube for at least forty minutes. She took me shopping to find a dress that hid my cast. She even bought me some cute little flower headbands, which she has customised into long daisy chains, to wrap around my crutches and make them all fancy.

I look so cool with my daisies and my flowing baby pink dress and my long blonde curls. It might just be because I haven't dressed up properly since Gia's wedding, but I feel so confident for it.

When Dean picked me up outside he said that I looked incredible but, then again, I suppose he hasn't seen me dressed up all fancy before, so I was bound to look different.

His cousin, Kirsty, is getting married at a hotel in Chester. Dean says it's exactly the kind of elaborate wedding venue you'd expect from someone who wanted to be a WAG. Harry, the man she's marrying, is a semi-professional footballer, I'm told. Dean says he's all right though, for a footballer, and that he makes his cousin happy.

Dean also casually informed me, on the drive over, that he has a room at the hotel if I need to go rest, but he also told me that he plans on staying sober all day so that he can drive me home after. I feel sort of bad that he can't properly enjoy himself, but I'm sure I'd feel worse if I took his hotel bed and he wound up sleeping on the floor.

There was an accident on the M62 that made us a little late, so we had to rush straight into the room where the ceremony was and sit down. We made it just in the nick of time, before 'Here Comes The Bride' started playing. We probably would've been OK, but it takes me so long to get around on my crutches. My wheelchair might've been annoying and clumsy, but at least I was faster when other people were pushing me.

Now I'm at the reception and, I have to say, I'm having an amazing time. The venue is stunning – we're in a big, old room with walls of twinkling lights and beautiful, classical music playing while we were eating. I've met lots of members of Dean's family and everyone is so nice. I'd wondered to myself if perhaps his parents might be divorced, to see if that might shed any light on why he's wound up so insistently single, but his parents have been married even longer than mine have.

Even his sister, Faye, who is sitting at the other side of me, has been married for eight years. She has two kids.

As far as Faye is concerned, I work in PR, live locally and broke my leg at a wedding – Dean keeps promising I won't do that again this wedding, something everyone finds hilarious. You can tell that his entire family absolutely adores him. I'm seeing a whole new side to Dean today; he seems like a real family man. He's dancing with his niece, wrestling with his nephew. I can't for the life of me understand why he doesn't want a family of his own.

'Dean said you had your first date at Treasure Island,' Faye says with an amused roll of her eyes. 'So like my brother to take a girl to Treasure Island.'

'He did,' I say. I suppose he did. 'I had a great time though.'

'We used to have to drag him off the penny machines when he was a kid,' she says. 'Only seven-year-old in the bay with a gambling problem.'

'I can believe that,' I reply. 'He got change for a tenner.'

'All right, stop making fun of me.' Dean laughs.

'He'd better get used to it, hadn't he?' Faye says.

I suddenly remind myself that we're not a real couple. It's so easy to get caught up in all the love and fun of the wedding. And Faye just seems so, so happy that her brother has found someone. She only wants good things for him and it's sweet that she's doing everything she can to make it happen.

'If you'll excuse me, ladies, I've promised my nephew I'll take him outside to see the swans.'

'You guys seem great together,' Faye tells me. 'Honestly, I probably shouldn't be saying this but after the . . . I just never . . . Ahh.'

'It's OK,' I tell her. 'He told me all about the divorce.'

I might as well put her out of her misery. She'd probably only worry she'd let something slip or made him look bad otherwise.

'Oh, phew,' she says. 'Honestly, Anna was awful. I didn't really get a good vibe the first time I met her, but you put these things out of your mind for the people you care about, right?'

'Totally,' I agree.

So her name was Anna. I feel like I've heard so much about her. It's weird to be able to put a name to her suddenly. It makes her seem more real.

'I think he just loved her,' she says. 'I think it was easy for him to ignore the issues. Honestly though, if I've learned anything, it's how important it is to have the talk about kids early on in a relationship, because if you can't give the other person what they want, things get messy.'

219

'Right,' I agree.

So did Anna want kids but Dean didn't? So she left him? I guess it really is important to have these conversations early on. I can't say it's a conversation I've ever had, but I've never had a relationship that lasted all that long anyway.

'I'm not saying you guys need to have it tonight,' she laughs. 'Just, you know, Anna hurt him. It wasn't just that she said she didn't want kids . . . it was the fact that she divorced him for wanting them, immediately met someone else and got knocked up in a matter of months. That's got to sting, right?'

Wow. I knew something must have happened to devastate him, but I had no idea it was that. How unbelievably awful, to tell the person you love that you want to have children, only for them to say that they don't, leave you and then go on and have a kid with someone else.

'It's just awful,' I agree, pretending I already knew this. Well, I did imply that I knew, and her heart was in the right place, talking to me about it. She just doesn't want her brother getting hurt again.

'So, what do you do?' I ask her as I notice Dean heading back towards our table.

'I'm a teacher,' she says. 'Oh, look, the boys are back.'

'It turns out that little James here, who wanted more than anything in the whole wide world to see the swans, is now terrified of them,' he tells us.

James hugs his uncle's leg sheepishly.

'I don't blame you,' I tell him. 'I was a bridesmaid at my friend's wedding, and she had a swan carry the rings. I was terrified of it.'

James, who can't be more than four years old, steps out from behind Dean. He's holding a buttercup in his hand, which he hands to me.

'Is that for me?' I ask.

James nods his head.

'Wow, thank you so much,' I tell him. 'I'm going to keep it forever.'

'Oh, look at that,' Faye starts. 'That's my husband dangling our daughter by her ankles because she's dripping with apple juice. I'll be right back. In fact, I'll take this little terror with me and clean him up before cake time too.'

'You're so cute with him,' Dean tells me when we're alone.

'So are you,' I reply. 'You'd make such a wonderful dad.'

I hope I'm not laying it on too thick, but he absolutely would make an amazing dad, and reminding him will show him that this wasn't all for nothing.

'Thanks,' he says, not showing a glimmer of emotion. 'Everyone really likes you, you know. Everyone keeps telling me how great you are, how I'm punching above my weight, how I've caught myself a good one.'

'That's because they don't know the truth,' I point out. 'A dating expert who can't practise what she preaches, whose friends all dropped her the second she needed them, whose work forced her into taking time off because they didn't think she'd look sexy in the office in a wheelchair – which I'm pretty sure is illegal. But they made it seem like it was for my own good, and my friends made out like they were just too busy, and as for the men I always seem to fall for, well, they are always the type of men who will convince you that you're a bore for trying to lock them down.'

'There's a lot to be said for being locked down. You just have to make sure it's with the right person. And you're not a bore and your friends don't sound like friends at all.'

I smile at him. He looks so amazing in his grey suit. It's the first time I've seen him in anything other than denim, T-shirts and denim or leather jackets. He looks like he's trimmed his beard even shorter than usual and his hair is neatly blown back. He scrubs up really, really well. I can't get over how gentlemanly he looks.

He might look like a gentleman today but I suppose he's always acted like one. I'm just starting to realise that.

'For someone who insists on living the bachelor life, that's a very sweet thing to say about the right person,' I point out.

'Well, when you've wasted so much time with the wrong person, you don't want to make the same mistake again.'

For the first time, Dean, the big, strong, sexy policeman who is all charm and sarcasm seems vulnerable. He seems like he could be hurt. It makes complete sense to me, why he's so scared to get into another relationship, and I don't want to be the person who makes him feel like he needs to rush into it. There is no denying what an incredible boyfriend and/or husband he would make, but it has to be on his terms.

'How are the cocktails?' he asks me, changing the subject.

'Pretty good,' I reply. 'How's the orange juice?'

'Pretty orangey,' he replies with a grin before taking a meaningful sip.

I bite my lip as the cogs turn in my head.

'Have a drink,' I tell him. 'Have a few. It's not fair – that I get to drink and you don't when this is your family's party. We can stay here tonight. We can figure out sleeping arrangements later.'

'We really don't have to do that, Lola. I don't need a drink to have fun. It's just so nice to see everyone, play with the kids, hang out with you . . .'

God, it's nice to hang out with him too. It really, really is.

'I want to stay,' I insist. 'I'm having a really good time.'

'Ladies and gentlemen, the bride and groom will be having their first dance now. Please welcome them to the floor,' the DJ announces.

Harry and Kirsty take to the dance floor to perform a suspiciously ambitious routine to 'Hello' by Adele. Honestly, do couples not listen to the lyrics of songs before deciding they are romantic? I'm not sure if this is better or worse than 'Careless Whisper' being my parents' song.

'Weird choice of song,' Dean whispers to me. 'Not very romantic.'

'I was just thinking the exact same thing.'

As other couples join them on the floor, Dean asks me if I want to dance.

'Me?' I squeak.

'No, the fake girlfriend behind you – yes you.'

'There's something I need to tell you,' I start seriously. 'I have *a broken leg.*'

Dean laughs. He looks so gorgeous when he laughs.

'I know that,' he replies pointlessly. 'But I'll carry you onto the floor and I'll hold you while we dance. To "Hello", by Adele, the queen of the break-up ballad. Singing a song that could definitely be interpreted as being about trying to reconnect with an ex.'

'Sounds perfect,' I say.

As Dean scoops me up in his arms – seriously, as an adult, you think you'll never be carried again and these days I feel like everyone is carrying me – a few people notice and begin cheering and applauding. I tense up in his arms, terrified that the bride will be fuming at us for pinching the attention, but Kirsty just smiles over at us. She seems so in love and so happy. It just goes to show that for most people the love is the most important part of the wedding day, not the dress or the food or what kind of animal you can get to carry your rings without swallowing them or breaking anyone's arm with their beak. And it certainly isn't a day for feeling like someone having a painful accident is an act of sabotage, nothing more than a thinly veiled attempt to steal the limelight.

I exhale deeply as I melt into his arms.

'This is nice,' I say. 'This is just . . . really nice.'

'Hey,' Dean says.

I lift my head and look into his eyes. I wonder if he's trying to look into my soul like he always does, but he closes his eyes and plants his lips on mine. We kiss for a few seconds, until Adele reaches the climax of the song. We finally part again once it's over.

'Wow . . .' I mutter.

Dean just grins at me.

It was an amazing kiss that sent shockwaves through my body. I can't help but wonder, is this a kiss for show, or because he wanted to kiss me? It certainly felt like a real kiss, and it felt like more than just a kiss – there was so much that came with it, feelings I don't even know how to process. You don't feel feelings like that from a show kiss, do you? And now all I can think about is doing it again, not just to check if it was real but because I've never felt anything like it in my life.

Chapter 40

This has honestly been the best wedding I have ever attended. Ever. And Ed Sheeran did a set at Gia's.

I may have come here under false pretences and I might not know anyone, but I've had the most incredible day with Dean. He's been charming, attentive, he's brought me drinks, helped me dance (well, a version of dancing at least). And then there was that kiss . . . When I think about it, I swear I can still feel his beard tickling my lips. Whether it was for show or for real, it felt real for me. Just . . . wow. I want to do it again, all night, maybe even for the rest of my life, it was *that* good.

After the party we head up to the room that we had never intended to sleep in. It's a gorgeous room with a stunning king-size four-poster bed. After sleeping on the sofa, and then the single in my childhood bedroom, it looks so inviting. For two reasons, if I'm being honest . . .

I know Dean was only ever supposed to be a client – not even a client, a charity case – but I feel like I'm falling for him . . .

'So, you'll be going home soon?' Dean asks. 'Not Marram Bay home, London home?'

'That's the plan,' I reply. 'But . . . I don't think I want to.'

'No?'

'No,' I reply. 'I'm loving being around my mum and dad; I've made some great friends. I don't really know what's waiting for me back in London. There's my job but . . . I don't know . . . I've kind of gone off that a bit too.'

'Oh?' he replies.

'Yeah, I'm not sure you can force these things,' I say. 'I suppose it kind of made sense for celebrities, royals and other miscellaneous rich people who like to have their associates carefully vetted but, in real life, the right people come into your life when you're ready, and you move at the exact pace you want to. If you want to be single, be single. Don't listen to anyone else. Not society or your family . . . or me.'

I plonk myself down on the bed as carefully as I can.

'You've changed your tune,' he says as he sits down next to me.

'I have,' I say. 'I've learned a lot about love and about myself . . .'

I've learned a lot about Dean too, but I keep that to myself.

'So you think you'll move back?' he asks.

'I'm thinking about it,' I reply. 'Even if it's just until I figure out what to do next. When I broke my leg I felt like I was so fragile. It turns out it was my life that was fragile. My leg will heal, but I'll never get my life back. I'm kind of tipsy now though, so ask me again tomorrow.'

Dean laughs. 'I'm kind of tipsy too,' he replies. 'I probably won't even remember to ask you.'

'All's well that ends well,' I say, for some reason, with a kind of manic laugh that fizzles out into the silence.

'So, it's late,' Dean starts. 'The bed situation . . .'

'Let's just share it,' I say. 'It's a big bed and . . . and . . .'

I don't think I'll ever be able to tell you who is the instigator, but we kiss again. This time, there's way more passion to it as all of the sexual tension that has been undeniably building between us bursts to the surface.

I am mindful of my leg but I don't need to be. Unlike Will – a medical doctor, may I remind you – who was slinging me around like a rag doll, Dean is way more gentle. It's gentle but passionate and I don't think I've felt such a gloriously subtle compromise of the two extremes before.

I wiggle off my dress as Dean hurries off his clothes. Neither of us says a word. It's like we both know exactly what we're doing.

As he presses down on top of me and kisses me, I completely push my leg out of my mind and just enjoy the moment. Without really realising it, I have wanted this for so long. I'm not going to let something silly like a broken bone ruin it for me.

Chapter 41

I wake up lying on my back with a pillow underneath my broken leg, just like I do every day. I wonder, for a split second, if what happened with Dean was nothing more than a delicious dream, until I glance next to me in the bed and see him lying there, sleeping contentedly.

I think it says a lot, that we're both in our underwear and there's a pillow placed lovingly underneath my leg. It wasn't just a case of wham, bam, thank you, ma'am before falling asleep. Dean helped me get ready for bed and made sure I was comfortable. He really is a dream come true.

It's as if somehow he knows I'm staring at him because he wakes up and catches me.

'Good morning,' he says.

'Good morning to you,' I reply.

Dean lifts himself up onto his elbow and leans forward to kiss me.

'How are you?' he asks.

'I'm pretty good,' I reply. 'You?'

'Yeah, I'm decent,' he says with a laugh. 'Fancy some breakfast?'

'Oh, that would be amazing,' I enthuse. I'm starving.

'Incredible,' he chuckles to himself. 'I leave you feeling "pretty good" but breakfast is "amazing".'

'Few can compete with pancakes,' I reason.

He nods in agreement. 'So, last night . . .' he starts. 'You said you were thinking of moving back home.'

'I did,' I reply. 'I am. I think it's time. I miss my family.'

'That makes sense,' he says. 'My ex really struggled being away from hers, especially when her dad was ill. They were all the way over in the States.'

'Oh, Anna was American?' I say curiously. 'I don't know why, I was imagining an English rose type.'

'Nope, she was about as all-American as you can get.'

Suddenly Dean cocks his head and stares at me curiously.

'What?' I ask as I watch his brow furrow and his smile vanish.

'You didn't know Anna was American . . .' he tells me.

'No, I didn't,' I reply. 'You never told me she was American.'

'I also never told you she was called Anna,' he replies.

Shit. I'm sure if I were better at this stuff it would occur to me to say something smart, but I feel so guilty knowing details he never offered me that it makes me awkward.

'No, well, your sister . . .'

'You were talking to my sister about my marriage?' he asks angrily. 'When you know I don't like to talk about it?'

'Well, no, she just started talking about it,' I say.

'And you didn't stop her? How much did she tell you?'

'I didn't get chance to stop her. She was just chatting and anything I didn't know, she'd said before I'd even realised it.'

Dean jumps out of bed and hurries into his clothes.

'What's wrong?' I ask.

'You and my sister, talking about my private life when you had no right to. She tells you some sob story about me and . . . you must feel so sorry for me, and when people feel sorry for people their feelings are . . . distorted.'

He seems so hurt and embarrassed and I feel so bad. I wish I'd stopped Faye talking before anything came out because there's no way my feelings changed just because I felt sorry for him.

'Sure, I saw a different side to you last night, but I definitely didn't feel sorry for you. I'm seeing more of your soft side lately – not just yesterday – and I like it. If anything, I shouldn't be kissing you at all because you're a client.'

I'm about to tell him just how much I like him when a whole new realisation washes over him.

'You're right, I am just a client,' he says. 'Just some poor guy who can't get a girl without playing the sympathy card.'

'Oh my God, Dean, no,' I start. 'What I meant is that I shouldn't be kissing clients at all – that I would never, but, I just felt so strongly about you and, well, you're not even a client. Your sister isn't paying me to help you; she just asked, and I said yes.'

'Wait, what? All this time I've been coming to your classes because I thought Faye had wasted money on them, and I needn't have bothered?'

'She didn't think you'd come if you knew,' I point out.

'I've had enough people lie to me,' he says softly as he heads for the door. 'I don't need any more.'

I want to go after him, but pulling myself up out of bed and getting ready takes me far too long. I'm only just struggling my shoe on when there's a knock at the door.

'Faye, hi,' I say.

'Morning Lola. Dean said he had a police emergency and had to rush off. He's asked me to drive you back to Marram Bay with us, if that's OK?'

'Oh, OK, yeah, sure, thank you,' I babble.

Dean has obviously spun her another story so I'm not about to upset him by doing anything other than going along with it.

'Can I help you get ready?' she asks. 'Dean said you might need help?'

'Yes, please,' I say softly. 'Just having a bit of trouble with my shoe.'

'Was he OK?' she asks me. 'He could hardly look at me. He practically stormed past me, only stopping for a second to ask me to drive you.'

'I think he was just worried about the work thing,' I say. 'It must be a scary job.'

'Yeah, I don't think he likes to talk about it,' she says. 'He doesn't like to talk about anything all that much.'

Faye helps me hop back to the bed before assisting me with my shoe.

'It was so nice to have you here with us yesterday,' she tells me. 'And being here with Dean. Maybe I'm just an overprotective sister but he's been so lonely for so long, and since he met you, it's like you've tapped back into the old Dean. He'd kill me for saying this, but it really seems like he's falling in love with you. I just can't thank you enough for giving me my happy brother back.'

I don't know what's worse, the fact that I've hurt Dean so much when he was obviously having strong feelings for me, or the fact that I think I might be falling in love with him too . . .

Chapter 42

I have gathered my parents at the breakfast table to tell them some news.

'You're not going home early, are you?' my mum asks, horrified at the thought that I might take off anything up to three days earlier than I told her previously.

'No, bigger news than that,' I say. 'Do you think I would sit you down to break that kind of news to you?'

'Oh, is it sit-down news?' my mum says. 'I didn't realise it was sit-down news. What do I do?'

'Stay sat down I suppose,' my dad tells her with a laugh. He doesn't seem worried; he's way too chilled out for that.

'You're not . . . not pregnant?' my mum says.

'I am not pregnant, Mum, not even close.' I sigh. 'I'm moving back to Marram Bay.'

My parents jump to their feet with joy and hurry around the table to hug me.

'Really?' my mum says. 'You're not pranking us?'

'Pranking you? No.' I laugh. 'I just want to come home. I've loved being around you and there's nothing in London I want to go back to. I'll give my notice and then . . . I don't know, I'll think of something.'

'There are plenty of single people in Marram Bay,' my mum reminds me.

'Yeah, maybe . . . or maybe I'll try something else. But, either way, I'm coming back so . . . can I live here for a bit please?'

'Of course,' my dad says.

'Live here forever,' my mum adds excitedly.

It's nice, to make them so happy.

'I'll go get some champagne from the bar,' my dad says, leaving me alone with my mum.

'Is this why you've been quiet since you got back from the wedding?' she asks.

'I didn't realise I'd been quiet,' I say.

'Yes, because you were miles away,' she replies. 'Did you not have a very nice time?'

'No, it was really nice,' I say. 'I had a great time.'

I did have a great time yesterday; it was this morning that ruined it all.

My mum sits down on the chair next to mine and reaches out to take my hand in hers.

'Do you think you'll keep trying to find Dean someone, now that you're staying?' she asks. 'You've done such a brilliant job with everyone else – Kim and Robbie are on a date right now. He's taken the day off. They've gone to Marram Bay Comet Con.'

I don't know what amuses me more, that Marram Bay has a Comic Con or that my mum calls it Comet Con – I wonder what she thinks it is.

'I don't know about Dean, Mum – I might give up.'

'I thought you might end up with him,' she says. 'I thought that might have been part of the reason you're moving back home.'

'I'm moving back home because I want to see you guys more,' I insist.

'Well, we won't want to see you if you're miserable,' she (hopefully) jokes.

I fidget with the placemat in front of me, lifting up one corner before allowing it to drop back down onto the table.

'Are you annoyed because you didn't set him up with anyone or are you annoyed because it isn't you?' she asks.

I suppose, when you're a mum, you don't need to be a brilliant detective to know exactly what's going on with your kids. My whole life she's always been a few steps ahead of me, waiting for me when I arrive home later than I said I would, getting to the post before I had chance to intercept letters from school, and now, knowing when I'm holding something back.

'Maybe it's both,' I say.

'Champagne,' my dad announces as he walks back into the room with a bottle. He shakes it theatrically before realising his mistake. 'Maybe we'll wait a minute.'

'Don't give up just yet, Lola,' my mum whispers to me. 'It's Valentine's Day tomorrow – you never know what will happen.'

Oh wow, I had no idea what date it actually was. Valentine's Day, eh? Maybe I won't give up just yet. Maybe I've got one last trick up my sleeve.

Chapter 43

I hover by the Hope Island Abbey, shifting my weight back and forth between my crutches. I texted Dean, told him I'd be here, and asked him to join me, but I haven't heard back from him yet. With my arms growing tired I slip them out of my crutches and lean my body back on to the wall behind me. I don't know how much longer I should wait here before I give up.

It's Valentine's Day and, here in Marram Bay, we take matters of the heart very seriously. For the annual Valentine's Day Festival, the local restaurants usually take it in turns to host a special romantic meal. This year it is the turn of Yorkshi, Hope Island's (if not the world's) only Yorkshire sushi joint. Well, that's what they call it, but it isn't raw fish, it's just local favourites served sushi style. I visited once when I was here for Christmas a few years ago. We had Wensleydale and smoked salmon rolls, fish and chip Nigiri . . . We even had these tiny little cooked breakfasts that looked just like the real thing, with scrambled egg wrapped in black pudding.

Tonight though we're not actually in Yorkshi; Yorkshi have set up a pop-up restaurant in the abbey ruins. The place is completely transformed with fairy lights to make it look pretty and heaters to keep everyone nice and warm. Everyone is dressed beautifully and sitting at cute little tables for two, which are decorated with fresh red roses. It's a romantic dream come true. Well, for everyone but me. I've been stood up.

'Would you like to take your table, miss?' a waiter asks me.

'Actually . . .' I start.

'I'm here,' Dean says as he hurries over in a suit – a different suit to the one he wore to the wedding. This one is black. I don't know why I didn't expect him to have more than one suit, but he looks even better in this one that he did in the last.

Dean might be looking good but he doesn't look very pleased to see me. It's cold, standing just outside the walls of the abbey away from the heaters, but it's even frostier now Dean has turned up.

'Let's get this over with,' he suggests, which floors the waiter. I suppose all the other couples are loved up, so this must be very confusing for him.

We sit down at our table and order a couple of drinks. All Dean wants is an orange juice, which makes me think he's about to take off. I order the same.

'I understand that you might want to talk to me, but did you really think this was the right place to do it?' he asks once we're alone.

'Will you just hear me out please?' I ask.

Dean nods, but I can tell that his usual patience is absent.

'First of all, just to clear up what happened, I did promise your sister that I wouldn't tell you she wasn't paying me to help you. She asked me if there was anything I could do for you and I said that I would try. I just heard something in her voice . . . something that told me how much she loved you and how much she wanted to help you. But she asked me not to tell you that she wasn't paying me because she didn't think you'd take it seriously if you didn't think there was something on the line.'

'Well, yeah, I guess she's right about that,' he says. 'If I'd thought it was optional there's no way I would've come. When she told me you had a money-back guarantee, I figured if it didn't work

– which I was certain it wouldn't – I could get her money back for her at least.'

'Well, no money changed hands, so you were never a client. I just really wanted to help you, and to me, it always just felt like we were friends.'

'I suppose I felt the same,' he says, looking down at his hands as he fidgets with his napkin. 'I guess I forgot that what we were doing was supposedly your job and then, when you reminded me, it all felt a bit . . . I don't know.'

'I know what you mean,' I say. 'And I know you don't like people knowing your business and I know that you don't like people feeling sorry for you but it's impossible not to feel sorry for you. Not to pity you, but what your ex did to you was awful. How can I not feel for you? Especially after what happened with me and Patrick, and especially when I care for you so much.'

'Sorry,' he says softly. 'I was embarrassed. It's embarrassing! Anna divorced me because I wanted to have kids with her and then went off and got pregnant with someone else. It's *me* she didn't want to have kids with. I was the problem.'

The emotion in his voice makes me feel awful for him all over again, but I try not to show it because I know he doesn't like it.

'You don't know that,' I tell him. 'You won't ever know that. You can't ever know that, because even if she told you that wasn't the case you probably wouldn't believe her anyway.'

Dean looks me in the eye, nodding thoughtfully. He always seems like this big strong man, but to see so much hurt and vulnerability in his eyes – it's terrifying. He's supposed to be this untouchable police officer. I suppose we're all humans with feelings, at the end of the day. Even big, strong Yorkshire men.

'Dean, you are an incredible man. You deserve a family of your own and there will be someone out there who wants to start one with you; you just need to let them in. You were so quick to push me away . . .'

Even now, sitting at the table together, it feels like we're sitting miles apart. I don't know if it's my imagination, but it seems like Dean is leaning back in his chair. I start to feel like I'm getting somewhere, but it's like he'll never quite let me close enough.

'Because I don't know who or what I can trust,' he says. 'I don't know what's real – I thought my marriage was real. I don't want to get back into anything unless I know it's real.'

'But you can't know that until you do it,' I tell him. 'I know you're scared, but you need to take a leap at some point. Date someone – it's not that bad. Take a look around you, at all these couples. Being in a relationship with someone is just stuff like this, going for dinner, hanging out together. OK, sure, every now and then you help them out because you care about them, and you'll wind up at a few family parties but, seriously, Dean, it's not that bad. It's actually really, really nice.'

For a moment, Dean just laughs. He laughs and shakes his head in disbelief before massaging his temples.

'What?' I ask.

'All that stuff you just said,' he starts, leaning forwards in his chair.

'Yeah?'

'You just described us,' he points out. 'Hanging out, going to dinner, doing each other favours, going to family parties together . . . That's what we've been doing. Have we been dating?'

'Oh . . . well, yeah, kind of . . . I suppose we have, yeah.'

'Huh,' he says thoughtfully.

'Has it been awful?'

'No, it's been kind of great,' he says. 'Happiest I've been in a long time.'

'Well, I guess that's because there's been no pressure or expectation. I didn't realise we'd been dating either.'

'I thought you were working,' he says.

'Dean, I think pretty much from the second the Pirates scored their first try, I stopped working and started just having fun. You were there for me through Will, through my parents' drama,

238

helping with my leg stuff . . . You binned off your big work bust for me!'

'Well, yeah, because you're more important to me,' he says. 'I can't believe how important you are to me.'

'Well . . . do you want to keep dating?' I ask. 'Because I'm definitely moving back here.'

Dean reaches forwards and takes my hand. On a chilly night like tonight, I feel the warmth that comes from him more than ever.

'I'd like that,' he says with a smile. 'So, you're going to quit your job and start again back up here?'

'Yeah, I might start my own business, or I might try something else. I hear there's a lot of really boring crimes that need solving.'

'One of these days something awful is going to happen in Marram Bay and you're going to feel really guilty.'

I laugh. I highly doubt anything bad is going to happen here.

'So . . . we're dating?' I ask.

'We're dating,' he says. 'I can't wait to tell my sister – and mean it this time. Finally have her stop sticking her nose into my business.'

'Is that the only reason you're doing this?' I ask. 'Because I'm only doing it to meet your dog.'

'I've heard of worse reasons for couples being together,' he replies.

Our waiter approaches and places our drinks down. He nervously removes a pad from his pocket, ready to take our order.

'It's OK,' I reassure him. 'We're friends again.'

'More than friends,' Dean adds.

I can't believe we've been technically dating all this time and neither of us noticed. I suppose we were just having a good time and that's all that matters really. Sure, it's important to want the same things in the future, but you talk about it and you figure out what you want to do as a team when the time is right.

Maybe Dean and I have a future together, with marriage and babies and even more dogs – I would love that – but now isn't the time to put our names down for it. It's about growing our relationship together and seeing where it takes us.

A wise man once said that, when you want to spend the rest of your life with somebody, you want the rest of your life to start straight away. That's all that matters. Starting our life together and seeing where it takes us.

Chapter 44

'I love you so much, I don't ever want to leave you,' I say in a sickly sweet voice. 'Who is the most handsome boy in the world? You are, yes you are.'

'I feel like a third wheel,' Dean says as I scratch Rufus the Labrador's ears.

I spent the night at Dean's house last night and, while it was an amazing end to a wonderful Valentine's Day to spend the night with him, I have to admit, I am a little bit in love with his dog.

I reluctantly say goodbye to Rufus, content that I'll be seeing a lot more of him, and I get into Dean's car so that he can drive me home – to my new home, which is actually my old home. I thought it was going to be weird, moving back in with my parents, but since I arrived back in Marram Bay, drama aside, I've never been happier. Especially now. I am so deliriously happy now.

Some chatter comes in over the police radio in Dean's car. I don't know what it means. It sounds like it's in code. I don't know. I wasn't really paying much attention.

'Oh no, has someone's lawn grown too long for the Neighbourhood Watch?' I ask sarcastically.

Dean looks at me gravely. 'No, this is serious.'

'Oh?'

'In fact, I'm going to take you there. I think you need to see that, sometimes, scary stuff is going down in this little town, and people like me are the only thing keeping you safe.'

My eyebrows shoot up. Gosh, I was only kidding. I don't want putting in actual danger just because I don't know when to let go of a joke.

'Carole, it's DC Gardner here, how many of them did you say?'

'Nine of them,' she replies.

'I'll take this one. I'm in the area, maybe two minutes away.'

'Are . . . are you sure?'

'Yes.'

Nine of them? And we're going alone? Even the woman on the radio seemed shocked at the idea of Dean going alone – and she doesn't even know he's got me with him.

Dean hits a button in his car that turns on blue flashing lights and a siren. I didn't even realise this car had them; they're sort of hidden.

After a minute of fast driving down a quiet country lane, Dean turns the siren off.

'We're approaching the scene,' he says. 'Time to be covert – we don't want to spook them, not if there's nine of them.'

'What?!'

Dean pulls up behind some trees and gets out of the car. He runs around to my side and opens my door for me.

'Come on,' he says.

'No way,' I reply. 'I get it, we have scary gangs here. I don't need to get killed today.'

'Lola, I'm not leaving you alone here – come on.'

Suddenly scared to be left alone, I get out of the car.

Dean sneaks back around to the boot and gets something out.

'Here, put this on,' he says placing something over my head.

'What is it?' I whisper back.

'It's a stab-proof vest,' he tells me. I shoot him a look. 'You were right; you don't need to get killed today. Now, follow me.'

'Dean, I am on crutches,' I remind him.

'It's OK,' he whispers back. 'We'll go slow.'

Unsure what else to do, I hop along behind him. Dean slows down as we approach a road to turn a corner. As we do he stops dead in his tracks.

'Carole was wrong,' he says. 'There's at least twelve of them.'

I catch him up and brace myself for what we're about to be confronted with, only to see twelve geese blocking the road, and three cars' worth of traffic parked behind them.

'Oh, you bloody idiot,' I say, laughing with relief. 'Are we here to move some geese?'

'Yes,' he says. 'You're right, nothing awful ever happens here.'

'So, the stab-proof vest?'

'Oh, no you need that,' he insists. 'Geese can be pretty angry, and their beaks are really strong. I've been pecked before.'

He says the last part as though he were a soldier recalling an old war story.

'I suppose I don't mind, that you're the world's most boring policeman,' I tell him. 'I'd rather you had rubbish stories about getting pecked by geese if it means you're safe.'

'Aww, Lola, I didn't know you cared,' he says as he leans in to kiss me.

One of the drivers stuck in the traffic jam holds their hand down on their horn, causing us both to jump out of our skin. The geese, however, don't move an inch.

'Oops.' Dean laughs. 'I'd better go do this. Maybe you should wait here, ma'am, where it's safe.'

'Oh, I certainly will, Officer.'

I watch Dean as he chases the geese around the road, trying to get them to move out of the way. He looks so funny, and not policeman-like at all.

I smile to myself as I think about how the rest of my life is starting today. Well, only if Dean survives the angry goose that is chasing him . . .

Acknowledgements

Massive thanks to my editor, Abi, and the HQ Digital team for all of their hard work with this book.

Thank you to everyone who takes the time to read and review my books – without you, I wouldn't still be doing this.

Thank you so much to all my family and friends for all of their constant love and support. Thank you to the fantastic Lynsey, the Blair to my Serena. Shout-out to the wonderful Rebecca and Belinda, my Aussie beauties. Thanks to Kim and Aud for always being incredible. Thanks to Joey and James for being the best, I don't know what I'd do without you. Finally thank you to my fiancé (I can't believe I get to say that!) Joe, for absolutely *everything*. I love you all.

Falling For You

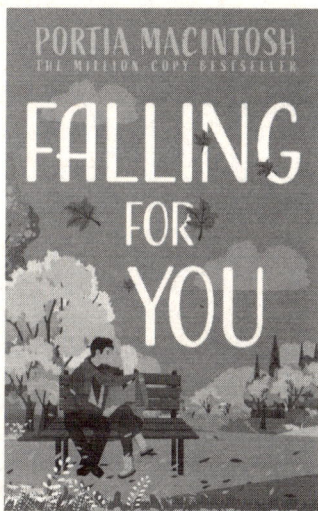

Thirty-one and oh-so single, Lily Holmes is ready for a fresh start. The charming seaside town of Marram Bay – glowing with autumn leaves and crisp sea air – feels like the perfect place.

She's determined to make her new deli a success and give her son a happy home. The only problem is that the locals aren't exactly welcoming to a city girl. Then there's the infuriatingly handsome cider farmer next door. With golden orchards and warm smiles, he might just be the key to winning over the locals – if Lily's past doesn't catch up with her first.

As the nights grow colder and sparks fly, will she finally find the fresh start she's been dreaming of?

Snow Love Lost

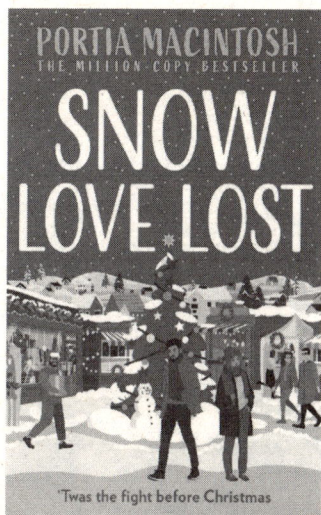

Ivy, the owner of a year-round festive store, loves Christmas. When her mother passed away, Ivy vowed to take over her mother's store and keep the Christmas spirit alive in the idyllic seaside town of Marram Bay, and she's been running the place single-handedly ever since.

The only thing missing in Ivy's life is a dash of romance – something her twin sister, Holly, will not let her forget.

As Christmas approaches, an enigmatic businessman moves to town, threatening to bulldoze her beloved shop to make way for a holiday complex. Ivy must fight to save the store. But could this intriguing newcomer be hiding a softer side, one that just might grant all her holiday wishes?

Here Comes the Ex

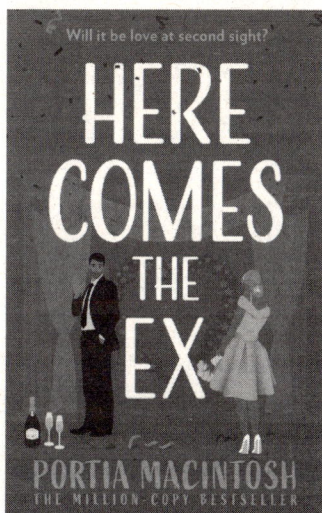

Luca is used to being 'the single one' – which is partly why she dreaded going to the wedding of an old university friend. Surrounded by faces she hasn't seen in 10 years, Luca can feel herself being sucked back into the immature, decade-old gossip that no one seems to have forgotten.

But when Tom walks in, Luca's heart stops. He was her 'almost boyfriend', and she had been completely swept off her feet by him… but he's currently standing next to the girl he broke her heart with at a party all those years ago.

As the evening draws on and the champagne continues to flow, it's clear that Tom can't take his eyes off her. Will Luca's luck in love finally take a turn?

Dear Reader,

We hope you enjoyed reading this book. If you did, we'd be so appreciative if you left a review. It really helps us and the author to bring more books like this to you.

Here at HQ Digital we are dedicated to publishing fiction that will keep you turning the pages into the early hours. Don't want to miss a thing? To find out more about our books, promotions, discover exclusive content and enter competitions you can keep in touch in the following ways:

JOIN OUR COMMUNITY:

Sign up to our new email newsletter: hyperurl.co/hqnewsletter

Read our new blog www.hqstories.co.uk

𝕏 : https://twitter.com/HQDigitalUK

 : www.facebook.com/HQStories

BUDDING WRITER?

We're also looking for authors to join the HQ Digital family! Please submit your manuscript to:

www.hqstories.co.uk/want-to-write-for-us/

Thanks for reading, from the HQ Digital team